Praise for Abbie Williams

"Williams populates her historical fiction with people nearly broken by their experiences."

— Foreword Reviews (Soul of a Crow)

* Gold Medalist - 2015

— Independent Publishers Awards (Heart of a Dove)

"Set just after the U.S. Civil War, this passionate opening volume of a projected series successfully melds historical narrative, women's issues, and breathless romance with horsewomanship, trailside deer-gutting, and alluring smidgeons of Celtic ESP."

— Publishers Weekly (Heart of a Dove)

"There is a lot I liked about this book. It didn't pull punches, it feels period, it was filled with memorable characters and at times lovely descriptions and language. Even though there is a sequel coming, this book feels complete."

— Dear Author (Heart of a Dove)

"With a sweet romance, good natured camaraderie, and a very real element of danger, this book is hard to put down."

— San Francisco Book Review (Heart of a Dove)

Second Chances

a **SHORE LEAVE CAFE** *novel*

Abbie Williams

central
avenue
publishing

2016

Published by Central Avenue Publishing, an imprint of Central Avenue Marketing Ltd.
www.centralavenuepublishing.com

SECOND CHANCES

978-1-77168-106-3 (pbk)
978-1-77168-007-3 (epub)
978-1-77168-055-4 (mobi)

Published in Canada

1. FICTION / Romance   2. FICTION / Family Life

To being brave enough to take a second chance...

Prologue

THEY SAY YOU ONLY FALL IN LOVE ONE TIME IN YOUR LIFE.
Thank God that's not true.

I can only tell you what I know about it and that is this: love engraves both your mind and your body in countless irreversible ways. It happens most often when you least expect it. It pitches stars into your eyes so that everything, even ordinary, everyday things take on a luminescence you never noticed. At first it is indistinguishable from lust. Lust is the scent of the warm skin of your lover's neck, a look in his eyes that makes your belly weightless and your entire body tremble. It is a thousand and one murmured words and soft sighs and intertwined fingers. It is fascination and daydreams. It is hot and sudden as lightning on a humid July night, slick and swift as the endless rivers in your blood. It propels your sensibilities, sparkling, into the air.

Love is getting up in the middle of the night through cobwebs of exhaustion because your child is crying. It is the responsibilities and details, both trivial and momentous, the memories of a shared lifetime. It is jagged as shattered glass and dense as lead. It is a thing of endless contradiction and infinite speculation. No one can explain it, including me.

But I will tell you this: it is not something that only happens once in your lifetime. That is one thing I know for certain.

Chapter One

Landon, MN - August, 2013

"Go after him?" Jilly repeated, disbelief raising her voice about a half-octave.

I lifted my head from her shoulder and curled my arms defensively around my bent legs. I wore our grandmother's robe, my feet bare and chilly in the predawn damp, unwilling to be swayed by my little sister's incredulous tone. Instead, resolute in my decision, I rested my chin on one knee and studied the smooth, inky surface of Flickertail Lake, bathed now in muted starlight. The eastern horizon bore a slim stripe of pale saffron, slowly brightening. Though not normally unwilling to voice his opinion, Justin Miller, seated on Jilly's far side, wisely held his tongue.

Finally Jilly could stand my stubborn silence no longer and prodded, "Joelle, what in the hell are you thinking? You can't possibly follow them to Oklahoma. You have to let him go, for now, anyway."

At that I found my voice, ragged though it was from tears and exhaustion. "I won't."

I sensed my sister softening; her next question emerged more gently. "Jo, what did he say when you talked to him?"

It stung me to my core to repeat Blythe's words, but I did, whispering, "He told me that he wasn't good for me, that there were things about him that I didn't know." And then, realizing that Jilly certainly possessed information I did not, I demanded, "What did Rich say earlier? You must have talked to him."

Jilly shifted and raked her right hand through her short golden hair, creating a spiky mess. From the corner of my gaze, I saw Justin curve his hand around her thigh and pat her twice, a calming gesture. For a moment I didn't think she was going to elaborate, and I dropped my feet to the dock and turned to implore her.

"Jilly, please tell me," I whispered, studying her familiar profile.

My sister bit her lower lip and then turned to face me, the blue of her eyes evident even in the meager light. She said, "Rich called about two hours after you'd gone to bed. Mom talked to him. He bailed out Blythe and then told Mom he was taking Bly back to Oklahoma. No ifs, ands, or buts. It was part of the condition anyway, since Blythe has to face charges there. Now, if Jackie decides to press any here, then Blythe will be in extra trouble."

I curled my hands together and pressed against the ache in my belly. Jackie could most certainly decide to take that option; Blythe not only knocked him down twice, but Jackie was now also missing an incisor from his toothy grin. I closed my eyes, better to block out that image. Instead I saw Blythe's eyes, deep blue-gray and wounded, as he told me he loved me, but that he wasn't good for me. That there were things I didn't know about him. I struggled to draw a deep breath, my heart thumping painfully; I was the one to end our relationship just a week ago, believing I was doing the right thing.

Jilly paused, studying my face now; I sensed more than saw her concern. She added, even more softly, "I think—and Jo, I promise I'm only saying this because I love you and I am fucking worried about you—I think you should stay here. I don't think it will solve anything if you try to go there. What can you do?"

"Show him that I love him no matter what. I let him down, don't you see?" I whispered fiercely, not caring that Justin was hearing all of this, too. To his credit, he didn't clear his throat and excuse himself, didn't so much as shuffle his feet. Instead he studied the lake, keeping his hand wrapped gently around Jillian's leg.

Jilly asked, not unreasonably, "Wouldn't a phone call accomplish that?"

I shook my head, unable to respond through the emotion clogging my throat. I couldn't convey to Jilly just how much I needed to find Blythe, to see this through. He needed me, it was that simple. I finally whispered, "I won't stay long. I'll be back before school starts." Necessity would pull me home before long anyway, the necessity of motherhood. But I understood what I must do, which was go after Blythe, even if it meant he would send me away for good. I needed to know the truth, for better or worse; otherwise I would forever torture myself with the wondering.

"Jo, sleep on it, at least," Justin finally ventured, his tone gentle.

"I will," I whispered, again bending my knees and threading my hands together around them. I didn't mention that it wouldn't change my mind.

The three of us made our way back up the shore a minute later, me in the lead, Jilly and Justin a few yards behind, walking with fingers loosely linked. I climbed the porch steps and then turned to watch them amble along, so glad for my sister's happiness that I spent a moment soaking in it; Jillian was widowed twelve years ago, and only just recently began seeing Justin Miller, a longtime friend of our family. They continued on past the porch, where I stood with my hips pressed lightly to the top rail. Jilly called over her shoulder, "Stay there, Jo, I'll be right back."

I stayed on the porch, obeying her, watching as sunlight tinted the sky with amber hues. The birds were very much awake; the shore echoed with their lively chatter and conversational chirps. The lake itself remained secretive in the last of the silvery dimness of dawn, level as a mirror with no wind to mar its surface. I studied the familiar sight in all its clear-morning beauty, thinking about what happened since yesterday evening.

Blythe was in trouble. I didn't know all of the details, but I vowed to find out. Just over a week ago, I'd told him that we had no future together. Despite everything my heart was screaming to the contrary, I felt as though it was wrong to ask him to stay, to bind himself in any permanent way to a mother with three girls of her own, one of whom was expecting a baby in February. For the countless time, my heart seized with the realization of Camille's pregnancy. My oldest daughter, conceived when her father and I skipped the last half of senior prom to have sex in his car. No protection, just heat and desire and crossed fingers; roughly nine months later we were legally wed, living nearly a thousand miles from our hometown of Landon, Minnesota, and in possession of a newborn.

No matter that Jackie's mother insisted we marry; we were in it for the long haul, I thought back then. And once upon a time, I'd loved my husband dearly, back when those damnable first-love stars clouded my vision. It wasn't until over a decade and one gorgeous new assistant at my husband's law firm later that the foundation of my marriage began to crack and crumble. I ignored it for years, purposely, and by the time I realized I better start paying attention, the whole relationship, foundation to rafters, lay in rubble around my ankles.

I'd come home to Landon this past spring, a place steeped in memories, most centered upon my rambunctious, freewheeling childhood and high-flying teenage years. As a teenager, the thought of settling permanently in this one-horse town seemed loathsome, despite its familiarity and the presence of the women who'd taught me everything I knew about life, love, and the pursuit of independence. I came from women who prided themselves on their ability to avoid relying on men, who equated happiness with that very principle; no man was ever granted ownership of our family business, the Shore Leave Cafe, since its founding in the 1940s. Never mind the legend of the family curse concerning our menfolk.

My great-grandmother Myrtle Jean Davis established and opened Shore Leave after her father died and left her, his only child, the lakeshore property. She'd built a business from the ground up; nothing fancy, just a diner with a porch, a place for Landon locals and the droves of fishermen who flooded our town every year, serving beer by the mug and in the batter of her fried fish. Myrtle Jean was married for a brief time, later divorced, and single-handedly raised two daughters, Minnie and Louisa; in turn Louisa, my grandma, married young, gave birth to my mother and my aunt Ellen, and then raised them solo after her husband's voluntary departure from Landon.

It was a long-standing and distinctly bittersweet joke that our family of women maintained difficulties holding onto its menfolk, thanks to an ancient curse supposedly cast upon the Davis women. My mother, Joan, carried on the tradition of producing two daughters close in age, though my father, Mick Douglas, vanished from our history while Mom was pregnant with Jilly. The only men who'd ever been permanent fixtures at Shore Leave were Rich Mayes, Blythe's step-grandfather who had worked in the kitchen since before my birth, and Justin's dad Dodge Miller, who ran the filling station on the lake and stopped out for breakfast every morning. Dodge was the one to pull our dock out of the water every fall, in preparation for winter, for as long as I could remember; by the same token, he dutifully hitched it to his tractor and hauled it back into Flickertail each May. And now Jilly was dating his son, after a lifetime of knowing one another from afar.

As though my thoughts conjured her, Jilly bounded back from the direction of the parking lot, where she'd spent a few minutes bidding farewell to Justin. I sank onto a chair at one of the porch tables, propping my bare feet on the opposite seat. Seconds later Jilly lifted my ankles and claimed the space; I settled my feet comfortably in her lap. She braced her elbows on the tabletop, chin on one fist, and regarded me with somber blue eyes.

"What?" I demanded. I didn't have to sigh.

"You might be able to placate Justin, but not me," she said. "Sleep on it, my ass. You're set on your decision, I can see it in your eyes." She tipped her head slightly to one side and then asked, "Do you want company? You know I'd go with you in a heartbeat."

It was tempting, but in the end I knew it was something I must do alone, and Jilly sensed this truth.

"Don't worry about the girls," she reassured me. "They'll understand. And I'll keep them out of trouble."

I shook my head. "It's not that," I whispered. "I'm counting on you to explain why I have to do this."

She was about to ask me why, to explain it to her, too, but then she sensed the depth of what I was feeling, and asked, her voice very soft, "You really do love him, don't you?"

I closed my eyes, seeing only Blythe, and then I reached across the table and gripped my sister's already outstretched hand. I squeezed it, and she returned the pressure.

"I guess so," she said finally.

We sat for another few minutes in companionable silence, watching as the sun crested the treetops on the eastern horizon and spread its wings over the lake. The sky was powder-blue in the dawn's wake, cloudless, and voices traveled to meet our ears from the direction of the lake path, which wound back to our house and the detached garage with its second-floor apartment that Jilly shared with her son, Clint. My own girls were crammed, quite literally, into the upstairs loft in the house, the same home in which I'd lived my entire life in Landon, and of late they began to voice complaints about the situation; they would just have to live with it a little longer, until I found us a place to live in town.

One thing at a time, Joelle, I reminded myself, scraping a hand through my tangled hair. Right now the first thing on my list was coffee, then a shower; at the moment I was certain I looked more than a little depraved, my eyes red and swollen from weeping, my hair in snarls, dressed in an old bathrobe, the hem of which was far too short for my legs.

Mom and Aunt Ellen climbed the steps on the far side of the porch, Mom reaching behind herself as she walked to braid her long hair, its blonde length now liberally streaked with silver. Ellen always wore her own curly yellow hair short, and it currently resembled a flower gone to seed, fluffy and errant despite her best efforts. Ellen was just a year older than Mom and I thought of her as a second mother. To be truthful, Ellen's stoic demeanor and ability to listen quietly led me to her side more often than my own mother's over the years. She was the first person besides Jackie to know about my prom-night pregnancy, and coached me on how to break the news to Mom, all those years ago.

That thought stuck in my mind as I watched them, two slightly plump middle-aged women with freckled skin and wide hazel eyes, wearing jean shorts and Shore Leave t-shirts, Mom decked in hot-pink hoop earrings with circumference enough to be bracelets. They caught sight of Jilly and me at the same moment; Mom hesitated, but Ellen marched ahead and joined us at the table, setting down the large stainless steel bowl she'd been carrying. It was loaded with a whisk, two clean towels, and a pepper grinder.

"What're you powwowing about, girls?" she asked, no hint of teasing in her voice.

"Jo is going after Rich and Blythe," Jilly told her without preamble, and I rolled my eyes in exasperation, though they'd have to know sooner or later.

Ellen didn't respond, only turned her concerned gaze to my face; stubbornly, I kept my eyes on my hands, folded over each other on the tabletop. Mom overheard this, of course, and I sensed more than saw her lips purse in disapproval.

"Jo, Rich will take care of things, don't you worry," Mom said, coming near but not sitting with us. I braced myself for the coming onslaught of guilt that Mom was so famous for dishing out. Like a helping of mashed potatoes that would sit, brick-like, in your stomach.

"Mom," I began carefully, aching with tiredness but determined to speak my piece. I was not a teenager any longer, though Mom's expression reminded me of those years. I squared my shoulders and continued, "I am going to Oklahoma and finding them. I need to do this."

Ellen patted my hand, Jilly tipped her chair on its back legs, and Mom must have heard the conviction in my voice, because she low-balled, asking, "What are the girls going to think? What will Jackie think? He'll be back out here today, and you can bet he's not going to let this all slide."

"Not after getting his ass handed to him," Jilly said, laughing a little, her rich, deep laugh with its capacity to make everyone in hearing distance smile. I did, just slightly. Ellen, whose back was to Mom, winked at my sister and our mother frowned like a great-horned owl.

"Jillian, that is not funny," she bitched, and I lifted both hands in defense, though I hadn't made the comment.

"Seriously, I have never seen Jackie lose a fight, and he used to get in them all the time," Jilly continued. "But Blythe cleaned his clock. Jackie had it coming, even you have to admit, Mom."

Mom always adored Jackie and tended to stand up for him before anyone else, despite everything he'd done. She surprised me by saying, "That is beside the point, Jillian. I agree that Blythe was in the right, but it doesn't excuse what he did. Jackie was furious when you left last night, Joelle."

I didn't want to think about my cheating husband who was missing a tooth, courtesy of my former lover. The man I was in love with, Blythe Tilson, was this very moment being driven south and farther from me with each passing second. My hands and legs twitched with impatience; it was all I could do not to run to my car and peel out immediately. But there were a few things I needed to do first, this being number one.

"I'll settle things with Jackie, Ma, don't worry," I said. "He'll simmer down and head home to Lanny." To my surprise, a name that used to set my teeth on edge and my heart thudding no longer seemed to have power over me. Lanny was the woman for whom Jackie left me; the woman he claimed to love and wished to marry. Again, the thought didn't faze me. If Jackie were here before me at the moment I would gladly sign the divorce papers he'd hauled with him from Chicago.

"But what will you tell the girls?" Mom continued, and I struggled not to rub my temples, feeling the light headache I'd suffered since last night intensifying, but Ellen saved me.

"Joan, she's in love and she's taking this chance," my aunt said quietly. "Do you think life offers chances like candy?"

"Like jellybeans," Mom muttered sarcastically, but she backed off, and Ellen touched my hand briefly before gathering her cooking supplies and heading into the cafe.

An hour later, fortified by a strong cup of coffee, I was able to sit down with two of my daughters at one of the booths. Tish and Ruthann, both sleepy-eyed but snapping with curiosity, sat facing me, forearms lining the table's edge, elbows bumping. Tish's close-cropped hair, which had grown out over the months here in Landon, was currently adorned by a row of bobby pins holding bangs out of her cobalt-blue eyes; Jillian's eyes, bestowed on my middle daughter. Ruthie, whose eyes shone a soft hazel flecked with gold, dark curls hanging in a braid down her back, studied me intently; both of them wore pale-blue Shore Leave t-shirts, Tish's with her name written across the left pocket in permanent marker. Camille, my oldest, was still sleeping, exhausted of late; being roughly a month pregnant did that to a person.

For a moment my conviction wavered; how could I contemplate leaving my pregnant child behind while I drove cross-country? What if her morning sickness got worse? What if she had a question about something?

"Mom, you look terrible," Tish observed in her usual blunt fashion, snapping me momentarily from my worries.

"Thanks, dear," I responded drily, lacing my fingers around my coffee cup.

It occurred to me that in the past two months, since the advent of a boyfriend into their big sister's life, Ruthann and Tish were more often in each other's company. Camille had moved on for the time being, however unwittingly, forced ahead into adult life, and they were a little bereft in her wake. Ruthie, even with her scattering of freckles, suddenly looked more like an almost-teenager than my baby. When had that happened? Both Camille and Tish were olive-skinned, like their father, but Ruthie inheirited my coloring all the way, save for the dark, luxurious curly hair that Jackie kindly passed to his children. My own hair was straight and light, hanging now over my back in reams of tangles. I supposed my make-up was under my eyes and probably I should have brushed my teeth at some point. Ruthie, also my sweetest child, amended, "No, you just look tired, Mom."

"Well, I am a little tired," I said, and then lowered my chin to study them with serious eyes. "Girls, you know what I told you last night, about Blythe?"

They both nodded, expressions equally solemn.

"Well, Rich and Blythe left Landon last night, to drive to Oklahoma. Blythe has to face some charges there, and I am going to drive down there and see if I can help." *And bring him home with me, ideally to stay forever.* His name tasted sweet in my mouth, and I pressed my lips together as though to keep it there a moment longer. I was relatively proud of holding it together so well, when everything inside of me was shrieking, aching to run to the car and go, to find Blythe and get my arms around him.

"You're leaving?" Tish gaped at me. "For how long?"

"Just a week or so," I reassured, reaching to take her hand. For once she allowed it, curling her long, slim fingers with their short, unpolished nails around my own, like when she was a little girl. I said with quiet intensity, "I wouldn't go if I didn't love him, you know. But I do love him, and I can't let him go away from me forever, without trying to stop it." I hurried to add, "I won't stay long, no matter what. And I'll call you guys every night."

"But why can't you just call *him?*" Tish continued. "Why do you have to go there?"

"I want to see him, Patricia," I said, studying her eyes, attempting to impart the seriousness of my words. "I have to see if we are meant to be."

"Like, meant to be married?" Tish asked, drawing her hand from mine and then gripping the edge of the table with both hands. Ruthie bit her bottom lip, not speaking, but the question was clear in her eyes. When I didn't instantly respond, Tish slapped the table with the bottom of her palms, a gesture of pure frustration.

"This is bullshit!" she snapped, daring me to call her out for cursing. "Dad is marrying that dumb woman from his office, and now you're marrying Blythe? What about us?"

Tears sparked into her eyes, and it hurt me physically to see this. She was justified in her anger, I understood that. I needed to make her see that I wasn't choosing Blythe over them, that I would never do that. But the ground here was incredibly shaky, totally unknown territory for me.

"Dad is a cheater," Tish said, some of the steam leaving her tone, replaced by a sadness that hit me much harder than the anger.

I regarded my middle girl, who swiped at her nose with a knuckle, roughly, the way a boy would. I said carefully, "Tish, honey, I know this is hard to hear—" She began to interrupt me, but I held up a hand, warning her with my eyes. I drew a breath and went on, catching Ruthann in my gaze, too. "But you're both old enough to understand that sometimes people fall out of love. Dad fell out of love with me, and it hurt me really badly. You guys saw that. But don't you think it would be worse to stay married to someone who doesn't love you anymore? Wouldn't that be living a lie?" I was pleasantly surprised at the sincerity of my speech; I wasn't saying these things to pacify my kids, but truly meant them.

They considered my words, though Tish studied the tabletop and Ruthie directed her gaze out the window at Flickertail. I prodded, "Right?"

Ruthie finally nodded, looking back at me. She smiled her sweet smile.

"Mama, we just want you to be happy," she added, and my heart melted with relief.

"Yeah," Tish grumbled, unconvincingly. But then she managed a little half-smile. "We do, Mom, honestly."

"Thanks, you two," I whispered. And then, because I needed to know, I asked, "What did Dad say after I left?" Just remembering what took place on the front porch last night caused me to cringe, Blythe and Jackie in a fist-fight. Jackie, whose hot temper landed him in numerous such situations in high school, had never come out on the losing end, but this morning he was surely worse for the wear, and missing a tooth. Had Blythe been hurt? I hadn't noticed any physical damage to him last night, and it was hard to imagine since Jackie barely landed a single punch, but still. The thought of Blythe hurting in any way only aggravated my desire to get going.

You've caused him more hurt than anyone. You, no one else.

I know, I acknowledged painfully. *And that's why I have to go to him.*

"He talked to Camille mostly," Ruthie said, playing with the sugar boat, absently stacking and restacking the little pink and blue bags of sweetener. "He told her he's not mad at her, and he told us we could come to live with him in Chicago if we wanted, and—"

My heart nearly came out of my chest. Ruthie saw the horror in my eyes because she cut herself off and assured quickly, "But we wouldn't do that, Mom, you know."

I swallowed and said what necessity required, though my throat was dust-dry. "You know if you girls want that, I wouldn't… I wouldn't stop you. I know you love your dad, and miss him." The speech cost a lot of my bravado and I drank a long sip from my coffee, which was now lukewarm and unpalatable, simply to hide my face.

Please, please never let them want to do that, oh please, please.

Tish said, "Mom, we love it here. We want to live in Landon, with you."

"I like Chicago, but I can't imagine not living with you, Mama," Ruthie said, and I felt a fraction of the tension leave my shoulders.

"Okay," I allowed. "And you're willing to give Blythe a chance?"

They both nodded.

"We wouldn't have to call him 'Dad' would we?" Tish asked, and I rolled my eyes at her.

"No, just 'Bly,' like you have been all summer," I said. *If he comes home with me, if I can make him see.*

"Dad said he's coming over later today. He wants to talk to you, too," Ruthann added, her eyebrows quirked with concern.

"I know, sweetie, it'll be all right," I said. "And I'm sorry about everything last night. I hate that Dad and Blythe got into a fight. Blythe was just worried about me, but Dad would never hurt me that way, you know that."

"It was pretty scary," Ruthie admitted. "Blythe looked so angry, I was worried for Daddy."

Jackie would writhe in shame at that statement, though Ruthann only meant it with compassion. I said, "I know, honey, Blythe was just really mad. And he felt bad for hitting your dad." Maybe not immediately, but there was no need to be that specific.

Clint suddenly bounded over to our booth, squeezing against Tish to displace her on the seat. He was holding a plate loaded with pancakes and syrup.

"Quit shoving me!" Tish complained, but moved aside gamely enough. She grabbed a napkin-wrapped trio of silverware from the tabletop and shook it open, snatching the fork and then helping herself to his plate. Clint playfully stabbed at her hand with his fork, and Ruthann, now pressed against the wall, took the easy way out and ducked under the table, popping out on my side.

I snuggled her close and she observed, gently, "Mom, you kinda smell like you need a shower."

"Point taken," I said, smiling against her soft hair.

Three hours later I'd showered, dressed in clean clothes, packed a bag with enough supplies for a week and a half—the longest I could figure being absent from my children—and withstood the blame Mom attempted to ladle over me. She followed me right up the steps and into my bedroom, despite the fact that lunch would begin in the cafe in a less than an hour and that she'd been on my case without relenting almost since I'd ended my conversation with the girls.

"Jo," she continued, sitting on my unmade twin bed and watching me with somber eyes. I did my best to politely appear to be listening to her, all the while rooting through my drawers and tossing things into my travel bag. She persisted, "I truly don't understand this. Why can't you call him? Wait a while, see how you feel in a few weeks. A month. Maybe this was just a rebound kind of thing."

My hackles rose at that, but I knew she was only trying to be reasonable.

"Seriously, I know he's a nice boy," she said. "But chasing after him this way, Jo…"

I finally rounded on her, cheeks hot. I stood still and faced her squarely, pressing my hands against my thighs to still the trembling. With extreme effort I knocked the edge in my voice down a peg or two and spoke quietly, but with emphasis. "Mom, I appreciate what you're trying to do, but he's no boy. He's a man, an amazing man, and I love him. *I love him.* I am going to find him and tell him so, because I owe him that. I owe myself that." My voice emerged hoarsely, but I meant every word. "If he sends me away then I'll let him go, but I have to find out."

Mom's lips softened a little, though her eyebrows knitted. She reached a hand in my direction, fingers splayed, but then let it drop back to her lap when I remained stubbornly unmoving. She said, "Joelle, this isn't like you."

"Then you know what, Mom, maybe you don't know me as well as you think you do," I said, my tone flat, and venomously resumed packing.

"Maybe so," she allowed. "But I know you better than you think. I know you're moving on from Jackie, but I hope you've considered the odds in this relationship, too. It's going to be so hard, honey, think of that."

"Well, I'll never know if I don't try," I said, my back to her and a catch in my throat.

"All right," she finally relented, rising and clutching me in a hug. I stood motionless in her embrace, angry, but at the last moment turned and hugged her in return, breathing against her familiar scent. She rubbed my back, and then requested softly, "Call us every night, all right?"

"I will," I assured her, and managed a small smile.

Camille was helping out with the lunch rush as I entered the cafe later, craving the familiarity of routine to get me through until tomorrow morning. I intended to leave with the sunrise; Mom promised to help me plan later this evening, including making a call to Christy Tilson, Blythe's mother and Rich's stepdaughter. I meant to go to Christy first thing. I kept my cell phone in my apron pocket, some part of me hoping that somehow, despite everything, Blythe would call me. I craved the sound of his voice so much that I could hardly bear it; I touched my phone yet again, caressing it as I had all of the nights for the past two months when he'd call me in the early hours of the morning as I lay in bed. I would be warm, with his scent all over my skin, my arms and legs aching from being wrapped around him the entire night before, and he'd call to tell me good-night. I breathed hard through my nose, hearing his deep voice in my memory, remembering the sweetness of those moments as my gaze lingered on the kitchen, where Blythe worked this past summer.

"Jo, light a fire!" Jilly said as she bustled past with a tray of drinks. "You just got a five-top outside!"

I kept busy until late afternoon, but when a lull fell, a restless energy began to creep back into my thoughts. No matter how very much I wanted to be on the road to Oklahoma, I was realistic enough to know I'd be exhausted if I left now. I needed a good night's sleep, or as much of one as I could manage at this point, and then I'd leave at dawn. Right now I possessed both a road map and a feverish urge to drive south on I-35.

"Jo, sit with me awhile," Gran ordered from her seat at one of our porch tables. The cafe was nearly empty of customers, the sun slanting over the lake on its westward descent. I braced my tray against one hip and slung upon it the bar towel I'd been using to wipe down a tabletop. I obeyed without question, sitting with a sigh. The air was laden with humidity and sweat skimmed between my breasts and collected along my hairline. I brushed at loose strands and then braced my elbows, meeting my grandmother's direct hazel eyes. Her face was stern, and dear, dearer to me than nearly any other in my life. I knew if I were to look back at pictures of her from my childhood she would appear much younger, but it seemed somehow as though she never changed. Her entire face was shaded under the brim of her straw hat, her knobby knuckles curled around a mug of coffee, even in this heat.

"You be careful down there," Gran said, as though I was heading into a war zone. I knew she really meant *be careful of your heart.*

"I will, Gran, I promise." My voice sounded more sure than I felt.

"You remind me so much of myself at your age, Joelle," she said, surprising me. She'd said many times how she thought I resembled Mom, but I understood that she wasn't referring to looks right now. "Even though Minnie was older than me, I sometimes felt like the older sister, the one who protected people. That's you, Jo. I admire you for going after young Blythe. But I worry about you. You have so much to be responsible for."

I dropped my gaze first to the tabletop and then looked out over Flickertail, glistening like a living creature in the sunlight. I closed my eyes, seeing the same scene superimposed upon the inside of my eyelids, this time painted over in oranges and reds. Finally I whispered, "I would never think of putting them second, Gran, you know I wouldn't."

"I know that," Gran said, again with uncharacteristic softness in her voice. "But I saw how Blythe looked at you all summer, lovesick like I've never seen. You two thought you were hiding things so well, but I knew, and your sister knew. Joanie…well, I'm not sure she knows yet."

I giggled a little. "Mom still thinks I should be with Jackie, even though she won't admit it."

Gran snorted, sounding more like herself. She took a long sip from her mug and then said, "I love my daughter, but she wears blinders when it comes to certain things."

The sound of the porch door swinging open halted our conversation, and I turned on one elbow to see Jilly headed our way, a tub of silverware that needed rolling in her arms. She joined us with a huff of breath and asked, "Jo, you don't mind getting this tub rolled before you call it quits for the night, do you?"

"You know I don't," I returned, and turned to the mindless task. "And I did plan to help until close, you know."

"Good deal," my sister said, and gave me a one-armed hug.

Chapter Two

I KEPT BUSY, JUST LIKE I'D PROMISED, ATTEMPTING TO ENjoy the gorgeous evening that settled over the cafe. The intensity of the day's heat fizzled away with the sinking sun and the air became totally static, lending Flickertail a smooth, glass-like serenity. The western sky blazed with colors reminiscent of the inner curve of a seashell, somewhere between orange and peach. The lake reflected the hue, wrinkled only by a group of mallard ducks that glided over the surface. The dinner crowd dwindled, leaving only a few regulars at the bar, and a group of four lingering over a last round of beer on the porch, admiring the incredible view. I checked on them for Jilly, leaving their bill, before untying my apron and making my way out to the dock to sit and contemplate tomorrow.

I left my shoes on the shore, rejecting the glider in favor of the dock boards and sinking my legs, bare beneath my cut-off jeans, into the lukewarm, slightly murky green water that lapped at the moorings. I untied my hair from a ponytail and shook out its length; I was finally getting used to the feel of its formerly shoulder-length strands on my back. I hadn't let my hair get long since high school, and as I ran my hands through it I imagined Blythe doing the same thing, his big, caressing hands that could be so gentle and hold me with such tenderness. Again I missed him so much I felt ill, inhaling a deep breath and holding it.

"Jo," said a quiet voice from behind me, from the end of dock. He hadn't made his way onto the boards because I would have felt the reverberations. I sat still as a threatened spider before turning and studying the man whose voice I knew so very well.

Jackie appeared expressionless as our eyes met. He, too, seemed rooted in place, wearing crisp, khaki-colored pants and a polo shirt, impeccable even on a casual summer evening. So different than how I remembered him from summers past, always clad in swim trunks, shirtless, and with bare feet. Behind him, up the gently-sloped incline from the lake, the windows of Shore Leave reflected the setting sun in a blinding array of golden-red.

"Can I join you?" he asked finally.

I shrugged one shoulder without offering a word, stubbornly. I heard him sigh, but he joined me in the next moment, though he chose to take a seat on the glider. I kept my gaze focused away from him; it was so strange to be sitting here under circumstances like this, a place we'd sat together a million times in our past, where we'd occasionally made love, dripping and giggling under the stars after skinny-dipping. When minutes ticked away and Jackie hadn't spoken, I finally gave in and tilted my chin over my left shoulder to look at him.

He sat with his forearms braced on his thighs, gazing out over the lake with a distant expression, as though his thoughts were perhaps running in a similar direction. He hunched his shoulders and met my gaze, his own frank and serious. But then he softened a little, and even smiled.

"Your tooth is fixed," I said, without thinking, and his smile dissipated as instantly as fog with the sun.

"I drove into Bemidji and insisted," he explained tightly, jaws clenching.

"I am sorry about that, Jackie," I said, after a few seconds of awkward silence. "I never wanted any of that to happen. You *know* I always hated when you got in a fight."

"So where *is* Lover Boy?" he asked, trying and failing to restrain a note of maliciousness.

I shifted uncomfortably, not wanting to tell him anything. But shit, he would know sooner than later. I bit back a sigh and said, emphasizing his name, "Blythe and Rich are driving back to Oklahoma. And I'm heading down there tomorrow."

Jackie's back straightened and displeasure curled his upper lip. He snapped, "What in the hell are you talking about?"

"Jackie," I warned. "What I do is none of your business."

"Damn right it's my business!" he cried, his voice just shy of thundering.

"Keep it down!" I insisted. We glared at each other for a long moment before I asked, slightly more kindly, "What do you want from me?"

His face was familiar to me in nearly all of its emotions, but whatever rolled across his handsome features just now wasn't something I'd ever observed. He looked uncertain, and somehow fearful, before smoothing these expressions away behind a mask of anger.

He stormed, "What about the girls? I'll bring them back home with me if you go after that—"

"You will absolutely not!" I raged, pulling my legs from the water and rising to my feet, the better to face off with him. To my extreme relief, no one flew out of the cafe to watch this scene. Not like last night.

"Joelle, they will *not* stay here—"

"This is their home!" I yelled at him. "It's *my* home! And I will be back within a week."

Jackie stared at me, bewildered. He asked, "What the hell happened this summer?"

"What do you mean?" I hedged, no longer shouting since he was not. I even allowed my hands to slip out of the fists I'd planted on my hips.

"You look different," he observed in a new tone of voice, studying me in a way he hadn't in years. The sunset light bathed his tanned skin, played over his dark curls, so very like our girls' hair. He elaborated, "The way you used to look."

My heart stuttered at these words. It was because I *was* myself again, thanks to Blythe and his incredible love. I thought, *Blythe, sweetheart, you should be here. Why was I so blind?*

Finally I whispered, "I feel like myself again." And then I couldn't help but take a jab at him, clarifying, "No thanks to you."

Jackie's mouth twisted a little. He shifted his shoulders in a gesture of discomfort and said, "I truly am sorry about everything, Jo."

"How long?" I asked, watching him intently.

He knew exactly what I meant, and a deep sigh came through with his response as he admitted, "Since she started."

I turned away, still stung at being cheated upon for all those years, as if our marriage meant nothing to Jackie. I whispered, "I knew it, you know."

"I knew you did, after a while," he replied, his voice just as quiet. "And I hated that you didn't do anything about it."

I spun around to gape at him. Realizing how I must look, I snapped my mouth shut.

"You could have shown me you cared that I was messing around," he explained, his eyes boring into mine with a mixture of petulant hurt and anger.

I was too stunned to reply. Was this a petty, retaliatory way of trying to make this *my* fault?

"After the first few times I didn't even feel guilty anymore," he reflected, as though in the presence of a marriage counselor. I wanted him to stop speaking, but somehow the words wouldn't come to me. He seemed to take my silence as permission to continue. "And when you caught us last Christmas, at that stupid fucking party, I was actually relieved. But I am sorry you…well, you know…"

"Saw you fucking another woman?" I supplied, bitterness in my throat. "Yes, that was so…*relieving*."

"Dammit, I'm trying to be honest with you, Jo," he said. "I am truly sorry about that."

"Will she be good to the girls? Because I'll kill her," I said, and he rolled his eyes at me.

"She wants kids of our own," he said. "She's only twenty-seven."

I let that one slide, unwilling to respond. After a moment Jackie steered the conversation in a new direction, asking quietly, "What about Camille? Ben Utley's little brother is the father? She won't tell me anything."

This was safer territory and certainly something we needed to discuss. When Jackie scooted over and indicated that I should sit beside him by tilting his head, I did. Again it was a bizarre sensation; where once I would have tucked myself against his side, I now sat stiffly, slightly uncomfortable with the proximity of our thighs.

"Yes. His name is Noah and he's a little bastard," I said.

Jackie actually laughed and I sensed him shaking his head, though I kept my gaze directed over the water. He added, "I should probably go and have a come-to-Jesus talk with him. Joan told me the kid plans to go back to college this fall as though nothing happened."

I was still incensed over this, explaining, "He's smug, I thought that from the first. And he won't even talk to us. And Milla won't tell me how she really feels. I do know she was totally smitten with him this summer." Again, I was overwhelmed by my own culpability. I heard myself admit, "I should have been watching her more closely. I blame myself, Jackie, I really do, and I'm sorry about that. I didn't pay enough attention."

Jackie surprised me by snorting. "Hell, Jo, she's almost an adult. You can't guard her every move."

"I know," I said, but my heart still ached for our oldest, whose life would never be the same. We knew that better than anyone, I guess. I mourned, "But it's *Camille*. She's so smart, and she was going to go to college, Jackie, oh God…"

"I know, her whole world will be different now," Jackie said. "I'm glad she's got your family. I don't know how I would handle a pregnant kid in the house." I knew it. At least he was being honest. He turned my way and added softly, "Hey, no matter what I will always be there for our girls. Even if you live in Landon and I live in Chicago. You know that, right?"

I sighed and braved a look into his eyes. I said honestly, "I know, Jackie."

"How has she been feeling?" he asked.

"She's just been sleeping all the time. She won't talk to me, either. She keeps everything so close to her heart."

"She's always been that way. Tish tells us everything, at least." And his smile was fond.

"That's true."

"How are they taking it? Ruthie seems pretty excited, actually."

We were conversing normally for the first time in nearly a year. I felt a ribbon of relief stream through me as I replied, "She is excited, now that a little of the shock has worn off. Tish is still dealing with the fact that this means her big sister had sex."

When Jackie cringed visibly at my words, I added, "Sorry."

"She's my baby," he said. "And she's having a baby. It's too much. I wasn't ready for this yet."

"None of us were."

"It's how our folks felt, back when. My dad was ready to brain me for getting you pregnant when we were still in high school."

I said, "But we won't make them get married. I won't do that to Camille." About this I was adamant.

Jackie continued to study me in the gloaming light. He asked, his voice low and soft again, "You wouldn't have married me back then?"

I kept my eyes away from his as I said, "I don't know. I can't answer that anymore, and the decision was out of our hands anyway. We can't change that now."

He looked away and said, "Yeah, it was. But I will make that kid pay her child support."

I felt a rush of gratitude that he was taking this in stride, ready to stand up for his daughter. Despite his failings as a husband, he'd always been a good father to our girls, and for that I was grateful. From above, up on the porch, the screen door suddenly creaked on its hinges and Tish called, "Dad! Phone's for you in the cafe!"

Jackie and I both turned to look over our shoulders, almost knocking heads, to see Tish framed in the door, holding it open with one shoulder, the porch light bathing her in a yellow-orange glow. He called back, "Who is it? I have my phone right here—" He reached for his pocket and then added, "Guess I don't."

"Caller ID said 'Chicago,'" Tish informed.

"Better get that," Jackie muttered, rising to step around me.

I didn't bother to respond, instead reaching for the zillionth time to touch my own cell phone, imagining how close I was to hearing Blythe's voice, if I dared to call that number. My heart sent anxious blood and concentrated longing through my body; I missed him so much. I rose and followed in Jackie's wake, but headed around to the far side of the porch to see if Mom was free; we needed to discuss a few things, too.

It was after ten and Ellen locked up the cafe, leaving Jilly and me on the porch. Mom and Gran were already home, along with Ruthie and Camille, who could barely keep her eyes open an hour ago. Tish, Clint, and Clint's best friend Liam sat around the fire pit along with the dogs, roasting marshmallows. Their conversation, punctuated by an occasional laugh, was a pleasant murmur in the background. The air remained motionless, save for the constant hum of mosquitoes buzzing near our ears; I sat with my feet propped on an adjacent chair while Jilly leaned her hips against the railing, blowing lazy smoke rings at the lake.

"Justin's coming over in a bit," she said, after we'd enjoyed the night in companionable silence.

"I'm glad, Jills, so glad for you guys."

She smiled around her cigarette and then roughed up her spiky blond hair. Her eyes were blue as cobalt, clear as crystals, with the kind of sexy shape that people called 'bedroom eyes.' I'd always been jealous of my sister's beautiful eyes, fringed in naturally thick, dark lashes. Jilly blew a long trail of smoke and said, her voice sweetly sincere, "I never thought I'd feel like this again."

Christopher Henriksen, Clint's father, was Jilly's husband for just a few short years before he died in a snowmobile accident the winter Clint was three. I lived in Chicago then, but Jilly's grief was palpable, reaching me even across the miles separating us physically. She vowed never to love again, and for a long time I was sure she meant to keep that promise.

"I'm so happy for you," I whispered. "Jilly, you deserve to be happy."

"So do you," she returned and glanced over her right shoulder at me. She said, "I saw you out there talking to Jackie earlier."

I paused for a beat. "Yeah, we were talking about the kids a little." I wasn't sure why I was suddenly hesitant. Jilly's gaze sharpened instantly, an expression I interpreted as a warning, and I added, speaking too quickly, "He seemed weird. Reflective. He said…he actually told me he wished I would have shown him I was angry that he was cheating. It's like he was hurt that I didn't *do* anything about it."

Jillian ground out her smoke in the ashtray and then sat near me, her face intent and focused, assuming what I thought of as her mind-reading expression. She didn't seem inclined to speak and so I babbled on, "He told me that he was actually *relieved* when I caught him last Christmas. He implied he didn't have to keep up the charade anymore."

"He *was* the limping horse," Jilly said finally, as though to herself, and tapped the index finger of her right hand against her lips.

"What the fuck does that mean?" I asked, but my tone was curious rather than scathing, despite my choice of words. Even though I knew it was about a dream. Jillian and her precognitive flashes; I learned over the years to take them with a grain of salt, though Great-Aunt Minnie was also possessed of the gift, and no one dared to be skeptical of her. Not even Mom.

Jilly closed her eyes as if peering inward and explained, "Last night after the fight, I dreamed about a horse limping across a field. A dark brown horse, limping like it was favoring a leg. I woke up speculating it was Blythe, but now I know it was Jackie."

"Shouldn't the horse have been missing a tooth?" I asked, sounding bitter. I swallowed that away and then said, for no real reason other than to irritate her, "Did you know that Jackson's parents named him after the Johnny Cash song?"

Jilly shot me the annoyed look I'd been expecting, her eyes crinkling at the corners and lips looking as though she was trying to bite through an apple seed with her incisors.

"Yeah, I guess you do," I said, listening to Tish and the boys goofing off in the background. "That used to be our favorite song. Jackie would sing it in the shower."

"He's limping to make you feel sorry for him," my sister warned.

"I know," I admitted, lacing my fingers and fitting my thumbnails together.

"He'll keep limping, Jo."

"What are you saying?" I asked, sounding more accusatory than I'd intended. But Jilly was silent, putting on her enigmatic face.

"Jillian Rae, I would never fall for a lame horse," I insisted. God, did she think I was that pathetic?

At last she sighed and then reached over with one hand to hook her fingers through mine. She said, "I know, Jo, but I had a shiver for a sec there."

"Then put on a sweatshirt," I suggested. I wasn't sure if I meant that to be bitchy or not; fortunately Justin's silver truck suddenly beamed its headlights across the parking lot and Jilly chose to ignore my comment. She sat up straight, fussing with her hair once again.

Uncharacteristically, she wondered aloud, "Do I look all right?"

"You look amazing, like usual," I said, then teased, "What does it matter what you look like just to go have sex?"

Jilly whapped my shoulder as she rose to her feet, slipped on her sandals, and called good-bye to the kids.

Clint called back, "See you, Mom!" in his usual cheery fashion.

"Have fun," I chirped.

"See you in the morning," she added, over her shoulder. "I'll get up to say bye."

"Thanks, Jilly Bean," I said, utterly sincere.

Justin climbed out of his truck to catch Jilly in a hug, then called hello to the kids and me. I waved back and then helped myself to the pack of smokes that Jillian left abandoned on the table. I lit one as the truck pulled out of the lot, just in time to hear my middle daughter's voice calling over, "I see that, Mom!"

"Dammit, go to bed!" I yelled, only half-kidding.

But, heartless teens that they were, all three just laughed.

I ambled back to the house, but found I wasn't ready yet for bed. I stood for a time in the wedge of light from the fridge before finally closing it without finding anything worth eating, my thoughts flowing back to the night less than a month ago when Blythe and I crept back to the house during Shore Leave's annual Fourth of July Eve party to make love in the kitchen. I leaned on the same countertop now, resting my forehead against it, thinking of him.

What if he tells you it won't work? What if he tells you to go back to Minnesota and forget about him for good?

My heart scattered panicked blood around my body at the thought. I lifted my head and felt dizzy, almost ill. If I tried to go to sleep now I would just lie awake for hours, worrying. At last I fumbled in the dark kitchen for the old gray hooded sweatshirt that Mom kept hanging on the hook by the back door. Slipping into its ratty warmth, I decided that I'd sit and stargaze until I felt ready to face my bed.

On my return trip to the cafe, I met Tish, Clint, and Liam walking back to the house.

"Jeez, Mom, aren't you going to bed?" Tish asked.

"I'm just going to sit for a little bit longer," I explained. The boys were trying to put one another in a headlock, Clint with his unmistakable hee-hawing laugh. He sounded just like his dad, and in the darkness he could have been Chris; it gave me a little bit of a shiver. I refocused on Tish and said, "I'll come up and say good-night."

"K, Mom," she agreed, and then embraced me for just a second, but tightly. I kissed her curly hair, which smelled familiarly of her favorite strawberry-scented shampoo.

"G'night, Aunt Joey," Clint added, breaking free of his friend to kiss my cheek.

"Aw, good-night, Clinty," I returned, and then they all took off at a gallop.

And I continued on through the stillness of the night.

Sometime later I came awake with a jolt, realizing I'd dozed off on one of the porch chairs. A mosquito tickling my left temple with its bite woke me and I slapped at it in irritation, glad I was at least wearing jeans and the hooded sweatshirt. Shit, I was still probably bitten in two dozen new places. I stretched, noticing the moon was in a new position on the black backdrop of the sky, hearing the high-pitched trill of the gray tree frogs, the grunting bass of the bullfrogs and the fiddling crickets harmonizing in a grand cacophony of night sounds. Their noise always seemed to escalate after midnight; likewise, a breeze blew in over the lake, cooling the air but not strong enough to chase away the mosquitoes. I knew sleep would come if I went back to the house now, but decided to have one last smoke before heading that way.

I was standing against the porch rail, exhaling slowly, watching the lake as it lay hidden in the muted shades of night when someone just behind me asked, "When did you start smoking again?"

I simultaneously gasped and startled so hard I dropped the butt, whirling around to confront Jackie as he appeared unexpectedly for the second time this evening. He stood with one foot on the bottom step, watching me, more disheveled than he'd appeared earlier. He was also drunk. A slow-burn kind of drunk; obviously he'd been imbibing for hours. I pressed a hand to my chest in an instinctive reaction to calm my galloping heart.

"Where is your car?" I demanded, scanning the parking lot, not wanting to think about why he was here at this time of night. Goddamn limping horse.

"Walked," he explained succinctly, still watching me. His eyelids were hooded and his voice just this side of slurring.

"All the way from your uncle's?" I snapped.

"From Eddie's," he clarified. "Left the car there."

I stared at him in complete frustration, before deciding that action was the best thing. I spun around to unearth the hidden key to the cafe; my hand was oddly shaky and I tried two times before I inserted it correctly into the lock. Once within the dark interior of Shore Leave, I ignored my jumping innards, my unease at dealing with my sodden husband on a night when I shouldn't have been seeing his face at all. Damn him, he was doing this on purpose to torture me. I fumbled in my purse, which was stuffed under the counter, finally locating my car keys. From across the dining room the screen door creaked open and Jackie was coming through it. I hadn't bothered to click on any lights, and he called, low, "Jo? Where'd you go?"

"Over here," I told him. "Getting the keys to get your drunk ass home."

"Not yet," he said, now headed my way, though rather slowly. I was struck again with disconcerting familiarity; how many times in our past had we met in this very same place on hot summer nights, under cover of darkness, finding any excuse to make love? He'd bent me over this exact counter on more than one occasion.

Jackie leaned over that same counter on his elbows and grinned wickedly at me, looking too much like the teenaged boy I'd just been trying to banish from my mind. I gripped the keys in my right hand and ordered, "Let's go."

"Let's not," he whispered. He reached and closed his fingers around my wrist, loosely, but when I tugged impatiently, he kept hold.

I hissed, "Stop it, Jackie, I mean it."

"Come here," he said in his same old inviting tone, and I yanked hard then, freeing my arm. He cajoled, "Jo, come on."

"*No*," I told him, my voice firm. I was so angry that he was behaving this way that I could have decked him. I moved around the counter but he followed, cornering me and this time slipping his arms around my waist, clutching my ass and drawing me flush against him. Before I could react he bent his head, sending the sharp scent of bourbon rolling over my face.

"Jackie!" I yelped, and shoved him in the chest with both hands. "Stop it! What in the hell are you doing?"

He stumbled back and regarded me as though through a haze, his eyes unfocused even in the darkness. He was more shitfaced than I'd realized and I relented, shifting position and hooking his arm over my shoulders. He leaned heavily against me, reeking of booze, and I ordered, "Come on, you can crash on the couch."

"Can't," he murmured, and suddenly his knees seemed to liquify. With alarm, I realized he had passed out.

I grunted with the effort of keeping him upright, but then gave up and just sank to the floor, bringing him with me. He was like a cooked noodle, flat on his back before I could help it. Kneeling at his side, I studied his familiar profile in the dimness, with something close to stun, trying to make sense of what he was doing here. What it meant.

"Shit, shit, shit," I muttered. Now what? I couldn't possibly haul his inert body across the lake path to the house. Nor could I wake Mom or Ellen to help me.

At that moment headlights beamed across the windows, flashing over me like a lighthouse beacon. Justin and Jilly, thank God. I darted out the screen door and waved at them. Jilly bounded out of the truck as soon as they parked and called, "Jo, what are you still doing up?"

"I need your help," I informed them. "I killed Jackie and need to dispose of his body."

Justin laughed heartily as he hopped out of his truck. Moments later they joined me on the porch and I insisted, "Come and see for yourselves if you don't believe me."

Inside Shore Leave Jilly clicked on the lights, making us all abruptly squint, and said, "Well, shit. It's true."

Jackie was horizontal on the floor beside the row of stools along the counter, his chin pointed at the ceiling, feet flopped outward. He might have been dead but for the rip-sawing snores that were making his chest rumble at intervals. I shook my head, suddenly exhausted, as Justin asked, "What in the hell?"

"He showed up here drunk just before you guys got back," I explained. "Drunk as shit."

"Where's his car?" Justin asked.

I thumbed in the general direction of Eddie's, while Justin and I continued staring at my husband. Jillian, however, trained her suspicious gaze upon me.

"The bastard," she muttered. "He tried to kiss you, didn't he?"

I squirmed and finally admitted, "He tried, but I shoved him away."

"That effing limper," she said. Justin shot her a questioning look, though I understood her words. Jilly continued, angrily, "He's doing this because he's a big jealous baby, that's what. He can't handle that you found someone new."

"Pretty much," I agreed. I knew that's what motivated this bullshit, more than anything. Go figure; the irony of the situation wasn't lost on me.

"Well, I say let him sleep right there tonight," Justin suggested, chuckling, and I looked his way; from a particular angle his livid facial scars weren't even visible, though the longer I'd been around him this summer, the less I noticed them at all. He snorted and said, "He'll pay for it in the morning."

"Yeah, but what if the girls find him?" Jilly asked. "Or Mom? Christ, we'd hear about it for weeks."

I giggled a little, and then reflected, "Gran would just step over him and start the coffee."

Jilly giggled, too. "But she'd be sure to poke him with her cane a few times. Not hard, just enough to bruise a rib or two."

"Fine, he can come home with me," Justin grumbled. "Help me load him up."

Anyone watching would have assumed we actually were disposing of a body; Justin hooked his arms under Jackie's torso and hefted him up, while Jilly and I each snagged a leg. He was ragdoll-limp between us as we hauled him, haltingly, across the parking lot and then with great difficulty into the passenger seat of Justin's truck. For a moment, after we settled him, Jackie came to, his gaze catching hold of me, and he murmured, "G'night, Jo, love you," before his eyes rolled backward in his head.

I froze, unduly troubled by that statement. Jillian slammed the door, effectively cutting off my thoughts. She said, "Come on, let's get to bed. You have a long drive tomorrow."

And I let her lead me home.

Chapter Three

Morning dawned thick and silver with cloud cover. I bent over each of my girls in their beds in turn, cupping their cheeks and kissing them, assuring them that I'd call each night, that I'd be back soon; before they knew it. Jilly was the only one fully awake, bundled in her quilted pink robe, a travel mug of coffee in hand. She brewed it for me in her kitchen, and I clung to her under the heavy, early morning sky. She kissed me and whispered, "Bring him back."

"I will, and I'll call every night," I whispered against her hair.

I climbed into my loaded car, turned the key. A few drops of rain spattered over the windshield as I rolled down the window with a touch of a button and reached out to my sister. She clutched my hand extra hard. Thus fortified, I pulled from the parking lot, slowly, then drove around the lake and back through Landon, before turning out onto the main highway, heading for the interstate.

By midmorning I cleared Minnesota and entered Iowa under a clear blue bowl of sky. I'd hauled along a carry case jammed with my favorite CDs, and was listening currently to Bon Jovi, the old stuff, the music from my youth. I kept the windows down, despite my speed, my heart unsettled by a wild rush of conflicting emotion. Exhilaration and terror, mostly, but a ribbon of pure thrill wound through me, too, at the fact that I was doing something like this. Going after what I wanted for myself, instead of sitting by and letting life happen to me. I felt alive, in a way that I hadn't in over a decade.

Blythe, Blythe, don't be angry that I'm coming, I thought, my breath catching a little at just the thought of my lover. *Come back with me, we'll make it work. Somehow, we'll make it work.*

I couldn't bear the thought of the alternative.

The interstate hummed beneath the tires as I drove south past mile upon mile of rolling green hills, cornfields a month from harvest. Driving solo invited reflection and my thoughts spun back to the nights in Blythe's old black truck, sneaking away into the darkness to find a few hours alone. I revisited the night we met, playing over that moment again. I'd just arrived at Shore Leave from Chicago, kids in tow, to discover that my mother hired an ex-con. Angry, exhausted and emotionally drained, I'd walked into the cafe that night expecting…well, certainly not the future love of my life. I'd been almost too shy to shake his hand. And afterward, during those first few weeks, I'd tried so hard to ignore my feelings for him, but it was useless, out of my hands, my initial and intense attraction slowly replaced by something more. The last thing on earth I expected was to fall in love. But then, that's the way of it…

I'd believed myself in love once before, totally under the spell of Jackie Gordon's smile. It still rankled me this morning that he could so casually, in last night's drunken state, speak any words of love to me. The man who'd told me just a month ago that he was in love with another woman and wanted to marry her. The man I'd fallen out of love with long ago (though it took almost equally as long to realize it), when our marriage began to wither on the vine.

To be fair, when I was a young girl Jackie was my ideal: charming, sexy, tan and lanky, never wearing a shirt during our long, hot summers on the lake. He'd been a fan of settling his neon-tinted sunglasses atop his head, squinting into the sun, his toothy grin constantly flashing. He teased me all the time, untying my bikini top, slipping his hands over my stomach, always ready to make love, and in those days I was always willing.

I bit my bottom lip now, all these years later, remembering the morning I realized I was pregnant and that I must tell Jackie. How abruptly our virtually carefree relationship came screeching and grinding to a halt.

"Pregnant?" he'd repeated on that spring afternoon, May 1985, roughly three weeks after our senior prom.

I nodded, my insides knotted and heaving with tension, though I held it together reasonably well from all outward appearances; even Jilly hadn't suspected the truth. Jackie and I sat on the arbor swing in his parents' big, shady yard, alone but for the lazy spring sunlight and about a million birds, Jackie keeping the swing in motion with one foot. When I revealed my news, he stopped it with a jolt. His eyes were dark and serious on mine. But despite everything he took my right hand between both of his.

"Are you sure, Jo? You did a pregnancy test and everything?"

"Yes, and yes, I'm sure," I said, desperately willing away the ocean of frightened sobs threatening to hurricane through my body. "Oh, Jackie, Gran will *kill* me. She'll murder me. She's warned me about this for so long."

And he'd smiled at these words, a little hint of his grin, teasing, "Warned you about me?"

I glared at him for trying to make a joke at this moment, and his grin slipped away. He said, "Tell Ellen first, for sure. She'll help your mom and Louisa understand."

"What about your parents?" I worried, chewing at my thumbnail. Greg and Patricia Gordon were both pretty uptight for having such a wild only child.

"We'll tell them together. It'll be okay, Jo," he whispered, drawing me close to his chest, kissing my hair. And I'd believed him.

Our wedding took place a month and a half later, after our high school graduation, and I'd been too ill with morning sickness to do any real celebrating. Mom was furious with me (though she hid that fact in front of anyone), Jilly heartbroken; Gran, Aunt Ellen, and Great-Aunt Minnie (who'd still been alive in those days, dishing out both fried fish and heaps of advice) had all resigned themselves to the inevitable—the inevitable meaning my departure from Landon. Gran attempted on two occasions to talk me out of marrying Jackie. They were sick at the idea of me moving all the way to Chicago, but at the time it made sense; Jackie was already accepted into college and I would stay home with the baby. Which I did, and then did again, and finally for a third time.

"Dammit, Jackie," I murmured, blinking behind my huge sunglasses into the bright sun of an Iowa morning, over eighteen years later. Why hadn't I listened to my gran? Why had I believed in Jackie? But that was a pointless question, and besides, without having moved to Chicago I wouldn't now have either Tish or Ruthann, the lights of my life. My trio of girls was the best thing I'd ever put out into the world, and in any case, I'd always have wondered about Jackie if he'd gone off to college and left me behind. Better to have experienced the failure than be constantly second-guessing.

I need a smoke, I thought, groping for my purse to find the pack Jilly stashed there for me. I extracted one and then used the same hand to engage the car lighter. I promised, *After this trip, no more. Totally done smoking.*

I drove for another hour before pulling into a gas station. Again I spent a moment marveling at this trip I was making, alone. Five years ago I wouldn't have considered such a thing. Even six months ago. But even Jackie noticed the change in me this summer. I had found my old self, collected up the scraps that scattered all apart during the past difficult years, reemerging as the Joelle I used to know, the one who'd been tucked deep in my heart. But stronger now, and wiser. This time understanding what love was all about. I rolled my eyes as I couldn't help but hum the Madonna song with the same phrasing. But it was true…and I needed to act on that love or else I would never know what might have been. And that was a What If that I refused to live with.

Blythe, Blythe, just wait. I was so wrong to drive you away. Please be glad I'm coming for you, please don't think you're not worth it. My sweet man, you're so worth it, so worth everything.

Fifteen hours of driving was what we'd estimated. I would arrive in Missouri by early afternoon, and intended to be in Brandt, Oklahoma, Blythe's hometown, late tonight. By early evening, I was roughly fifty miles from the Oklahoma state line, and my nervous energy about put me over the edge. My entire pack of smokes was gone, my hands were on a slight tremble, and I made a sudden decision to stay the night in Wichita, Kansas. It was vanity more than anything that motivated it; I couldn't bear to confront Blythe reeking of cigarettes and with such deep shadows under my eyes. What's more, he didn't even know I was on the way.

In a small, tidy room at a hotel just off the interstate, I stood under a jet of just-shy-of-scalding water, bracing my hands on the shower tiles and letting the anxiety seep down the drain along with the travel dust. Afterward, I coated myself with peach-scented lotion, trying not to think about how much Blythe loved the scent on my skin, then snuggled into my robe and twisted my hair into a single clip on the back of my head. Slightly calmer now, I carried my cell phone to the small balcony outside my third-floor room and sank onto a plastic patio chair. The Kansas sky shone clear and wide and yellow-tinted with the first hints of sunset as I called Shore Leave. Gran answered after three rings with her unmistakable "*Hel*-lo," lots of accent on the first syllable. It was more of a demand than a greeting and I said, "Hey there," and drew a deep breath.

"Joelle, where are you?" she asked immediately. It was Sunday, so the cafe would be relatively quiet. I imagined Gran leaning over the front counter with its toothpick dispenser and ancient till that chimed a cheerful bell with every sale.

"Wichita," I said. "I decided to stop for the night. I'm exhausted."

"Rich called today and talked to Joanie for an hour or so," Gran informed; she sounded a bit like she was tattling. "She told him you were on the way."

Of course Mom did, I should have known, but my heart still clattered at this news. I whispered, "What did he say?"

"He wasn't surprised. He promised not to tell Blythe until you were already there."

My heart ached at how close I was to him, to Blythe. Only a few days since I'd seen him…but it felt immeasurably longer. And we'd parted with such uncertainty. I finally said, "I'm glad Rich understands. And I'm so nervous to meet Christy."

"Aw, she's a sweet girl, and understanding," Gran reassured. "And it's not as though you forced her boy into something unwilling." She squawked a laugh. "Ain't that right?"

My face flooded with heat. I said, "Gran, come on."

"Here's Camille," Gran said then, and a second later my oldest's voice came over the line. It always startled me to hear my children's voices on the phone; they sounded too grown-up.

"Hi, sweetie," I said. "How are you feeling today?"

"Ugh, not great," Camille responded. Away from the phone she added, "Thanks, Gran," and then I heard her taking a long sip of something. "Soda," she explained. "Why don't they tell you that morning sickness has nothing to do with mornings? It's all day, Mom, seriously."

I laughed. "I remember. But it goes away from one night to the next and then you'll just be starving."

"When is that?"

"I'd say for you, in about three or four weeks. Try some of those oyster crackers Gran has in the cupboard."

"I did," she said, sounding pitiful. "No help. Clint and Tish just drove the golf cart into town to get me some strawberry yogurt. It's the only thing that has sounded remotely good today. At least there hasn't been the fried fish smell all day."

"Oh, Milla," I empathized. "I was just like that, too. But I promise you'll feel better in a few weeks."

"I hope so," she muttered. And then, "Here's Ruthie. Love you, Mom."

I blew her a kiss and my youngest chirped, "Hi, Mom!"

"Hi, love," I responded. "Did you have a fun day? What's Aunt Jilly doing?"

"She's out with Justin," Ruthie told me. "They took out the paddle boat after Justin got done with work."

She chatted about the rest of her day, and before she hung up I requested, "Honey, have Aunt Jilly call me later, all right? And say 'hi' to Tish and everybody."

"K, Mom," she said. "Talk to you later."

"I love you," I told her. "Good-night." And then I leaned and tossed the phone back into the room; it bounced off the bed and landed on the floor, but I didn't have the energy to retrieve it.

The sky became streaked with mackerel clouds in shades of lavender and violet. I inhaled deeply; someone was using a charcoal grill in the vicinity and it smelled fantastic. I realized I hadn't eaten since mid-morning and was debating whether to order a pizza or go in search of an actual grocery store when my cell phone buzzed from inside the room, signaling an incoming call. *Dammit.* I figured it must be Mom, or maybe even Jilly, but when I picked it up from the floor the name on the display read *Blythe*.

Hot, frantic blood swamped my veins. I made a sound in my throat that was part longing, part fear. In the end I debated a second too long and it went to voicemail. With shaking fingers I pushed the redial button, imagining my heart as the dynamite at the end of one of those long detonator cords. But in this case, the flame was racing at the target, not inching.

And then his voice was in my ear, so warm and immediate and intense. "Joelle," he said. "Joelle. Oh, baby, where are you?"

"Blythe," I breathed, sinking to sit on the bed. My heart thumped so intently it almost drowned him out.

"Gramps told me you're on the way here. Joelle, where are you? Are you close?" He sounded agitated, as though he might be pacing.

"Blythe," I said again, my throat raspy with emotion. "Are you all right? I've been so worried."

"Aw, sweetheart," he said, low, his throat likewise rough. "Don't worry about me. You have enough to worry about."

"I'm in Wichita," I told him, and longing for him swelled through my body, now that I'd heard his voice.

He exhaled in a rush. "You're only two and a half hours away. I would come to you but I can't leave the state. Can you come here tonight?"

"Yes," I whispered. "Yes, I'll come."

"Rich and I are at the Arrowhead Motel, just outside of Brandt. It's a straight shot, and you'll see the motel from the interstate. Is Mom expecting you tonight?"

"She was," I said. "Will it be too late once I get there?" I was already up and throwing things back into my bag.

"No, no, not at all," he said. "Call me if you can't find it."

"I will," I said. "I'll be there soon." And I hesitated for a split second, desire and hope and so many other things rioting inside me.

"Hurry," he said then. His tone sent trailers of heat spiraling down low into my belly. "Please hurry. But drive safe."

"I will," I said again. And then I hung up and tornadoed through the room, grabbing my shampoo and make-up bag from the bathroom, brushing my teeth, shaking out my hair and running my fingers through its length, stumbling in my haste to get dressed. Jeans, tank top, sandals…I barely remembered to check out before I was jogging to the car. The girl at the front desk was kind enough not to charge me for the night.

The sky was huge and glinting with the first couple of stars as I slid behind the wheel, reenergized. He wasn't angry, he hadn't told me to go home to Minnesota and forget about him. So much for Rich keeping my secret. But I didn't care. In less than a few hours Blythe would be in my arms. I ached with the need to hold him, to cup his face and kiss him like he'd just returned from battle. I flew south as a moon waxing to full beamed down like an ivory smile.

I let the radio seek until it found a local station, and a country song came crooning into the car, reminding me of the nights that Blythe and I would dance to the radio in his truck, out at the old state park campsite. I curled my hands around the steering wheel and kept it on that station, volume low, nerves jittering as I crossed from Kansas into Oklahoma. I reflected that I'd never been farther south than southern Illinois. The sky grew spangled with stars and I passed only a few other cars on the road on this August evening. The western rim of the horizon, visible out my passenger-side window, still held a streak of orange, but it melted into darkness by the time I'd navigated past Oklahoma City. Within a quarter-hour, I saw the first green road sign announcing *Brandt, 37 miles.*

My phone vibrated again, from the central cup holder where I'd stashed it, and I saw that Jillian was calling this time, but I ignored it, too keyed up to talk. She left a no doubt lengthy voicemail, and I promised myself I would call her tonight. I needed to hear her voice and she would be angry if I didn't call. The road flashed away beneath the tires, my heart rate increasing with each passing mile. Twenty-four, then eleven, then three…and then I saw it off the interstate, just as Blythe said. A neon-pink sign advertising the Arrowhead Motel, complete with a flashing arrow that quite literally pointed the direction to its parking lot.

I signaled for the right turn, slowing and at last braking completely at the stop sign. The Arrowhead Motel was the only building on the appreciable horizon, a low-slung structure that housed maybe three dozen rooms. I turned left and drove a few hundred yards before making the final turn into the parking lot. There were outside lights on, and vehicles parked at intervals all around the motel, including Blythe's old black truck.

I was here, for better or worse, and put the car into park.

Chapter Four

Brandt, Oklahoma - August, 2003

Blythe's truck was so familiar to me that merely the sight of it induced a response throughout my body; so many hours he and I spent there, falling in love. My next breath lodged behind my breastbone as I sat there, clutching the steering wheel, dying to run to that motel—Blythe was there, just beyond one of the closed doors. And then, as though my thoughts conjured him, the door to room 17 crashed wide and there he was, striding across the parking lot, his eyes fixed on my car. I don't remember opening the car door. It seemed later that I simply flew into his arms. He ran to meet me and I clung, my arms tight around his neck as he lifted me up and close, my legs bent parallel to the ground as we clung. Blythe buried his face against my neck, his breathing ragged. I gripped his skull and stroked his hair, tears flooding over my cheeks and getting him wet as he covered my face with kisses, each word stroking my skin like a touch as he said, "You're here, oh, Joelle, you're here. Oh God, come here."

"I'm here," I said, half-weeping, cupping his face to better study it. He brought his forehead to mine, his eyes with an expression of certainty and pain. "I had to come, I had to see you."

"But you shouldn't have, baby," he whispered, sliding his hands gently over my shoulders, coming to rest around my waist. "You shouldn't have to go through this. I don't want this stress for you."

At that moment I noticed Rich hurrying our way from the direction of the same motel room. Blythe clutched extra hard before releasing me; together we turned to face Rich, and I reached to hug him.

"Joelle, honey," Rich said, gathering me close. I breathed against his shoulder, clad in a worn flannel shirt, imbibing the scent of tobacco and his perennial aftershave; Rich was as much a father to me as anyone I'd ever known, and I allowed his familiarity to comfort me. He patted my back twice before drawing away, and as he did Blythe moved near again and wrapped an arm securely around my waist. I couldn't bear to stop touching him either, and snuggled into his side, pressing my face to the scent of him. He kissed the top of my head.

"Mom said you'd talked," Blythe said, nuzzling my hair. "C'mon, come inside, sweetheart."

"Jo, Bly, I'm going to have a smoke," Rich said as we made our way along the sidewalk. "I'll be in after a few."

"All right, Gramps," Blythe said over his shoulder, then let me pass in front of him and carefully closed the door behind us. The moment we were alone I turned to face him, heart thumping painfully, heat and tension racing through my blood with equal fervor. I looked up at the man I loved. He studied my eyes, his so intense that I could hardly breathe. He moved so suddenly I gasped. I was in his arms and against his huge chest, my legs around his waist, before I even knew he'd lifted me. I wrapped my arms around his shoulders, unable to get close enough to satisfy my need for him.

"Joelle, Joelle," he groaned against my mouth before claiming it, one big hand cupping my head, tipping it into his hungry kisses. I curled my fingers into his loose hair. He tasted sweet and salty, as though my tears were caught between our mouths. Blythe pressed soft kisses along my neck, my jaw, coming to rest with his lips against my left temple. With a graceful movement he turned and seated us on the bed, keeping my legs woven around his waist. From six inches away I drank in the blueness of his dear, beautiful eyes, my hands resting on his wide shoulders.

"I'm so glad you're here, you have no idea," he whispered, smoothing hair from my cheek. He stroked his fingers all along the side of my face, tracing over my bottom lip. His voice low and hoarse, he admitted,

"When you left the jail that night, I thought there was a chance I might never see you again. The drive down here about killed me, thinking that."

"Oh, Blythe, sweetheart, I'm so sorry," I said. I'd thought the same thing, lying in bed that night.

"But you're here," he said, with wonder in his tone. "I've been pacing like a caged animal since we talked, you should have seen me. I still can't believe you're here." He caressed my neck, his fingers trailing in my hair, which hung loose over my back. With gentle motions, he combed through it. "You're so soft. God, I've missed seeing you, making love with you at night. All I could think about this week was the last time we'd been together back in Landon."

"I've missed you, too, and I'm so glad you're happy I'm here. I was afraid you would send me away," I whispered, tears in my eyes again. He thumbed them away as they streaked over my face, and I continued, determined, "I got up in the middle of the night and knew I needed to come after you. I love you and I want you to come back to Landon with me, for good."

He closed his eyes and inhaled slowly through his nose. He whispered, "I wish I could, I so wish I could."

"You can," I insisted. "Remember how you said you knew I belonged there? You were right, and you belong there, too."

The sound of Rich's footfalls drifted through the window near the bed, propped open to the night air. I moved, with great reluctance, to sit in a less intimate position beside Blythe on the bed, keeping a decent distance between us. He sent me a look that said our conversation was nowhere near done, and Rich tapped lightly on the door before entering the room, surveying us with concern in his eyes.

"Joelle, I'm glad you made it here safe, honey," Rich said as he took a seat on the single chair near the window. I shifted position to slip off my sandals and then sat cross-legged on the mattress, folding my hands together like an obedient elementary school student. Blythe reached over and curled one big hand around both of mine, and I entwined my fingers through his from either side, returning the gentle pressure.

"What's happened since Friday?" I asked, directing my question at Rich.

Rich exhaled an elongated breath through pursed lips, an age-old habit and one I recognized from my childhood. He plucked at the slim pack of cigarettes in his shirt pocket, almost unconsciously, before his right hand roamed back to join the left and he began twirling his thumbs around one another, another familiar gesture. At last he said, "Well, we got in Saturday afternoon. I rode down with Bly, but I'll fly home when it's time. We spent last night at Christy's but there just ain't any room there, which is why we're here now. Christy seems to think that the charges will blow over."

"I talked to Dale yesterday," Blythe said quietly, squeezing my fingers again, as though he needed reassurance. "He's my parole officer. He says we can probably get before a judge by Tuesday or Wednesday. He told me to lay low until then."

"Jackie won't be pressing any charges," Rich said, and I looked his way in surprise.

"Did you talk to him?" I asked.

Rich shook his head and then clarified, "No, but Jillian and your mom did, just this afternoon. He was out to Shore Leave to see the girls. It sounds like he's sorry for how he acted the past few days. He said to tell you he's sorry about last night."

I nearly gritted my teeth, wishing that Rich had the foresight to deliver this news without Blythe hearing. It wasn't that I wanted to keep any secrets, but I'd already put Jackie's obnoxious behavior behind me; his alleged apology meant next to nothing now.

Altogether I was glad Jackie was over a thousand miles away as Blythe's eyebrows drew slightly together and he asked, "What?"

I sighed a little and said, "He showed up drunk at the cafe and was acting like a jerk again."

Blythe grasped my hands a little more tightly but his tone was calm as he said, "I'm sorry I wasn't there."

"It's all right," I assured him. "We needed to talk about the girls anyway. He told them they could come to live with him and Lanny in Chicago, but they don't want to. And it was an empty promise anyway. I know they couldn't handle three teenagers, plus a new baby."

Blythe's expression softened as he asked, "How are the kids doing? I miss them, and Clint. I miss the whole place. It was so hard to walk away. God, I was dying."

"They miss you, too," I said, my eyes absolutely devouring him. I loved Rich dearly, but holy hell did I wish he had his own motel room. I clung to Blythe's hand and tried to redirect my thoughts.

"They don't think I'm an asshole for punching out their dad? God, Joelle, when he flung you against the wall I was ready to kill him."

"Now, Bly," Rich interrupted.

I said, "No, no, I know you were just angry. And protecting me. But honestly, Jackie was just caught off guard because I slapped him. He wouldn't ever hurt me. I mean, not physically, not on purpose." I was babbling, the strain of the past few days shredding my control. I closed my eyes and inhaled slowly, collecting myself. When I opened them again, Blythe was looking at me with such love, such concern, that it took all of my willpower not to leap into his arms and take him backward upon the bed.

I refocused, not without effort, and then quietly asked Rich, "So what next?"

Rich settled his ankle on the opposite knee and considered. At last he said, "I think it will be all right, sweetie, I do."

I didn't get the feeling that he was trying to pacify me, but he was definitely worried, more worried than he was letting me see. I wondered if Blythe knew him well enough to notice it, too. Shit, and now a small moth of fear beat its wings inside my stomach, growing larger with each second. Blythe sensed my sudden agitation, because he moved with his easy grace, shifting so that he sat behind me, his long legs on either side of my folded ones, his strong arms around my waist, his chin against my right temple. His huge chest bracketed my entire body, and it felt so good that I shuddered with pleasure, all at once enfolded by his warm safety and strength.

"It'll be okay, Joelle," he said low, squeezing me for emphasis. I clutched his forearms, letting him offer me this reassurance. We were together, and that was all that mattered in this moment.

"I know," I whispered. "I know, sweetheart."

Rich's phone rang. He extracted it from his pocket and informed, "It's Christy," before answering.

While Rich was occupied chatting, Blythe murmured in my ear, "I'm so happy to have you in my arms. Nothing in the world could feel better."

I turned my face a fraction, so that my nose rested against his chin, curling my fingers over his forearms, possessive and urgent.

Rich hung up and said, "Your mom needs a ride home. Her car isn't starting."

"I told her yesterday she needed a new battery," Blythe said with affectionate irritation. He kissed my temple and decided, "We'll go get her and then she can meet you, love."

"Where is she?" I asked, reluctant not only to move out of his arms, but because I was terrified to meet Christy Tilson, despite everything.

"Her job," Blythe explained, bending down to collect my shoes. He set them side by side on the floor and then teasingly caught my bare feet in his hands. Kneeling, he studied my expression of unease and teased, "You coming?"

I rolled my eyes, bracing one hand on his shoulder as I slipped into my sandals. "Wild horses couldn't stop me."

Minutes later we rolled along under the starry sky, back onto the interstate for a mile or so, and then Blythe took the exit into Brandt. I clutched his free hand in my left, lifting it to press my lips to his knuckles, each one individually.

He angled a grin my way. "I love having you back in the truck with me. It's so empty in here without you, baby. Nothing was right without you."

"I love being here," I replied, folding his captive hand between my breasts, thrilling to his sincere words. "I have so many amazing memories of this exact bench seat."

"Come here," he ordered, his voice low and sweet as he hauled me against his side and wrapped his right arm about my waist. He kissed my hair again, murmuring, "You smell so good, just like a peach. God, I want to bite into you."

I smiled against the side of his neck. But I couldn't allow myself to melt away just yet, not when our next stop was to pick up his mother from the bowling alley where she worked evenings. I bit his earlobe lightly, with a promise for later, before sliding back to my side of the seat and taking a moment to observe his hometown through my open window.

"It's just like Landon," I murmured, and it was; one stoplight guarding what was certainly the busiest intersection, in this case the juncture of Main and First Streets. The downtown buildings were constructed of brick, square and with flat roofs, reminiscent of a town built long ago. Most were closed for the night, although down a side street a number of bars advertised their unmistakable presence with the welcoming glint of beer lights; cars were crowded nearby like ants at spilled sugar.

"Except without the lake nearby," Blythe said. "I got so used to Flickertail that it seems like it should be just there, at the end of the road."

The streetlights appeared old-fashioned, stands shaped like hourglasses with round lamps perched atop, glowing amber. Every dozen feet or so, all along the sidewalks, whiskey barrels spilled over with petunias. Benches waited patiently under awnings in front of nearly every business; when we passed a small appliance shop, closed for the night despite the fact that its OPEN sign glowed in the front window, Blythe smiled and commented, "Looks like Rusty forgot to click out the light again. His dad'll have his hide."

"Your accent is adorable," I teased him. And it was; it must have been his home territory that kicked up the hint of a southern twang that always lingered just beneath the surface of his words. Blythe snorted at my observation.

"Why, thank ya, darlin' girl," he responded, with extreme exaggeration. "Might I observe just how all-fired gorgeous y'all look this evenin'?"

"You may," I told him.

"An' might I dare ta hope, darlin', that later you might be willin' to… well, a gentleman don't like to be so blunt…" I laughed, feeling the warmth of it spread all through my body. Despite the late hour and my worry over everything, I laughed so hard that it overtook Blythe, too. When I dared to look his way he winked with such a devious expression that I was lost again, swept away on waves of mirth until my belly ached.

"Are you satisfied now?" he teased, when my laughter reduced itself to periodic giggles. He reached and cupped his right hand around my left leg, just above the knee, where he knew I was ticklish as hell. "Or do I have to keep up with the 'adorable' accent?"

"No, please," I gasped as he squeezed lightly on my leg, sending another fit of laughter over me. "Please, don't!"

"Now, I don't like ta make a lady beg," he began again, sounding like an over-the-top Rhett Butler. "But in this case…"

I laughed until I could scarcely breathe; he was merciless. He was also laughing hard enough that we were probably in danger of driving off the road. I was trapped in the car with his relentless tickling, my protests totally ineffectual, my hands rendered weak and helpless by that strange phenomenon that comes from being tickled. At last he parked and bent over the steering wheel, shoulders shaking as he hooted at my expense. But at least he'd stopped with the torture. I caught my breath and then poked at his torso, which was like iron beneath my fingers.

"See how you like it, you bully," I said.

"Joelle," he gasped out through his laughter. "I'm not…ticklish."

"You are!" I insisted, using both hands now, and he moved swiftly and caught me close, pinning my arms to my sides and then taking my earlobe gently between his teeth. A tremor ran through me and I was breathless from far more than laughter as I insisted, "You are."

He rubbed his jaw, prickly with a day's growth of stubble, against the side of my neck and I shivered again, as though feverish. He moved with deliberate slowness to nip my other ear, my chin, and finally my lower lip. I trembled in his grasp, ablaze with desire. He kissed my mouth with infinite gentleness before drawing away and whispering, his voice ripe with teasing, "You'll have to wait until later for more, sweet girl."

My eyes flew open, indignantly. But then I realized we were parked in front of Bob's Bowl, the place where Christy worked. I moved immediately to my side of the truck, straightening my hair, nervous as hell now that we'd arrived. And I couldn't help but nag, "You're *such* a bully."

We climbed out into the warmth of an August night; I felt a sudden rush of disorientation as I leaned against the truck door and studied the stars. I left Landon at dawn and was now over a thousand miles away, but as Blythe rounded the hood and took my hand, the feeling washed instantly away. He curled together our fingers and led the way. I would bring him back to Landon with me, no matter what it took; I glanced up at the waxing moon and vowed it, right then.

The inside of Bob's boomed with country music and the clatter of bowling balls flying down the lanes. The crowd was rowdy; the bar side of the building was dimly lit, complete with a neon sign reading 'Striker's Lounge' visible through a haze of cigarette smoke, while the gaming side was brilliantly awash in revolving lights. Bob's Bowl was obviously a hot spot in Brandt. We hadn't walked ten feet before an older man with impressive sideburns and a full beard came directly to us, clapped Blythe on the back and declared heartily, "Junior, good to see you!" He was heavyset and jovial, and reminded me a little of Dodge.

Blythe drew me against his side and said, "Hey, Bob, what do you know? This is my Joelle."

Bob adjusted his wide-framed glasses with one hand and reached to shake my hand with the other. He said, "Pleased to meet you, Miss Joelle. We've heard all about you."

I was mildly startled by this statement, but smiled back at him and said, "Good to meet you, too."

"Ain't you lovely," Bob observed, and winked at me before turning and calling, "Christy, your boy is here!"

My nerves jittered as a woman came from behind the bar, in the process of wiping her nose with a tissue. She caught sight of us and her face broke into a smile, a truly welcoming smile. I tried to return it but my lips were stiff; it took all my willpower not to fidget. Blythe seemed amused and squeezed my hand as Christy approached us. It had been a damn long time since I'd met anyone's mother in this context.

"Hey, Mom," he said easily. "Your battery is out, huh?"

She took another swipe at her nose and stopped before us, studying me with forthright curiosity. The first thing I noticed about Christy Tilson was that her eyes were exactly like Blythe's, beautiful, long-lashed, and the color of faded denim, a warm combination of blue and gray. She was petite, at least six inches shorter than me, slim and fine-boned; her reddish-blond hair probably accounted for half of her overall weight. It hadn't changed appreciably since the 1980s, I would have bet money, with corkscrew curls, thick bangs, and a lot of aerosol spray holding it all in place. Her face was darkly tanned and delicately constructed; I realized at once that it did indeed register in my memory. She wore jeans, a black server apron and a black t-shirt with *Bob's Bowl* scrawled across it in neon green.

"Hi guys," she said, and her voice was low and mellow; it suited her. She went on, her accent far more pronounced than Blythe's, "And Junior, I know you-all told me about that damn battery, but I didn't have time today. You can switch it out tomorrow."

Everyone here called him Junior; so where the hell was Blythe, Senior?

"I will," he promised. And then, with bashful pride, "Mom, this is Joelle Gordon."

"I figured," Christy said, smiling again. "And I do remember meeting you years ago, Joelle, when I visited Rich and Mom in Minnesota. It's good to see you."

"Hi," I responded. "I remember you, too. And thank you."

"God, you must be exhausted," she said, abruptly moving into action. "Let's get you home for the evening. I don't live far." And so saying, she retrieved her purse from behind the bar, called good-bye to a handful of regulars, and then shepherded us back out into the night.

Blythe opened the passenger door for us, and I insisted on taking the rear seat, allowing his mother the front. We drove through town and then about a mile into the darkness, before Blythe turned left into a trailer court whose gravel road curved through an opening in a tall, wrought-iron fence. The sprawling place appeared cozy in the darkness; most of the trailers shone with glimmering lights, whether from within, or solar-powered yard lanterns, or here and there strings of twinkly white lights framing window sills, reminiscent of Christmas. Blythe braked before a yellow double-wide and as I studied it from my seat in his truck, I realized this was where he had been raised; my heart beat harder just imagining him growing up here.

Not that my own childhood home was so fancy, or spacious, and I was certainly no snob. But still. It hurt a little to think that all of his youthful memories were centered around a place called Gatehouse Court, where the yards seemed to consist of slim borders of scraggly grass that stretched the length of three steps to meet the gravel road which curved through the entire place, where you could probably hear every fight and smell every joint being smoked by neighbors whose homes were roughly five feet from your own.

I climbed down after Christy, noticing how she made the place homey. Tiny lanterns glowed in candy colors from the awning over the front entrance. On either side of the cement steps rising to the little porch, huge terra cotta pots overflowed with bougainvillea in brilliant magenta. There was a woven green welcome mat and two cats who met us as Christy unlocked the door and clicked on a lamp with a torn shade; its golden spill illuminated a space that was minuscule and tidy. We entered into the front room; the kitchen was just around the corner to the right, while a short hallway to the left no doubt led to bedrooms.

A television set with a bowtie antenna perched on a kitchen table covered by a fringed yellow tablecloth, sharing the space with a stack of mail and a trailing ivy vine in a squat, indigo-blue pot. The floor beneath our feet was carpeted in an atrocious brown-and-orange fleck, and there were framed pictures everywhere; I curbed the urge to go and look at every one of them. As Blythe entered behind me, the space seemed instantly smaller. I could not imagine my 6'4" lover inhabiting this place. He ducked his head to get in the door.

His hand was warm on the small of my back, and I wanted to curl up with him in his old full bed, which we'd laughed about back in Landon, and was no doubt far too tiny for the both of us, but I didn't care. He would curve around so that I fit against his chest and wrap his arm and one leg over me, and I wanted it so much that I could hardly tear my gaze from him. My limbs felt heavy and my nerves on edge; I knew he must leave, return to Rich at the Arrowhead Motel rather than spend the night here, and the thought made tears prickle behind my eyelids.

Pull it together, I scolded myself. *Dammit, Joelle.*

Christy bustled down the hall, away from us, calling over her shoulder, "Joelle, have Junior put your things in his old room. I'll be right back."

But the moment her bedroom door clicked shut Blythe enfolded me in his embrace and held tight, resting his chin on the top of my head and letting me cling to him. He smelled so good, indefinably himself, and he understood that I needed holding right now, more than anything.

"It'll be all right," he whispered, putting his warm lips to my ear. He brushed hair from my neck and kissed me lightly, and I quivered. "Don't worry, baby. I can tell you're worried."

I rubbed my hands over his ribcage, which was so tough and solid beneath my palms. I lifted my chin and he kissed my lips, again with gentleness and yet so much repressed passion that I trembled in his arms, and felt him grin against my mouth. I needed him so much, in every way.

"Blythe," I murmured, clutching fistfuls of his t-shirt now; knowing that his mother could come back around the corner at any second was the only thing that kept me from ripping it from his chest.

He kissed me again, this time much more deeply, cupping the back of my head with one hand to tip it where he wanted. The soft sound of a bedroom door being opened in a different part of the trailer was the only thing that brought me to my senses; when I pulled back, shaken and weak-kneed, his eyes were dark and hooded with desire. But he grinned again, letting me step back, and whispered, "Soon."

I turned just as Christy came into the living room, clad in a pink sweat suit, rubbing lotion into her hands. If she suspected we'd been making out like teenagers, she hid it well as she breezed through to the kitchen asking, "Joelle, would you like a drink?"

"Go, relax a bit," Blythe said, rubbing my back again with a gentle hand; he was so fond of doing that, and it calmed the fire in my stomach. "I'll grab your stuff, sweetheart."

"Thanks," I told him, standing on my extreme tiptoes to plant a quick kiss on his lips. Fortunately I'd thought to retrieve my bag before we left the Arrowhead parking lot.

Moments later I sat at the table with the fringed cloth, uncertain, though Christy was friendly as she hustled around the space, clinking ice into tumblers and pouring us each a rum and cola. She topped these with lime wedges and slid one in front of me as Blythe appeared in the archway and leaned one shoulder on the wall. A smile lifted the right side of his incredible lips.

"Junior, we'll be just fine," his mother insisted, curling one leg under herself as she took her seat.

"I know," he said, his deep voice soft. "I'll be back bright and early."

"See you in the morning," I told him, keeping my voice as neutral as possible; his smile widened ever so slightly, and he came fully into the kitchen and reached to take a strand of my loose hair between his fingers. He rubbed it gently, like some men might rub silk or even gold.

"'Night," he murmured, and then Christy rose and gave him a quick squeeze. I watched him go, my insides humming with equal parts yearning and tenderness. The truth was he understood something that Jackie never fully had.

That something was me.

Chapter Five

After his truck fired to life and drove away, I faced Christy at the table. She regarded me with a disconcerting frankness, spinning her drink in slow circles between her palms. Now that I'd commandeered her attention, I floundered. She didn't strike me as a judgmental person, but still; I was closer to her own age than her son's, and the thought made me squirm, though outwardly I sipped my drink with moderate composure and made small talk with her for a few minutes.

Finally she said, "I remember what fun you and your sister had that summer I stayed with Mom and Rich." She lifted her drink for a long swallow, before continuing, "What a pretty place, the restaurant on the lake. I loved it. I think I spent half the summer lying on that beach."

"It is great," I agreed. "I love it there, too."

"I was so happy that Junior got hired up there, and a chance to move away from this place. Rich looks out for him so much, and he's not even his real grandpa. But that's why Mom loved him." She paused for another sip, and then said, "My son is a good boy. He's always worried about me first, even when I didn't deserve it. Too damn bad his dad wasn't the same way."

"Where is Blythe's dad?" I asked, but she needed little prompting, launching into the story with a sense of unburdening herself.

"Junior is named for him, you know. Blythe and me met in high school, but we didn't date until a few years later. We were together for about a year, while I worked at the bowling alley and he was in the National Guard. We never got married, but after I got pregnant I thought we finally would. I found out at Halloween. I remember calling Mom to tell her and she was making pumpkin pie. God, she was so mad at me. I figured Blythe would be so excited…" Her voice trailed off, her slim shoulders sagging a little.

I knew exactly how she felt. The same expectant hope coursed through me when I'd been pregnant the first time. I wanted to touch her hand but held back, instead lacing my fingers together and listening as she continued her story. "But he wasn't thrilled. I should have known. He left right after I told him, and I was almost eight months along by the time I saw him again. It was in the spring, and he seemed to have made up his mind that we'd make a go of it, and so we moved in together into this place. That was April, 1980. Junior was born a couple weeks later, on May tenth. Blythe always called him 'Junior,' and so does everyone else around here. Blythe tried at first, I think, but it was hard on him. He was working nights then, and he couldn't sleep with a baby crying all day…"

"I'm sorry," I said softly, and I was. I knew. I knew exactly.

"Would you like to see a few pictures?" she asked, as though reading my earlier thought, and I nodded eagerly.

She produced a couple of old leather albums and I opened the first to see Christy as a much younger version of herself, grinning and cradling a newborn. My heart lurched; that was my Blythe, of course, and the next snapshot was of Christy and the man who was clearly Blythe, Senior. He was tall, towering over Christy as they stood together in the sun over two decades ago, and good-looking, but in a scruffy, disreputable sort of way, with thick sideburns, a goatee, bushy dark hair and mirrored aviator sunglasses. He was smiling with a lot of teeth, and I found myself struggling to find a glimpse of my Blythe in him. Even if I hadn't heard the story Christy just told, I'd have guessed he was an asshole. I turned the page and there he was again, no shades this time, and I could see Blythe a little in his features, though his eyes were dark and he was less handsome than his son. Christy looked over my shoulder as I flipped the pages, gesturing with her glass as she made observations.

"Junior's dad left us before he even went to kindergarten. Mom and Rich wanted me to move to Minnesota so Mom could help take care of him, but I never could get enough courage to leave our hometown. I figured I didn't know anybody up there, and what would I do, live with Mom and Rich? But sometimes I wish I would have gone."

My heart melted to see Blythe as a little boy, adorable and chubby-cheeked, obviously well loved by his mother, despite their clear poverty and the lack of a father. I allowed myself to acknowledge that Blythe looked exactly as I'd pictured our imaginary little boy. Christy recounted making him Halloween costumes, and going to Christmas concerts, and visiting Landon in the summer of 1985, the last time she'd been north.

My heart stuttered again, imagining that…that was the same summer I married Jackie. God, that was weird as hell. I'd just graduated from high school in 1985, embarking on a hopeful new life; Jackie and I would have left Landon for Chicago just as Christy and Blythe arrived for their summer visit that year.

I sipped my drink and closed my eyes, again feeling the sense of disorientation. When I opened them, Christy sat in silence, studying me. No time like the present. I grabbed the bull by the horns and said, "I love Blythe. I love him with all my heart."

Her gaze shifted away and she pressed her lips together and rubbed them in the fashion of someone who has just applied lipstick. My heart wrenched, waiting, but then she fixed her eyes on mine, pretty blue-gray eyes so much like her son's, and said, "I know. He loves you, too. I've never seen him this way."

"You don't want to kill me?" I asked softly. "I have three daughters, you know, and if I thought for an instant—"

But she cut off that sentence by touching my left hand lightly with her fingertips, the brush of a bird's wing. Simultaneously she said, "No, of course not. When Junior is serious about something, I know it. He's a good man, and I get the sense that you're a good woman."

"But?" I prompted hesitantly.

She sighed. "But you and I both know it's not as easy as that. And he might have to go back to jail for a while. I don't know. Fuck, I hope not. He doesn't deserve it."

"What happened last spring?" I asked, relieved that she accepted the news so graciously.

Her face twisted and then her gaze shifted up and to the left as she stared into the past. Finally she said, "I was dating a guy I met at work, back then. Junior didn't like him, but I couldn't understand why until the night this guy slapped me for the first time. I didn't say anything because I knew Junior would be mad. He's always had a bad temper…that's what got him into jail in the first place, for taking Tony's car that day. Tony was his boss at the time, they worked construction together. Has he told you much about it?"

I nodded, though *not really* would have been a more accurate answer.

"Well, it was all tangled up. Blythe is not a criminal, and I'm not saying that because he's my son. He's just not one. Believe me, I've dated real criminals, so I know the difference." She laughed briefly, then nodded at my glass and asked, "Do you need another?"

"Sure," I said automatically, and she flitted around the kitchen, fixing us a second round. The digital clock on the microwave read 12:54, but I couldn't think about bed yet. And I still needed to call Jilly tonight.

Christy resumed her story. "Well, Blythe was dating Tony's younger sister at that time, Julianne. She was a pretty girl, seemed nice enough, but I didn't like her. I couldn't explain it exactly, just a gut instinct."

I'd heard about his ex-girlfriend Cindy, but this name was new, and there was a sudden part of me that didn't want Christy to keep talking. But I kept my mouth shut.

"Tony and Blythe weren't best friends, but they got along pretty well until this one time Tony accused Blythe of taking his tools. He didn't do it, of course, and it turned out to be a misunderstanding, and Tony did apologize, but there was a rift after that. A distrust. Tony would come over for barbeque some nights that summer, when Blythe would be here with Julianne, and they all seemed to get along, but I could tell it was different. And then, what do you know, Julianne got pregnant."

I felt as though she'd slapped me. Or thrown scalding water across my face. There was a roaring in my ears and then all I could hear was

Blythe, back in the jail in Landon, saying, *But there are some things you don't know about me.*

"Oh shit, he hasn't told you that," Christy said, pulling me back to the current moment. Her voice and face were both stricken. "Shit, I didn't mean to spring that on you. *Shit.*"

"He has a child?" I asked faintly. I thought of my blind presumption, the way I sat there in Landon in his truck, telling him he didn't know what it meant to be a father. *Oh God, oh my God.* My heart felt stabbed.

Christy's face twisted again, but this time with something akin to pain. She said, "No, but it's because Julianne went and got an abortion. Didn't even tell Blythe she was going to do it."

I felt a slice of air return to my lungs. But then the weight of Christy's words, and what they meant, stamped down upon my heart. I reached and curled my right hand around her left, kitty-corner from me on the tabletop. I said quietly, "I'm so sorry. What a horrible thing to do."

Oh Blythe, Blythe. I ached for him at this news, but was human enough to also wonder why I hadn't heard about it from him. But he certainly must have his reasons. And I was flawed enough, in my own ways, to understand that.

Christy went on, "He would have raised his child, even if she didn't want it, but she took the decision out of his hands. Went to Oklahoma City and then called Blythe after, to tell him the news. He went crazy. And there was Tony, her brother, freaking out because Julianne gave him this sob story that Blythe *made* her get an abortion, which was the furthest thing from the truth. They were at a job site, for Christ's sake, and Tony told Blythe he was fired and then punched him. They got into a fistfight and Blythe beat him pretty badly. And then he took Tony's car to go find Julianne. But he didn't make it because Tony called the police and they got him first."

A jagged lump formed in my throat as I examined the pieces of this story. It was far worse than Blythe alluded in the past few months. Now I finally understood why he didn't want to talk about it, why his hometown could never be the same, as he'd told me that night we took the canoes out for a midnight ride.

"Oh my God," I finally said, my throat dry in a way that could not be eased by my drink.

"He served three months of a nine-month sentence. And then was on parole for about a year. But nothing much happened until last spring when he came over here one night and Ron was drunk…shit, I was drunk, too…and Ron roughed me up, caught me by the hair. Blythe saw the tail end and he just reacted. He grabbed the lid off the charcoal grill and slammed Ron across the face." She covered her own face for a moment. From behind her palms she said, "It was awful. But in his way, Blythe was doing the right thing again, defending me."

"He would," I said, and it was true. He defended the people he loved. I wanted to run back out into the night and chase his truck, find him. My heart stung with the desperate need to find him.

"I managed to get Ron to drop any charges, the bastard," Christy went on, her hands back on the tabletop. Her mascara was smudged and she suddenly looked more her age. "But now that doesn't seem to matter, because of the parole violation. This is my fault and I'm so sorry, Joelle. I want my son to be happy more than anything, I can tell you that with all my heart."

I made a small sound, touched by her words. But at the moment I couldn't bring forth my own, the question I was dying to ask lodged like a husk in my throat. At last I managed, "Where is…Julianne now?"

"California," Christy said. "Her mother lives out there, somewhere. She's never been back here that I know of, and I honestly don't know about Tony. I hope never to see that son of a bitch ever again. I'd take a frying pan to his head. The girl's, too. Don't get me wrong, I believe a woman should have control of her body, but to go and do such a thing, when the father wanted the baby. Would have cared for it. Hell, I would have raised it if I'd realized she didn't want it."

"Christy, I'm so sorry," I said again, feeling grossly inadequate, at a total loss. "But thanks for telling me all of this."

"Are you angry?" she asked softly. Her eyes were so much like her son's.

"No, God no," I told her, and this was true. "I just wish he would have told me all of this."

"He will. It's just so hard for him, it still hurts him so much. He blames himself." She sighed, deeply, before adding, "I need to hit the hay. Thanks for talking, Joelle. It makes me glad to see my son so happy. He's never been in love before, I want you to know that. But he's in love with you."

My heart glowed at her words, forcing out some of the bleakness wedged there by her story. I said softly, "I love him, too."

She patted my hand and minutes later showed me to my room… Blythe's old room, which would be mine for the night. I took a moment in the tiny bathroom between the two bedrooms, brushing my teeth and washing my face like usual, studying my eyes in the medicine cabinet mirror above the smooth round basin of the sink. The whole bathroom was tiled in a stone-washed blue, and all of the towels were rich cobalt, though frayed at the edges. Christy must be fond of the shade, as her living room furniture was likewise covered in navy-blue denim.

Oh God, Blythe, my sweet, sweet man. Did you stand here that first night after you'd gotten home from jail and wonder what in the hell happened? And you spent those terrible nights in a cell knowing your girlfriend aborted your child without telling you. God, the baby wouldn't even be a baby by now… he'd be close to two years old, tearing around, calling you 'Daddy.' Oh, Blythe…

How did one move beyond that knowledge? In a million years, I would never have guessed that Blythe harbored such a memory.

Later I curled beneath the covers in his old full-sized bed. The room was small; it was difficult imagining him sleeping in this space. I smiled slightly at the thought, bending my legs against the mattress, gazing up at the ceiling light above the bed as Blythe had probably done a thousand times in this exact spot. There was a narrow window that faced west; I could see the moon in its descent to the horizon and stacked my hands under my head to watch it, despite how tired I was after everything that had happened in the past few days.

Chapter Six

THE NEXT THING I KNEW IT WAS MORNING, AND BLYTHE'S voice was coming from the kitchen. I rolled to one elbow and knuckled my eyes. The room was dim in the dawn light, but the uncovered window allowed me to see the pale sky with its promise of a sunny day. Blythe was saying, "Don't make breakfast, Mom, we'll go out," and Christy responded in a murmur too low for me to catch. A second later there was a tap on the bedroom door, and my heart turned a cartwheel; before I could speak Christy said, this time audibly, "Junior, don't you dare, Joelle is sound asleep. She and I sat up talking until the coyotes came out."

He laughed, just outside the door, and as much as I longed to call out to him, push back the covers and pull him into bed with me, I knew in a million years I couldn't do that. At least, not at the moment. Then Rich's voice joined the group, and I knew I better get my ass up and moving. I found my brush by leaning over and rooting through my bag, then grabbed my robe from the floor, snaking my arms into it before daring to emerge further, mostly because the window was uncovered. There was a small mirror on the wall above a chest of drawers, and I brushed through my hair; it was the consistency of cornsilk here in the dry air of Oklahoma, nothing like the humidity of the lake country back home. I debated wearing my robe to the bathroom, but felt too exposed, and in the end dressed in my clothes from last night, minus underwear, toting my overnight bag as I left the bedroom. I would shower and then change into something clean.

Everyone was gathered in the kitchen, talking, and I felt absurdly shy as three heads turned my way at the sound of the bedroom door opening. Blythe grinned and came over at once, and my shyness dissipated instantly, becoming gladness as he cradled me in a hug and whispered, "Morning, baby," against my left temple.

"Morning," I returned sleepily, as he drew back and used both hands to smooth my hair. I looked hard into his eyes, the memory of my conversation with Christy foremost in my thoughts, but I knew I needed to wait for him to tell me on his own. Or, at the very least, I needed to refrain from mentioning anything until we could be alone.

"You sleep okay?" he asked, his eyes all over me since his hands could not be just now.

From the kitchen Christy called, her voice full of teasing, "Bly, let her have some space. Jeez, son."

He wore faded jeans and a red t-shirt that advertised what was undoubtedly a local restaurant, a place called Brandt's Behemoth Burgers, his hair tied back in its usual fashion. He looked incredible. He said, "According to Gramps, this has to go today," motioning to his ponytail.

"What? Why?" I asked.

From behind Blythe, Rich responded, "He needs to look more clean-cut. Joan suggested it when we talked this morning." Leave it to my mother to horn her way into something over a thousand miles from her current location. I reached, again a little shy with both Rich and Christy looking on, and gathered Blythe's long, dark-blond hair into my right hand, twisting my fingers around a strand.

"You won't mind?" he asked, the right side of his lips lifting into a half-apologetic grin.

"No…well, maybe a little," I amended. "I do love your hair."

"Bly, it's a good idea," Rich said. "And it'll grow back."

Blythe winked at me and planted a quick kiss flush on my lips. "Hurry and get ready, and we'll go get breakfast."

Thirty minutes later we were seated at a diner in downtown Brandt; it was just like Landon was for me, in that everyone who tinkled the bell coming into the place knew Christy and Blythe and stopped to make small talk. Rich sat across from me and while Blythe and Christy chatted with a pair of elderly women, I leaned forward, my menu bent at an angle against the table.

"What else has Mom said?" I asked him, and the skin around Rich's kind brown eyes crinkled into a web of wrinkles as he smiled at me, knowing exactly what I meant.

"Honey, she's just worried for you. And your sister is angry that you haven't talked to her yet. But you'll hear all about that soon enough." He winked at me before lowering his gaze to regard his own menu, murmuring, "I'm missing Shore Leave and Ellen's breakfast right about now."

I felt a flash of homesickness as he spoke, but at that moment Blythe rubbed his hand along my spine, gently and almost absently as he continued his conversation with Christy and the grandmotherly women who stood by our table. His hand was warm, and singularly comforting, and I realized in the same instant that my idea of home had been altered. My daughters would always be mine, but they were growing up and would make their way into the world before I knew it. Here with Blythe was my home, so to speak, and I tipped my head against his shoulder for the length of two heartbeats.

Rich drove Christy home after breakfast, while I remained downtown with Blythe. First on our agenda was his haircut, which Christy arranged over the phone.

"I used to work with her at Bob's," Christy told Blythe while we were still eating breakfast. "You remember Maggie, right?"

Blythe nodded, his mouth full of toast.

"She'll do a good job," Christy reassured.

And so after breakfast, Blythe was seated in a swivel chair in a small, sunny salon. An old Faith Hill song played on a radio at the front desk, the radio sharing the space with a tall, clear-glass vase jammed with sunflowers. I stopped to admire them before settling onto a polka-dotted wing chair in the waiting area.

"You want it all gone?" Maggie asked, her tone incredulous as she held Blythe's ponytail with one hand, a pair of skinny, hot-pink scissors poised in the other.

Blythe, his long legs crossed at the ankle, arms braced on the edges of the chair, winced slightly. But he affirmed, gamely enough, "All of it, Maggie. Military short."

The vinyl wrap that covered him from neck to hips crackled as he shifted again, angling a glance my way and shaking his head. The expression in his eyes was one of defeat. I blew him a kiss.

"But Junior, you have such great hair," Maggie lamented, flipping his long ponytail this way and that. Her hair was wispy and feathered, highlighted with alternating tones of red from ruby to rust. She caught me in her gaze and added, "Don't you think it's a shame to chop it all off?"

"I do love his hair," I told her, and Blythe grinned at me, his slow, steamy grin that made my knees weak. If I hadn't been sitting, I would have faltered a little. I smiled back at him, primly, and asked, "Can I touch it one more time?"

I was half-kidding, but Maggie stepped back and spread her hands wide. I crossed the room and joined her behind Blythe's chair, turning him to face the mirror before I slipped the band from his hair and used both hands to gently comb it loose. He did have gorgeous, thick hair and I wanted to bury my face in it one more time. But I didn't dare with an audience. I looked up to meet his gaze in the mirror and arranged his hair over his shoulders.

"Shit, Maggie, you have to cut it before I lose my nerve," he said, catching my right palm and kissing it quickly.

"All right, but for the record, I'm against this," she insisted, gathering it back into a bundle. She offered me the scissors. "You want to do it?"

"No," I said firmly. "I'll just watch."

"Wait, I'll surprise you," Blythe decided. "No peeking."

I agreed and headed outside to window shop. The day was hot, angling toward scorching, and I was glad I'd chosen a sundress and sandals. There was a breeze, but it kicked up dust and did little to contribute to cooler air. I rummaged in my purse for my sunglasses and then proceeded down the sidewalk. There was a drugstore a few doors down from the salon and I entered under the tinkling bell. The floor was checkered in black and white, like an old-time diner, and two teenaged girls who reminded me a little of Tish and Camille worked the long counter, complete with an ice-cream case. I couldn't resist and went to check out the flavors; one of the girls said, "We've got fresh strawberry today," and her accent (talk about adorable), along with the heat of the day, sold me.

"I'll take a sugar cone, please," I told her, and ambled around the store as I ate it; I was admiring a display of baby gifts when a hand slipped over my belly and I squeaked a little, even knowing it was Blythe.

I turned in his arms and drew a sharp breath.

"Oh my," was all I could manage to say.

"You like it?" he asked, both hands around my waist now, and I nodded. Holy hell, I liked it. His cheekbones were thrown into prominence, the angles of his face in relief without his long hair. What was left was about two inches long, and Maggie arranged it with stylish indifference in mind. His hair looked darker without all of the sun-bleached length. Sunlight streaming through the wide front windows caught him from behind, further dazzling my eyes. I swore his eyelashes were long enough to cast shadows over his face. His blue-gray eyes crinkled merrily at the corners as he grinned and said, "Your cheeks are on fire, baby."

"And my ice cream is melting," I said.

"Here, let me," he said helpfully, plucking the cone from my hand and twirling it around on his tongue.

"Now you're just being cruel," I said, pretending to be irritated, and he grinned even more, his eyes truly devilish.

"Come on, I'll take you on a tour of my hometown," he invited.

"Have a good day!" one of the girls behind the counter called as we headed back outside.

"Oh, we will," Blythe murmured just for my ears, still licking at the strawberry ice cream. He caught my hand in his as we walked, asking, "So, it looks all right?"

"Are you just fishing for a compliment?" I teased, swinging our joined hands.

He angled me a teasing look, crunching on the cone now. "Of course not."

"You are gorgeous," I said. "But not just on the outside." For the first time since this morning I allowed myself to think about everything Christy told me last night. I thought, willing him to hear the plea, *Blythe, sweetheart, tell me yourself. Trust me enough to tell me.*

"Aw, baby," he said, finishing the last of the cone in one bite. He stopped and turned to me, tucking me close to his chest there on the sidewalk of his hometown, the sun beating down on us.

"You are, you know," I told him, and he tenderly smoothed hair from my forehead, inadvertently displacing my sunglasses.

"Thank you," he murmured, settling them back over my eyes and then punctuating the words with a soft kiss.

He drove me around for the rest of the afternoon, pointing out everything that I requested, from his high school to his first job (the local grocery store, called County Beef).

"They sell everything, not just meat," he explained, and I punched his arm.

"I tried wrangling one summer," he said, after we ordered chili fries from a drive-through window.

"As in horse wrangling?" I'd kicked off my sandals and sat with my feet propped on the dashboard, the greasy container of fries we were sharing balanced on my knees. Both of us were doing everything to keep the shadow of Blythe's appearance before a judge from our thoughts.

"Yeah, there's lots of ranchers in this area, and I worked at one of the local places before senior year. It was tough work. I'd never really been on a horse, but I thought it couldn't be that hard. Boy, was I wrong. There was this regular at Mom's work that helped me get the job. It was his brother's place and they needed extra hands."

"Did you wear a cowboy hat?" I asked, trying to sound innocent.

"Yes I did," he said, and I didn't have to look his way to know he was smiling.

"Do you still have it?" I asked next.

"What are you saying?" he teased, and I pinched his side, dripping chili on my thigh.

"Ouch," I grumbled; it was hot on my skin and I swiped my thumb to collect the spill. I licked my thumb and reflected, "I've never worked anywhere but Shore Leave."

"What about when you lived in Chicago?"

"My only job there was raising the girls," I said, feeding him a couple of fries, very carefully, trying not to dribble chili on him. He mumbled thanks around the bite as I added, "I probably should have found a job after Ruthann was in school. Even just for the sake of seeing other adults, making friends. To this day my best friend is still Jillian."

Blythe said, "I'd say she's about the best friend a person could have, other than you. I think you're lucky if you have *one* best friend, instead of a hundred that don't actually give a shit about you. Besides, she feels the same about you."

"Who would you call your best friend?" I asked, studying his profile, overcome with love for him.

He looked my way, mouth somber. So happy to be near him, I reached and stroked my fingertips through the soft hair that curled a little on his nape; I wasn't yet accustomed to its much-shortened length. He said, "Since I served time I haven't had many friends, one way or the other. The closest I've felt to having friends in a long time was back in Landon, with you and Jilly, and Justin. I…"

He trailed to a halt, forced to look back at the road as he drove, but I felt the intensity of his eyes, even still. I prompted softly, "You, what?"

"I had all these ideas about the four of us…you and me, Justin and Jilly, living close together…being a family."

My throat closed; I could hardly swallow the bite I'd just taken. Tears stung my eyes as I whispered, "That's what I want, too." He put his hand on my thigh and the tender sincerity on his face, the softness of his lips at my words, went straight to my heart. I slid across the seat and kissed the cleft on his chin. I whispered, "That's why you are coming home with me."

"I want that so bad," he said hoarsely.

I kissed him again, this time aiming a quick one on his lips.

He grinned. "You should have heard me before you got to Landon last May. I wasn't really very subtle, asking Jilly questions all the time, just to hear more about you. God, I was already fascinated by you, even before we met."

"You were?" I marveled, settling back on my side of the bench seat, resituating the messy chili fries on my knees. Blythe kept his hand on my thigh. I said, "I mean, you've said that before. I was fascinated the moment I met you, believe me. But then again I hadn't heard about you until the minute we arrived."

He said, "When you came into the cafe that first night it was like all the air went out of the room."

"I felt exactly the same, but I didn't dare acknowledge it. I thought about you every second and I felt guilty as hell."

"Every second?" he asked, half teasing, half extremely pleased. He grinned as he said, "I *thought* so, even if you ignored me all the time. But I sensed how you felt. You watched me when you thought I couldn't tell."

I giggled at his accurate observation, agreeing, "I did. I couldn't stop myself and it was like being tortured."

"That night I saw you and Jilly at Eddie's I pretended I just noticed the golf cart out front," he said, and his deep voice was husky with re-membrance. He laughed a little as he admitted, "But I was practically stalking you. That was the first night I thought there might actually be hope. The way you looked at me when I left…"

My cheeks heated at both his words and the memory. I said softly, "You said you would come get me if I needed a ride. That was so sweet."

His grin deepened, his caress moving just slightly higher on my bare thigh as he repeated, "Sweet? Yes, let's go with that. Never mind that I was imagining making passionate love to you right up against the build-ing outside. I could hardly force myself to leave without you."

Hot little thrills erupted all through me at his words. I shivered, which he felt beneath his questing hand. He continued, his voice caress-ing me as much as his fingers, "And then at Trout Days, that was the first time I actually touched you."

"You caught my elbow," I remembered.

"I wanted to kiss you so bad when you turned around," he said. "And then to watch you dancing all night. Talk about torture."

"You found me walking on the lake road the next night," I whispered, already afire.

"I couldn't believe it," he said. "I was dying to find any excuse to get you alone, and there you were, just walking along. I was like, *This is it, this is what you've been waiting for.*"

I set the chili fries on the floor mat, as I wanted both hands free. I scooted to his side and hugged his torso; he curled his right arm tightly about me. I kissed the side of his neck, simply because now I could, and I delighted in this as I whispered, "And then you kissed me, under the fireworks."

"It was so right," he said. "I knew I wanted you, but I had no idea how much until I kissed you." I held him close, resting my forehead against his neck as he said, low and intense, "Joelle, I'm so in love with you. I wasn't expecting to fall in love."

"Blythe," I whispered. I closed my eyes, blocking out the sunny late afternoon that stretched before the windshield of the truck.

He said miserably, "I don't know what will happen tomorrow. Or Wednesday, or whenever I go before a judge. I might get sent back to jail. I don't know. Fuck, I just don't know and I'm fucking scared."

I sat straight so I could see his face, determined to reassure him. I said intently, "I will wait for you, do you hear me? No matter how long it takes. I want you to know that. I don't care that you've been to jail. I only care because it hurts you." He drew a slow breath, holding my gaze. Hope and joy collided in his eyes as I said, "Because I love you, Blythe Edward Tilson. I want to make a family with you."

"Joelle," he whispered, catching a strand of my loose hair, twining it around his index finger. And in that moment I knew I had to tell him what I knew.

"Sweetheart, your mom..." I trailed to silence, heart thudding anxiously. A trickle of sweat skimmed between my breasts but I was determined to finish the sentence. I gathered my courage and said, "She told me about Julianne."

I saw his jaw tighten. Without a word, he accelerated and drove us out of town. I sat in tense silence even though he didn't seem angry; rather, on a mission. He took a side road after a few miles, heading west. Less than a hundred yards later the road twisted up the side of a small bluff lined with cottonwood trees. At the top of this ridge he pulled into a clearing and parked, allowing us a bird's eye view of Brandt in the distance, its old-fashioned silver water tower glinting in the slanting sun. We were utterly alone here. Blythe lifted my left hand and rubbed his thumb gently over my palm.

At last he said, "I'm sorry I haven't told you about that yet."

"Don't be sorry," I whispered.

"I suppose I should hate her, but I don't," he said, running his free hand through his hair, standing it on end. It was a trivial thing to notice, but I reflected how he wouldn't have been able to do that this morning, when his hair was long. He brought my hand to his lips and kissed it, as though gathering strength. He sighed a little as he said, "We dated the summer I was twenty-one. She was only eighteen, and my first serious girlfriend since high school. I met her through Tony—" and with that particular name his voice snagged on something sharp. "He was my boss at the time. We did construction, mostly framing and roofing. Julianne was Tony's little sister, and she would visit the job sites, it seemed like she was always around, and I finally asked her out. But I never loved her. I know that's not the point, but I didn't. I liked her, I wanted to have sex with her, but that's where it ended. Tony wasn't crazy about us being together…he thought she was too young. Shit, I don't even know how it happened. She was on the pill." He cut himself short and asked quickly, "Is it all right to tell you this? If you told me about having sex with another man I would want to kill him."

I laughed a little, a release of tension, and said truthfully enough, "I want you to tell me. Please. I really do. I would hate to think you felt like you couldn't tell me things."

"That's true," he said, enfolding my hand between his. Again he sighed, before saying, "But somehow she ended up pregnant. She told me and I was shocked, but I wasn't upset at her. That's the last thing I was that day. I would have done right by her, and she knew it. I would have supported her and our baby. God, she cried and cried, like it was the end of the world. Said her brother would kill her. I told her it wasn't Tony's fucking business, but she wouldn't listen. He was so protective of her, I should have suspected she might do something extreme. I found out later that she had issues with depression in high school. But I never thought she'd do what she did. Without even telling me." His eyes grew wet and it was like a razor over my soul to see the tears he wouldn't allow to fall. His voice raw with pain, he said, "I didn't see her for two days and I was really worried. Tried calling but couldn't get ahold of her. I went to their house and couldn't find her. And then she called me from Oklahoma City. And said she'd made a decision."

"Blythe," I whispered, aching for him. And in the back of my mind I could not help but picture Camille, vividly remembering the way she looked when she told me she was pregnant, hardly more than two weeks ago. My Camille, my first baby…

He continued, "I would have begged her to reconsider, but it was already done. She'd been in and out of some place there, I never found out where, but it was done. And I just went crazy. Screamed at her, swore at her. I'm sorry about all of that now, for saying those things. But that doesn't change the fact that I meant every word. Later I found out she'd told Tony that I forced her to get an abortion, that I'd *made* her do it. I was at work that day, and Tony grabbed my phone from me and he was yelling at her, and then he threw my phone like it was a grenade and punched me right in the face. He wasn't a wimp, either. I went down, but I was so angry, Joelle, all I could remember later was a red haze. Two of the other guys we worked with pulled me off of him and he was bleeding all over the place. His blood was all over my hands. It was like a scene from some stupid fucking movie. I ran to the work truck and took off, where to I don't know, I didn't have a plan. I just had to get out of there. And no more than ten minutes later the cops pulled me over, guns drawn, like I was some fugitive. Apparently there was a folder in the glove compartment with money Tony was planning to take to the bank, and so I was a thief twice over. He told them I stole his truck and his money, both."

Blythe was clutching my leg as though it was a life vest and he'd just come up for the third time.

"So I got arrested that day and later went to court. I suppose I should be grateful I was only sentenced to nine months, especially since Tony pressed assault charges, too. But I got out after three. It wasn't anything like you see on TV, but it was fucking humiliating. I still feel like such a loser, a criminal. And I never got to confront Julianne. She called me once, while I was still behind bars, and said she was sorry. God, I could hardly talk to her there was such a lump in my throat. I hung up on her. I spent all those nights in that cell on that piece of shit bunk and all I could think about was my child that I'd never get to meet. I have never felt so guilty. So betrayed and helpless. It was the worst time in my life." He fell silent and sighed for a final time. His eyes softened as he looked at me, lifting his hands and cupping my face with such tenderness that the tears I'd been trying to hold back rippled over my cheeks.

"I'm so sorry," I whispered, getting my arms around his neck. "Oh, sweetheart, I'm so sorry."

"Don't cry," he whispered. "It's behind me now. It still hurts, and I still think about the baby sometimes. I imagine what he or she would be like. He'd be almost two by now. You know what Joelle, my sweet woman, when I saw how much you loved your girls that made me love you all the more. God, I love you. I can't even tell you how much."

I sobbed, turning my face against the solid curve of his right hand. He pulled me close and I clung, sobbing for him and the story he'd just told, for my own daughter who was carrying the child of a man who wouldn't be there for her, and for this incredible love that I'd found when I least expected it. Blythe gave me so much more than he would ever know. And, God help me, I would do everything in my power to keep him with me.

"Shhh," he soothed, his lips warm against my temple. "It's all right."

"I'm sorry," I was finally able to say, choking back my tears and managing a deep breath. I lined his jaws with my hands, whispering, "And I'm so glad you told me. I understand so much more now."

He smiled his sweet smile, the one that lifted the right side of his mouth higher than the left. "I would have told you before now, it's just so hard to talk about. I don't want you to think that I haven't moved beyond it, because in most ways I have. And I try to have more control over my temper these days, I really do. It's just when I thought Jackie hurt you, I didn't think, I just reacted." His eyes were intent on mine as he said, "Joelle, what I feel for you is the strongest thing I've ever felt in my life. When I told you that night in Landon that you should go, I wanted to fucking die. And you came here anyway, you came after me." His voice was full of wonder. He smoothed his strong hands, his incredible touch, softly down my neck, my waist, before cupping my breasts with infinite gentleness. I wrapped my arms around his neck and held him like I'd dreamed about holding him all of those nights back home, after we first met and I couldn't acknowledge how I really felt.

He murmured, "You smell just like a peach."

I laughed again, with pure happiness. Against his neck I muttered, "You sweet-talker."

His thumbs made gentle circles over my nipples as he whispered, "Did you sleep all right last night? I was glad to know you were in my old bed, even if I couldn't be in it with you."

"I can't imagine you fitting into that tiny space," I said, fitting myself against his strong chest. He licked soft, teasing kisses along the side of my neck, both hands busy sliding under my sundress. He reached my panties and I shifted my hips so he could free me from them, kicking off my sandals and then hooking a leg over his lap.

"There's another place I'd like to fit just now," he said with a throaty sound of pleasure, eyelids lowering in the seductive way that made my blood become fire. I lifted my arms and he delicately pulled the dress over my head, swiftly unhooking my bra. I quivered as he brought me to his mouth and opened his lips over my nipples, which swelled against his tongue.

"Aw, baby, you're so beautiful. You taste so good," he said, his breath warm on my breasts as he lavished them with attention. I curled my fingers possessively into his short hair.

"It feels so different," I murmured, running my nails along his scalp, and he shivered, taking one nipple lightly between his teeth. I gasped a little. "But I like it."

"Good," he said, kissing the skin between my breasts, his hands spread wide over my naked back.

"I like it very much," I clarified breathlessly, tugging off his shirt.

Blythe shifted, hurrying to free himself from his jeans, my hands all over him. He was naked, and so hard, hauling me close, kissing me deeply. He groaned and bent a knee over my hips, then brushed my hair away from my flushed cheeks. Already I was like a torch, burning up beneath his hands.

His voice lowered to a husky murmur as he said, "The first night I kissed you I didn't know where it would go. But now I can touch you, and kiss you, whenever, wherever…" And so saying he lowered his lips to my throat, trailing kisses between my breasts and down my belly while his hands skimmed along my ribs, coming to rest behind my thighs, easing them apart, stroking his tongue between my legs until I was gasping, my head bent backward against the seat. He was so amazing at what he did, my world ceased to mean anything but desire for those moments. When at last he lifted his head his breath was ragged, his eyes smoky blue fire.

He moved back over me and I wrapped around him, clutching his shoulders, overwhelmed yet again by the sheer force of him, his beauty and strength. I ached with longing for him, and would still, even when he was deep within my body, even when he'd just left it. It was unending, and like nothing I'd ever known. I only knew that it was the same for him.

"I love you," he said against my mouth, taking my lower lip in his teeth. Our tongues met and stroked; I knew his taste, the contours of his mouth, better than my own.

I held his face in my hands, caressing his strong jaws, scratchy with stubble now that it was evening. I told him, "I can't live without you. Not anymore."

He said, "Aw, baby, you won't be without me."

"Blythe Edward Tilson," I whispered, just to speak his full name, thinking again of all the nights I'd curled alone in my bed in Landon, dreaming of him.

As though reading my mind he said, "I used to dream about this, lying there in Gramps' trailer after seeing you at work all day. I dreamed about how your skin would feel, and how your kiss would taste, and the sounds you'd make when I touched you at last…"

"Sounds I'd make?" I teased.

He grinned and said, "All those sounds you were making just now."

My entire body flushed. I hid my face against his neck and whispered, almost shyly, "You're so good at that."

He moved in a sensual, unhurried fashion, resting his lips on my belly in passing, brushing his nose over my pubic hair. I trembled as he ever-so-gently kissed the flesh between my legs, my hips jolting instinctively against him. He murmured, "At this, you mean?"

"Yes," I affirmed in a tiny, breathless voice. "Oh God, *yes*, that…"

He grinned and bent his head. I felt as though I might shred apart at the seams, coming in hard, fast waves until I lay spent, sweat trailing over my temples. Blythe was above me then, a condom in place, sliding home with a deep groan. I could hardly breathe, unable to do more than cling to him. He came with a cry that made me think I'd hurt him, if I hadn't known better.

Replete, wrapped in each other's embrace, we lay naked in the last of the afternoon sun.

Chapter Seven

THE SKY WAS AWASH WITH SUNSET BY THE TIME WE MAN-
aged to sit up and think about getting dressed. Blythe's window was open
and the sounds of crickets met our ears as I fastened my bra and then
leaned over his lap to admire the view. The western horizon appeared to
have been splattered with liquid gold and then dotted by indigo-blue
puffs of cloud slightly darker than the robin's egg shade of the rest of the
sky. The sun itself was a molten magenta, just the top half visible as it
sank inescapably into a fiery pool of light.

"That is a gorgeous sight," I murmured, resting my forearms on
Blythe's lap. He leaned back against the seat and gazed out the window,
too, rubbing along my spine with his warm hands.

"I do believe that Oklahoma has some of the best sunsets," he said.
"But Landon is a close second."

I nodded agreement.

"Shit," he observed a minute later, but in a lazy tone.

I looked over my shoulder, eyebrows lifted in question, and grinned at
the way he looked in the auburn light, his hair all roughed up from my
questing hands, his lips warm and soft, eyes so blue-gray beneath spiky
long lashes. I said, "You are one handsome man."

His grin matched mine, both palms gliding over my ass, which was
still bare. He said, "Watch it, woman, I can't promise I won't need to
make love again, right here, right now."

"Is that supposed to be some kind of threat?" I giggled. "And why did
you say 'shit' just now?"

"Mom and Gramps were expecting us for dinner," he explained, tipping forward to plant a kiss on my shoulder. "But I think dinner has come and gone."

"Yeah, and then some. Shit. Will Christy be upset?" I felt like a teenager, so caught up in her own world that she neglected everyone else's. I hadn't checked my phone all day, hadn't called my own teenaged girls…

"It's all right," he laughed, kissing my other shoulder. "I'll call her."

He did, apologizing, while I slipped back into my clothes and brushed out my hair. I'd stormed through such a range of emotions just today that I felt a little drained, not to mention starving. Altogether I was glad that Christy was gracious enough to tell her son that there was plenty of food left.

"Mom likes you," Blythe told me as we drove back through Brandt.

"I like her, too," I said, resting my cheek on his upper arm as he drove, our hands linked on Blythe's lap. "She's kind. And she loves you very much. What about your dad? Do you ever talk to him?"

"He comes around sometimes," Blythe said. "Mom won't admit it, but he's into drugs. Maybe even something worse than weed, which I know he used to use. He would hide in the bathroom with the fan going, like he was fooling anyone."

"When was the last time you saw him?"

"He was in town just before I left for Landon, actually. I saw him for a minute. He looked like shit," Blythe said. "Poor guy. I don't hate him, even though he wasn't around much for us. Mom still loves him. I wish she'd let him go."

"It's not always that easy."

"Your mom and Ellen seem to get by just fine," he observed. "And your grandma. I never saw such tough ladies."

"You know, though, Gran has always talked about my grandpa, how she wished he'd have called her one last time. He just up and left Landon and she never heard from him again. My dad, too, I guess. Great-Aunt Minnie used to joke that there was a curse on the menfolk in our family, isn't that awful? But then after everything with Christopher…" I shivered a little. I didn't usually talk about either of these topics, the curse or Chris's death, with anyone other than Jilly.

"That's Jilly's husband, right?" Blythe asked as he took the turn into Gatehouse Court. "The one who died?"

"Yeah, Clint's dad. Clint looks just like him. There was a long time when we all thought Jilly would never get over him." I chewed my thumbnail as I remembered those days, however unwittingly.

"She seems really happy with Justin," Blythe observed. "And he's wild about her, as anyone with eyes can see."

"I'm so glad she let herself fall in love. And Justin is totally over the moon for her," I agreed, and then, as we neared the trailer, kissed Blythe's cheek. I whispered, "Thanks for a lovely evening."

He stole one last, quick kiss as he put the truck in park, whispering, "You make it lovely, sweetheart."

Christy and Rich sat at the table drinking coffee when we came inside. Christy studied us for a moment, her lips quirked, and I was instantly concerned that my dress was crooked, or inside-out, or that the path of Blythe's hands and lips somehow glowed all along my body, visible to his mother's eagle eyes. But then she smiled gently and said, "There's a pot roast on the stove, and mashed potatoes. Thought I was crazy making all that stuff when it was ninety-something today."

"Thanks, Ma, my favorites," Blythe said, and planted a kiss on her cheek as we entered the kitchen, which smelled wonderful. I filled a plate and sat beside Rich, who snagged a piece of my pot roast and sent me a wink.

"I'm sorry we're late," I added.

"Nice hair, son," Christy said as Blythe settled across from me, his plate loaded.

"It'll take me a while to get used to it," he said, smoothing a hand along the back of his head. "Maggie didn't want to cut it."

"I know, she called and told me so," Christy said, then laughed. "But it looks good, it suits you. Don't you think, Joelle?"

I nodded, my mouth full of her delicious food.

"Jillian called for you earlier," Rich told me, helping himself to my plate a second time, stealing a piece of cornbread.

"I'll call her tonight," I said, with a backsplash of guilt; I told her I'd call every night, and we'd not spoken yet. Nor had I talked to Tish, or Mom—though, as I was still irritated with my mother, I didn't mind missing her phone calls. And Tish was probably too occupied with enjoying the last month of summer vacation to make much of a fuss. I pictured the cafe, and my daughters in it; I hoped Camille was able to eat something today, and that Tish was allowing Ruthann to tag along a little…maybe Mom could invite Dodge's grandkids, the triplets, out to the cafe for an evening…

"Sweetheart, you better go call them," Blythe said. I looked up from my speculation to see his eyes on me, his expression tender, a half-smile hovering around his lips. He explained, "I can practically hear your thoughts right now."

"You're right," I said, touched by his understanding. I dug out my cell phone, its little red message light blinking as if in reproach. Immediately I dialed Shore Leave and Jillian answered on the second ring.

"Well it's about damn time," she said by way of greeting. But she wasn't truly angry, I could tell.

"Sorry," I said, taking the phone with me as I went outside onto Christy's little porch. The hanging lanterns glimmered in a cheerful rainbow welcome as I sat on the top concrete step, smoothing my skirt beneath me. The air out here was warm and crackling-dry, but not unpleasant. From nearby trailers I could hear muted conversations and laughter, music from someone's radio or TV, an occasional dog. Someone pedaling a bike crunched along on the gravel path; he offered a wave as he passed me, which I returned. I asked Jilly, "Any other dreams?"

"No important ones," my sister said. "Jackie was out here yesterday and he told me to tell you he was sorry for acting like an asshole. That was his exact phrasing. I think he actually meant it. He ate dinner with the girls and Clint on the porch. Mom and Ell sat with them for a while, but Gran just peeked out the window."

"What about you?" I joked.

"I went out with Justin, so I wasn't there the whole time. I guess Jackie stuck around and chatted with the girls until it was dark. It was fine until they started talking about Noah, and Camille begged Jackie not to go and have a talk with him, but he was pretty adamant that he was going to, that it was his job as her father. She bawled and had a little bit of a hissy and then went back to the house, but surprisingly Jackie handled that all right. Mom said he just kept on talking with Ruthie and Tish as though she hadn't acted that way."

"Aw, *Milla*," I groaned. "Shit. Jackie's in the right, but I understand how she feels. It's so humiliating. How could she get pregnant by such a jackass?"

Jilly giggled a little. "Nice, Jo."

I wished I could tell her about everything I'd learned last night and today, but it wasn't the time or place. I shifted a little against the hard concrete, wishing I could smoke. But I'd run out of cigarettes and there was no point buying more when I was quitting. I sighed and said, "It just kills me. I know she was in love with that little bastard this summer and then not only does he knock her up, he breaks her heart. I just have a terrible feeling he'll never be there for her."

"I know. I get the same sense. But what do you say? She'll meet a man who deserves her. I know it."

"But—" I began, but Jilly cut me off with a shushing noise.

"No 'buts' for now," she added. "It's so pretty out over the water. I wish you were here to have a beer on the dock. What's the word down there in Oklahoma? What's it like?"

"Prairie town," I responded. "Brandt is a lot like Landon, except not so pretty. I miss the lake."

"How is Bly?"

"Good," I said softly, and Jillian snorted.

"I'll bet," she teased me.

"Damn good," I murmured, and then she laughed her deep, rollicking laugh.

"Hurry and bring him home," she said. "I miss you both. How did we ever survive with you in Chicago all those years?"

"I was just wondering that today," I told her.

"Hey, I've gotta go. Ellen is in the weeds at the bar," Jilly said, and I could practically see my sister craning her neck as she looked that way to notice.

"Okay. Are the girls around?"

"No, they're out on the lake with Clinty. I'll have them call your phone later though. Love you!" she said hurriedly.

"Love you, too, Jilly Bean," I replied, and hung up.

I sat in the pleasant darkness a little longer, hearing Blythe, Christy, and Rich chatting in the house. Their voices rose and fell, punctuated by a laugh here and there, mostly Blythe's, his deep laugh that made my heart vibrate with happiness. I curled my hands around my thighs and arched my back, studying the stars. At last I heard dishes clattering into the sink, and then Blythe came out the screen door and joined me on the step.

"How's everybody?" he asked, squeezing beside me and wrapping one arm around my waist. I leaned my head against his strong shoulder and cupped his knee, rubbing my palm on the denim, faded almost to the smoothness of satin.

"Good, I just talked to Jilly. The girls were out on the lake."

He sighed. "God, I can just picture it. I miss it there so much. In the evenings everything seemed to quiet down, get all still over the water."

"Jilly told me to hurry and bring you home," I said, tightening my grip on his leg. "I told her I'd do everything I could."

He kissed my hair, drawing me closer against his warm side. I hugged him as hard as I was able, inhaling the scent of him.

"Mom wants to know if you play cards," he said, nuzzling my neck.

"As in Go Fish?" I teased.

He cupped my jaw in one hand and kissed me, gently suckling my lower lip, before replying, "No, more like Texas Hold 'Em."

"I don't know how to play that," I whispered, all shivery from his kisses.

"It's not too hard," he said, and then snorted a laugh, as we kissed again, playing with each other. He nipped my chin, just lightly, as he murmured, "But *I* am, and it's really distracting…you want to get out of here?"

I giggled, closing my teeth around his bottom lip.

"You two planning to join us?" And Rich was right behind us, standing at the screen door; he cleared his throat, obviously teasing.

Two hours later I'd been visited by beginner's luck enough that Rich threw in for the last time, cursing good-naturedly.

"Dammit, that's it for me," Rich said, tipping his chair on its hind legs, reminding me of Tish and Jilly. He added, "I need some shut-eye. Bly, you about ready to head to bed?"

Blythe held my gaze for a fraction of a second, with so much heat that my cheeks felt scorched. But he sounded totally at ease as he looked over at Rich and replied, "Yeah, we should probably get going."

"You'll call Dale first thing?" Christy asked, rattling the ice cubes in her empty glass in a nervous sort of gesture, her voice on edge. It was the first we'd spoken of Blythe's impending court appearance all evening.

He nodded, rising to his feet. I stood, too, prepared to walk him to the truck. Blythe gave his mother a hug and then took my hand. Outside, the trailer court had quieted under the midnight sky. When we reached his truck, Blythe enfolded me securely against his chest. I clung, pressing my face against his red t-shirt, my hands spread over the hard muscles of his back.

"Thanks for listening today," he whispered against my hair, rocking us side to side.

"Thank you for telling me," I whispered. I tipped my chin against his chest and he bent his head to meet my gaze, cupping my face and stroking my cheekbones with his thumbs. The lanterns from Christy's porch threw a soft orange glow over his face as he looked intently into my eyes. A surge of sudden anguish struck, scaring me, and I tightened my grip. I said urgently, "I love you, Blythe. So much…" I didn't want to let go of him.

"My sweet Joelle, I love you," he said, cradling me, resting his forehead against mine. He promised, "I'll come over first thing. Try to get some sleep."

"You, too," I whispered. I wanted him to come back inside with me so badly that my body hurt, inside and out. But Rich was coming out the screen door and we were forced to draw apart. Blythe kissed me one last time, whispering, "Good-night, sweetheart. I'll be here in the morning."

I slept better than I thought I would, though just before dawn a strange dream caught me in its web. I woke with a jolt, blinking into the dim gray light of very early morning. Darn that Jillian, getting her animal dreams stuck in my subconscious. I sat up and scraped strands of hair from my face. I felt sweaty and restless; a trickle ran between my breasts, unsettling me. With a sigh I leaned back onto the pillows, readjusting them, trying to remember the fading scraps of the dream only just playing out behind my eyelids.

Horses, I thought, closing my eyes. *There'd been horses…*

A field, thick with mist. I *was* a horse in the dream, and I knew this bizarre truth without the benefit of a mirror or a lake, or any other reflective surface. I recalled a fleeting glimpse of long, hoofed legs protruding downward from my torso. The sound of fighting, just beyond me, maybe over a hill or in the thick cluster of trees to the left…and I was worried about the lame horse, the horse with the limp, fearful it would be badly injured, maybe even killed. And then I'd woken.

My teeth went on edge, my eyes opening, and in the grayness of Blythe's old bedroom I drew both knees to my chest. I thought about Jackie telling me that he wished I would have reacted more to his affair. As in, track down Lanny and claw out her eyes? I hated that I was second-guessing myself after all this time, but his words made me wonder; typical lawyer tactics, I supposed, calculated to gauge a reaction. But then again, he'd seemed sincerely upset that evening on the dock. Maybe I should have confronted him directly when I'd first suspected his cheating, but it was so much easier to pretend that I was wrong, that my gut instinct was somehow invalid. So much easier to believe that my husband, who'd given me three beautiful baby girls, would never choose to be unfaithful, even if the option was readily available. I rolled sideways, hugging myself as though I was a child needing reassurance.

I didn't intend to fall asleep, but the next thing I knew Blythe slipped under the covers, curling his arms around me and drawing me back against his chest. The room glowed with morning sun and I murmured gladly as he encased me in his warmth, settling his chin over my left shoulder and kissing my neck.

"Morning," he said softly against my hair. He added, "Don't worry, Mom's out for breakfast with Rich."

I turned in his arms, getting mine securely around him. From a few inches away I smiled into his eyes and snuggled in close. He kissed my collarbones, smoothing aside my hair to do so, then ran his palms down my back, hauling my hips closer to his.

"I like your hair," I told him, my hands all over him.

"I was hoping you'd mess it up," he said.

I wore a long t-shirt but nothing else, unable for most of my life to sleep in pants or underwear of any kind. Blythe discovered my partial nakedness and made a sound deep in his throat, his husky lovemaking sound. I shivered and unzipped his jeans.

"I can't believe this," he muttered, slightly breathless as I freed him from his boxers, firmly caressing all along his length.

"What?" I demanded, heart thrusting as he maneuvered swiftly out of his t-shirt and moved above me on the mattress.

He clarified, "The second time we get to make love in an actual bed and it's the one in my old room." He grinned and I pulled him close, almost roughly, needing him so much I could hardly breathe. He responded with a deep kiss, bracing above me on one forearm, sliding his other hand downward over my belly. He made another throaty sound, whispering against my lips, "You feel so good." But in the next instant he whispered desperately, "I don't have a condom with me."

"It's all right," I said, and curved my thighs around his hips.

He struggled to compose himself enough to respond, "Are you sure?"

"Just don't come inside me," I said, and he groaned softly, kissing me with all of his passionate intensity. I lifted against him, begging with my hips, but still he held back. I was impressed by his self-control; sweat was beginning to form on my temples and between my breasts.

"I won't," he promised. His eyes were so intent, true upon mine as he whispered, "But if I do ever get you pregnant, I would be so happy. You don't even know."

My heart ached with tenderness at his words. How sweet of him, how in character to say such a thing at this moment. I was so in love with him that my entire body seemed to be resonating to a new frequency with the energy of it.

"Blythe," I pleaded against his lips, and he grinned before kissing me, his wide shoulders arched like wings. I gasped as he slid deep and then took up a steady rhythm, twining my legs around his hips. He'd never been inside me without a condom and I held him as tightly as I could, feeling his heart thundering, matching mine. Long, sweet minutes later I could barely recall my name, and when Blythe took my lower lip between his teeth I shuddered with the force of an orgasm, finally taking him over the edge. He groaned, gasping my name, and pulled out not a moment too soon.

"I'm sorry," he whispered some time later, as we drifted back to reality, tangled together.

Blissful against his chest, I murmured, "About what?"

He grinned sleepily and said, "Coming on your stomach."

I giggled, muffling the sound against his warm skin.

"It was so good to feel you without anything in the way," he said, fingers moving lazily through my loose hair.

"It was," I agreed, and his arms tightened around me. I tried to pretend I didn't sense a huge, unmerciful stopwatch hovering all too near, ticking away—the reminder of time running out. I wanted to stay here with him, in this moment, and an old Elvis song was suddenly in my mind, absurd but totally accurate: "Make the World Go Away."

"Joelle," he murmured, sensing the direction of my thoughts. "I know I don't deserve your love, but I'm taking it anyway. I love you, baby."

"You deserve it," I scolded, drawing back enough to see his eyes. "Don't say that."

At that very moment the front door of the trailer opened. Despite the fact that the bedroom door was firmly closed, I froze.

Christy's voice carried through the space. She called, "Junior, I know you're in there, so there's no use pretending otherwise."

I felt a wave of giggles coming on and bit the insides of my cheeks. Blythe planted a kiss on my neck and then called back, totally composed, "Hey, did you bring us any breakfast?"

Christy laughed and said, "No, but I've got some coffee."

A half an hour later I emerged from the shower and could tell immediately that the good-natured banter occurring when I'd entered the bathroom was over. I couldn't pinpoint the exact difference, but I could sense the tension even though I wasn't in the room. And then from outside, where he must certainly be standing on the porch, I heard the muted sound of Blythe in a one-sided conversation on the phone.

I hurried to comb my hair and brush my teeth, meeting my own concerned gaze in the mirror as I applied a quick layer of mascara. I dressed in denim cut-offs and a green tank top, the one that Blythe said matched my eyes. Shit, and I was running out of clean clothes; it was a stupid thing to think about right now, but my mind needed distraction. I heard Blythe coming back inside and I flew out of the bathroom, my hair loose and damp over my shoulders.

"What is it?" I asked, keeping my voice steady with real effort.

He looked somber, shoulders tense as he shifted the cordless phone from hand to hand. His eyes held mine but there was no hint of a smile around his mouth. I thought of how we'd made love not even an hour ago and my heart pitched painfully against my ribs. I felt ill with vulnerability; his eyes told me he felt the same. Christy appeared in the arch between the rooms, drying a glass with a daisy-printed hand towel.

"Bly?" she pressed.

"That was Dale. We have a court date in two hours," he said, looking over at his mother, his deep voice steady despite the anxiety flowing just beneath the words.

"Okay, that's good, get it done," Christy said. "Rich, did you hear that?"

"I did," Rich answered from the kitchen. "And I'll bring you."

Christy turned back to the sink, where Rich stood running water into the coffeepot. I moved directly into Blythe's arms, where he wrapped me close and rested his chin on my head. After a moment he murmured, "You smell so good, Joelle."

In response I squeezed him all the more tightly. I said, "I'll come, too."

I felt him stiffen slightly at my words and drew back to see his face. He smoothed my hair with both hands. His blue-gray eyes poured into mine.

"You don't have to do that," he whispered, and the tone in his deep voice implored me to understand.

"I'll do whatever you want," I whispered, my palms resting along his ribs. "Blythe, whatever you need."

He said, "I just need you. That's all."

He changed into dark khakis and a pale dress shirt, complete with a tie. I'd never seen him dressed so formally and it did things to my insides. His hair was impeccable, despite my having messed it up quite effectively earlier. I ended up staying at the trailer with Christy; though I longed to accompany them, to go downtown to the courthouse and listen to every word, I could tell that Blythe was reluctant to put me through that. So I stayed behind, and then Christy needed to go into work anyway. By noon they still hadn't called, and I felt like a pinball rattling inside a broken machine, and just as useful.

Blythe had kissed me good-bye with a promise to call as soon as he could. He was strung with tension and trying not to let me see it. Rich hugged me, whispering, "It'll be all right, sweetie."

I wanted to believe him so badly.

I called Jillian. It was lunch rush back home at Shore Leave and she would be in the middle of it, probably too busy to pick up, so I was doubly grateful when she answered with, "I was just thinking about you."

"Are you busy, Jills?" I asked, settling onto the lone chair on the little porch; it was already scorching outside, dusty and dry and oven-like, but I was under the awning and couldn't bear to hang out alone in the stuffy trailer.

"Not yet. What's going on? You have that sound in your voice," my sister observed. She was over a thousand miles away but I could see her perfectly, her close-cropped golden hair and fingernails polished with some odd color, like lime green, her familiar eyes as blue as August afternoons and fields of blooming chicory. God, I missed her.

"Jillian," I sobbed out, before completely losing it. I held her voice against my ear for strength as I cried and cried, pressing my fisted left hand against my forehead, uncaring that the neighbors were no doubt peering out their windows and speculating what the hell.

"Jo, it's all right," she said, at intervals.

And at last I calmed enough to gasp, "I know, Jills…I'm just so… shook up."

"Where's Blythe?"

"Rich took him to his court date," I whispered, my insides all shuddery. I cleared my throat and my words poured like water from a kettle. "He's supposed to call me when it's done, but it's been hours now and I haven't heard anything. I'm so worried and I'm here all alone, which makes it a hundred times worse. We made love this morning and it was so beautiful, but I'm scared it'll be the last time I'll ever touch him. Oh, Jilly, I don't know why I feel this way, so fucking afraid…"

She finally interrupted, "Jo, get a damn hold on yourself. You've been through too much in the past few days, that's why. You're just fine, and Bly loves you, and he'll be *just fine*. Jesus Crimeny."

I giggled a little, scraping tears from my cheeks with my free hand. I whispered, "What a great motivational speaker you'd make."

"Thanks," she responded cheerfully.

"Do you think I'm pregnant?" I asked next.

Jilly paused for a moment; I could practically hear her thoughts swirling as she considered my words. At last she said, "No, you're not."

I was actually disappointed, stunning me a little. I finally asked, "How's everything back home?"

"Great except for how much we all miss you."

"But what?" I asked, hearing it in her voice.

Jilly sighed as she admitted, "But Jackie has been hanging out here almost constantly. It's starting to get on my second-to-last nerve. And to top it off, everybody seems to have forgotten that they're supposed to hate Jackie. Justin has actually been *hanging out* with him. Last night I was all like, 'Don't you have a job back in Chicago, Jackie?'"

"You'd think they used to be friends or something," I teased, not unduly troubled at this news of Jackie's acceptance in Landon; after all, it was his hometown, too. I added, "And you know it's good for the girls to see their dad. They won't for a while after he heads back to Illinois."

"He said he took some time off," Jilly explained. "Tish and Ruthann have been enjoying his company, that's true. And Mom, for God's sake. Jackie could always charm the pants off her."

I giggled. "She always fell under his spell. Like I should talk, I guess."

"Yeah, but you were a teenager."

"What about Milla?"

"She's been avoiding everyone lately, poor pregnant mama. Noah goes back to school in a few weeks and the little prick hasn't been to see her, hasn't even called. Who'd have thought an Utley would be such a jerk? His family is so nice."

"Has Jackie talked to him yet?"

"Not that I know of, but I'll ask. He's out fishing with Clint and the girls right now. And I'll have Camille call you later," Jilly promised.

"Thanks for being there," I whispered.

"Gimme a break," Jilly said. "I gotta go, it's getting busy. Call as soon as you know what's up."

"I will," I promised. "Love you, Jilly Bean."

Chapter Eight

I FELL ASLEEP ON THE PORCH, MY FEET PROPPED ON A STY-rofoam cooler Christy left outside, the phone lying in my lap. If Jillian hadn't just confirmed that I wasn't pregnant, I would have been more than a little suspicious. It was blazing hot and my throat burned when I snapped awake, realizing that my phone buzzed with an incoming call. I saw immediately that it was Blythe and sat straight too quickly, swamped with relief; my feet hit the porch floor with a dull thunk. I almost dropped the phone in my haste to answer, saying, "What happened, sweetheart? I've been so worried…"

"Joelle." But it was Rich speaking, not Blythe, and ice water filled my veins. He hurried to fill the hole of dread created by my silence, explaining, "Jo, honey, I'm calling you for Blythe right now, because he can't. He got sentenced to thirty days. His parole officer said we shouldn't worry and that he suspected that it would be more time, so this isn't the bad news you're thinking."

My heart was pulverizing my ribs. I tried twice to draw a full breath before demanding, "Where is he? Rich, where is he right now?"

"Well, they're booking him right now. He's got to go straight to the jail since he received a sentence. It's thirty days, no bail posted this time. Otherwise I'd be bringing him home with me right now."

"No," I whispered, tears stinging my eyes and nose. But I couldn't act like this right now; I had to pull it together. I wouldn't think about how I'd have to go home to Landon without him. Because I couldn't stay here that long…even if my heart shredded apart at the idea of leaving him behind.

And in a jail cell. Oh, Blythe, sweetheart…

"Can I see him?" I flew to my feet, unable to hold still.

"He made me promise I'd make that happen, so I'll do my best for the both of you," Rich said. "Sit tight, honey, and I'll come get you."

More than an hour crawled past before we were allowed to see him, at the government center in Brandt. I was told I would be allowed five minutes, no more, as an officer led me to a small room in the depths of the building, where he knocked briefly and pushed open the door.

"Tilson, you have a visitor," the officer said. He left the room but did not shut the door, saying over one shoulder, "Five minutes."

Blythe wore an orange jumpsuit and he was cuffed. My darling Blythe, who'd held me in those arms just a few hours ago, who told me how happy he'd be if our lovemaking resulted in a baby, was cuffed like a dangerous criminal. Agony beat at me as he stood slowly, staring at me as though I might just disappear into thin air; I wanted to weep, especially when I noticed that his eyes carried the faint aftermath of tears. I wanted to rip apart the walls and take him away, never to return to this shithole place. I'd never felt so helpless.

"Baby," I said, my voice cracking a little. Normally it was an endearment he used for me.

"Joelle, I'm so sorry," Blythe said immediately, his voice full of gravel, as though he'd been shouting at the top of his lungs, and I made a sound of protest at the apology, a little intimidated by this stark room and the fact that he remained rooted in place. But I pushed that away and flew to his side, reaching to collect his face in my hands. My heart felt stabbed as he closed his eyes and fresh tears leaked over his cheeks. He turned his face against my right palm with a low, choked sound, bending to me, shifting his arms over my head as best he could with both hands forcibly joined at the wrists. The chain between the cuffs jingled. I clung to him, his hard, hale body beneath that hateful orange cloth.

"Don't you dare be sorry," I said. His eyes were tortured as he looked down at me, red-rimmed. It killed me to see his sadness.

"I thought I'd get the sentence waived, I really did," he said, his voice rough. "Dale said I should be glad it's only a month for violating parole, but I still thought I'd get off without more jail time. I'm so sorry. Sweetheart, I'm *so sorry.*"

"Don't be sorry," I said again, tracing my fingers over his eyebrows, his straight long nose, the cleft in his chin, like a blind person feeling a face for the first time. "It's going to be just fine. It's just a month. But I have to drive home before you'll be out."

"I understand," he said, pulling me tighter within the ring of his arms.

"I'll come back at the end of the month and then you're coming home to Landon," I said. He sounded so defeated that my heart clenched up, and I insisted, "No ifs, ands, or buts."

He managed a half-smile. "I knew Gramps would pull through and get you here before they took me away. I told you earlier that I don't deserve you. I love you so much, Joelle, it hurts."

Panicky birds flocked in my gut but I couldn't let him see that. I gripped his jaws in my hands and looked deeply into his eyes, the better to imprint my words upon him. I promised, "I'll be here when you get out. Can you call me? How does it work?"

"Once a week."

"Then I'll live for those four days."

"I miss you already," he said, his throat hoarse. "I'm so happy we made love this morning."

"You just wait 'til you get out," I told him, trying for some teasing.

"Come back to me," he whispered, and tears spilled over my face; I could no longer contain them.

"I will," I said. "And I'll be with you the whole time you're in here, just like you'll be with me." I touched my heart and then kissed his chest, pressing my lips to the steady beating of his heart. I whispered, "Remember when you caught my kiss that night at the cafe?"

"I will never forget a second I spent in your company," he whispered, crushing me closer.

A knock on the doorframe made me jump and his arms were like iron, holding and protecting me.

"Joelle," he implored.

He kissed me hard and I clung, terrified now that it was time to go, my bravado spent. We broke the kiss just as an officer entered the room. Blythe carefully lifted his arms, releasing me, and I was forced to step back.

"I'll see you before you know it," I whispered, biting down on my lip to stave off further weeping.

"I love you," he said, his eyes intense on mine, and I could tell he was keeping his deep voice steady with extreme effort.

"I love you, too," I said, and though it was just about the toughest thing I'd ever done, I made myself turn and walk away.

Out under the sunny, late-afternoon sky I clung to Rich, sobbing as he patted my back.

"Jo, it's just a month, honey," he said. "It's just a month."

"But I'll have to…go home…without him," I wept. "I can't, Rich…I can't leave him here…"

"Your girls need you," he reminded me; kind, gentle Rich. "And you'll come back. You two have a love I've never seen the likes of, Jo, and it's going to be all right."

I finally reduced myself to shaking sighs, so grateful for his solid, comforting presence. I whispered, "Rich, I wish you were my dad, I really do."

"Aw, Joelle," he said, gruff with emotion, and kissed my cheek before drawing away. His brown eyes twinkled with humor as he said, "Your mother would have a whole lot to say about that, I'd wager."

I laughed and sniffled at the same time, knuckling under my eyes.

"We better go tell Christy what's going on," Rich said then. "Come on. Do you want an ice cream or anything?"

I was about to say no, but then thought better. "Yeah, that sounds good."

An hour later we sat around a high top at Bob's Bowl, Bob himself joining us. He let Christy have the rest of the day free in light of everything, and she was on her second draft beer, her eyes red, though she was past crying and in the angry phase now.

"It just figures that they used the police report as a character reference," she lamented yet again. Rich explained that part of what landed Blythe in jail this time around were the two separate reports involving fights, the first with Christy's ex-boyfriend last spring, and the second with Jackie. Despite the fact that no formal charges were filed from either incident, the officer doing the reporting here in Oklahoma had not minced any words, and this morning's presiding judge proved unforgiving.

"They made him seem so violent," Rich said. "Especially the one last spring. Bly used a weapon?"

Christy cringed a little and said, "Yes, he hit Ron with the lid from the grill. It's just that he's so strong, and he doesn't think when he's upset." She looked over at me and reached for my hand, asking for the fourth or fifth time, "How are you doing, honey?"

I squeezed her fingers and replied, "Better. I was angry before. But I'm trying to remind myself that it's just one month." Although it seemed like ten times that. But I didn't voice the thought. I reminded her, "I'll come back here when he gets out. I have to head home to Minnesota soon, though, my girls…"

"I understand completely," Christy said. "Don't you worry about Bly. I'll go see him as often as I can. He won't be far, just over in Oklahoma City."

"I wish I could stay here," I whispered.

"I know," she acknowledged. "He understands, honey, don't you worry."

Another thought struck me and I looked at Rich, almost afraid to ask, "What about when he gets out? Will he be able to leave Oklahoma?"

"We'll ask Dale, first thing," Rich said.

"He's a damn lucky fella to have you so worried about him," Bob commented, and winked at me.

"I love him," I said simply.

Bob laughed and tugged on his beard, further increasing his similarity to Dodge. He said, "Well, then Junior's luckier than I thought."

I would leave in the morning; there seemed no point in staying now, though as I lay in Blythe's bed that night, curled around my aching heart, I could hardly tolerate the thought. It wasn't that I was trying to be melodramatic; the fear I'd confessed to Jillian earlier in the day remained stubbornly coiled within my stomach. I rolled to my other side and likewise turned my thoughts to this morning, back to making love with Blythe in this same space, holding him as deeply within myself as I could, both in my body and my heart. I drew the sheet over my nose, imagining that it retained the scent of him.

Rich took care of calling Mom, and I had talked to all three girls earlier in the evening, and then Jilly. I shifted my legs, restless, feeling too hot under the covers, almost claustrophobic. I hated that I couldn't call Blythe, couldn't even hear his voice tonight. He was surely in Oklahoma City by now, in the correctional facility there where he would serve the thirty days. No doubt he was hurting and aching as much as I was right now; I thought about every terrible prison movie or television show I'd seen. Would the guards be cruel to him? I pictured their mean, beady little eyes, nightsticks poised in hands. What if someone stabbed him with an improvised blade? Didn't that kind of thing happen in those places?

Oh God.

Joelle, stop it, I told myself firmly, wrapping my arms around my belly and squeezing, forcing a deep breath and then another. I was being foolish thinking the worst. Instead I thought of Blythe telling me how he still felt like a criminal, a loser, for having done time. I would have to do everything I could to negate those ideas he harbored, once and for all. Once I got him home with me and back into my arms.

Soon, soon, soon, I promised myself. *What's a month? You'll go back to Landon and get the girls ready for school, and help at Shore Leave, and get Camille through this morning sickness, and it'll be into September before you even know.*

And at last I drifted to sleep.

Christy and I hugged good-bye under a low, gray, sullen sky the next morning. She kissed my cheek, then handed me my travel mug, which she'd filled with hot coffee. I also had in my possession an old sweatshirt of Blythe's, which I'd found in a drawer, a faded green one from his high school days; my favorite part was that it read TILSON across the back in white lettering. I'd expected Rich to ride home to Minnesota with me, but he elected to stay behind; he planned to remain at the Arrowhead Motel for at least another week and just knowing he was here, close to Blythe when I was unable, offered me reassurance.

"Thank you," I told Christy. "I'll be back in a month."

"You've got his address?"

"Yes, in my pocket right here," I told her, patting my hip. "I'll write him all the time and he said he could call once a week."

"It'll be collect," she warned.

"I would pay any amount just to hear his voice right now," I said truthfully. "And you'll visit him?"

"As much as I can," she promised as I climbed into my car. She added, "Drive safe, Joelle."

"I will," I said. I rolled down the window and waved to her as she curled an arm around herself and raised her palm in farewell.

And I left Oklahoma behind.

Chapter Nine

It was nearing midnight when I turned at last onto Fisherman's Street and drove past the pines and spruces that guarded the town since Gran and Great-Aunt Minnie's youth, and certainly long before. The familiarity of Landon reached out to embrace me and I breathed a sigh, releasing it slowly and deliberately. Downtown was quiet; only Eddie's beer lights and the small street lamps glinted into the otherwise still, black night. Jim Olson's rusted-out Chevy Celebrity was the only car parked on the street at this late hour, about a dozen paces from the front door of Eddie's Bar, of course. I drove past the Angler's Inn and then turned left around Flickertail Lake, onto the lake road that led to Shore Leave and beyond, rolling down the windows to inhale the scent of the lake. Shore Leave at last, and I smiled in sleepy satisfaction to have made it home without stopping for the night.

I was fantasizing about my bed, and long hours of dreamless sleep, before I spent tomorrow morning writing Blythe a long letter, and then getting my act together to find us a place to live. As much as I loved being here at the cafe, I couldn't begin to imagine Blythe sharing the twin bed in my old room with me, while Gran snored on the other. I giggled at the thought, but any hint of humor dropped from my lips as I pulled into the parking lot to observe Jackie's car hunkered beneath the lone street light, sharing the space with Justin's silver truck.

Dammit. What in the hell?

Jilly banged out the porch door as I put the car in park and plunged my hands through my hair, debating whether to just head to the house and avoid the cafe altogether. Jilly wasn't kidding that Jackie was hanging around here too much these days, wearing out what should not have been a welcome in the first place. My sister reached the car and cranked open my door, then practically pulled my shoulder out of its socket.

"You're back!" she crowed, hugging me.

I hugged her hard in return, asking quietly, "What's *he* doing here?"

Jilly sighed and rolled her eyes. "He and Justin are having a beer. To be fair, Jackie was hanging out with the kids until just a little bit ago. They finally gave up waiting for you and went up to bed. They'd been out on the water all day and even Tish couldn't manage to keep her eyes open."

"Well, I think I might just head to bed," I told my sister, and she nodded.

"That's fine," she responded. "You okay?"

I nodded firmly.

"You should come have a quick drink at least," she urged. "I'll have Justin take Jackie over to Eddie's if they feel the need. I want to talk. I'm wide awake."

"You didn't drive over a thousand miles today," I grumbled, but allowed her to lead me to the cafe.

Justin and Jackie were elbowed up to the bar when we entered under the tinkle of the bell; the lights in the dining room were extinguished for the night, but Jilly and I knew the space as well as any place in the world. Mom always kept a couple of strings of white, Christmas-style bulbs wound around the woodwork above the bar, and these were offering the only illumination in the place, except for a small lantern-style lamp behind the counter. I dragged my heels as we entered. Justin, closer to the front door, leaned to catch a glimpse of me and called warmly, "Welcome home, Jo!"

"Thanks, Justin," I said, not meeting Jackie's eyes, even though he sat there alongside Justin, studying me quite openly. Jilly moved swiftly behind the bar and grabbed me a glass; hand poised at the row of tap beer pull handles, she turned over her shoulder to inquire, "The usual?"

"Yes, please," I said, not wanting to join them, though Justin tipped his head at the open bar stools.

"No, we're heading out to the dock," I explained.

"Don't go leaving just because I'm here," Jackie said, though not in a confrontational sort of way. His voice held the sound of hours of drinking, but he wasn't drunk. Not like he'd been last weekend.

"It's not that, we just want to talk," Jilly explained as she came back around the gleaming wooden counter, pausing for a moment to twine her arms around Justin's neck and kiss his temple. He caught her lightly around the waist and kissed her more thoroughly before releasing her. Their playfulness made my heart clench and I turned away so that the sudden tears in the back of my nose wouldn't spurt into my eyes. I missed Blythe so much that my chest felt gouged; it would be weeks until I saw him again.

"Come on, Jo, you can't go to bed just yet," Jilly commanded, leading the way back through the cafe. "I'm too selfish. I need to hear what's going on." She handed off the beer to me and reached to grab two hooded sweatshirts from the coat tree as we made our way onto the porch, down the steps and then out onto the dock, our favorite place to talk. The stars raged madly in the sky and I took a moment to inhale the air and let its familiarity comfort me as I followed Jilly out to our glider.

"So, are you all right?"

I sighed, plopping down beside her. "No. I thought he'd be with me when I came home. I hate that I can't talk to him when I want. I hate that he feels like a loser, sees himself that way because he's been in jail twice now. He knows I don't care, that it doesn't matter to me."

"What's the secret?" she asked, surprising me, though I should have learned by now not to let anything Jilly knew catch me by surprise. She explained, "I just sensed it."

Despite the tiredness gnawing at my brain, I told her the story. All of it, and she listened without breathing a word. When I'd finished she said softly, "Wow."

I curved my left arm through her right, clinging to her, missing

Blythe with a white-hot intensity. I whispered, "I know. I couldn't believe it either. And that's why he landed in jail then, and why he's back now."

"Aw, Blythe," she murmured, squeezing my arm against her side. "I knew he had a big heart. What a horrible thing to go through. Shit, Joelle."

"I know," I whispered. "But this is it. In a month he'll come back with me if I have to hogtie him. And then I'm going to make an honest man out of him."

"I hate to point out that you're still technically married," Jilly said, and I grunted in response.

"Hardly," I said. "I'll sign those divorce papers and Jackie will leave me the hell alone. It's over between us."

"Don't count on it," Jilly said, somewhat ominously. "He's been getting sentimental this week, I can tell. Playing 'daddy' with the girls and feeling all nostalgic. I can see it all over his face."

"He's always been a good dad," I defended, not sure why I bothered. "I can't say he isn't, even if he's been a shit husband. At least, for the past five years."

Up at the cafe, the screen door creaked open and the sound of the men coming out onto the porch met our ears. Justin called, "I'm heading home!" and Jilly shifted position and slipped her sandals back over her toes.

"I'll be right up," she called over her shoulder. And then to me, "You gonna hang out down here?"

"No, I'm exhausted."

Jilly darted up to the porch to kiss Justin good-night (which, judging by their average, would last about ten minutes) while I went the longer way around the cafe to the parking lot, where I meant to grab my purse and travel bag, and lock the car. I walked with my head tipped down, studying the blacktop, and didn't sense Jackie until he was in step with me. I was mad at myself for startling a little. He saw that and laughed, low.

"Sorry, I didn't mean to scare you again," he said. "And I'm sorry about the other night."

"I know, Jilly said." I reached my car and clicked open the trunk.

"So, how was your trip?" he asked, sounding too innocent.

I looked over at him at that; he stood leaning on one hip against the far side of my car, both hands shoved into his front pockets. He wore jeans and a ratty t-shirt, a Bears ball cap over his dark curls. He appeared to have spent the day on the lake along with the kids. I finally spoke. "Why do you ask?"

He shrugged as though my answer meant nothing. "No reason. I just wondered."

I hefted my bag out of the trunk and shouldered the long strap, saying, "It's great that you've been hanging out with the girls. They've missed you."

"Do you want me to get that?" he asked, nodding at my load.

I rolled my eyes at him.

"I've missed them, too," he said, watching me with an expression I couldn't read. Or maybe I just didn't want to read it.

"Well, that's great," I said, slamming the trunk with a bit too much force. He seemed to get my hint and backed off, in the direction of his car.

"Good-night, Joelle," he said as I walked away, but I pretended not to hear him.

I allowed myself the luxury of sleeping in the next morning. Upon waking I rubbed my eyes and looked over to observe that Gran was up and about, her bed neat as a pin, like usual. I groaned, flopping back onto my pillow and then cast a longing glance at the cell phone on my night-stand. I needed to hear his voice. Just for a moment, just so I could hear he was all right; I knew when I saw him in the courthouse in Brandt that he was worried I wouldn't come back for him, even though he'd tried to hide this from me. He figured that I would get home to Landon and realize I didn't need an ex-con boyfriend complicating my life. I gripped the lower half of my face in one hand, horrified that he might let doubt dominate his thoughts, now that he had all this time on his hands.

Oh God, Blythe, don't think that. I love you. I'll show you just how much… I'll spend the rest of my life showing you. It'll be all right, my sweet man.

I couldn't stay in bed all day, tempting as that thought might be just now. I needed to face everyone, and hug my girls, and I wanted to write Blythe a letter and tell him that I knew how he felt and why he shouldn't worry.

But first some coffee.

Ruthann intercepted me on the lake path and I ran to catch her in a hug. She was wearing her hair up in a complicated twist; Camille must have done that for her, because I knew Ruthie couldn't manage such a hairstyle on her own. I rocked her side to side and planted a kiss on her right ear.

"Ouch, that was loud," she giggled, pulling away to hook her arm through mine. "I was just coming up to see if you were awake yet."

"Barely, but am I glad to see you," I told my littlest. "I missed you!"

"We missed you, too, Mom, but Dad has been out here almost every day hanging out. We've been having fun, even though Camille is mad at him right now," Ruthie explained, reminding me of Tish. Usually Tish was my informant.

"I know, Aunt Jilly told me," I said. "How has Milla been feeling?"

"All right. She's *soooo* grumpy," Ruthie added. "Mama, how's Blythe? Grandma said he went back to jail. Why?"

Ugh. I decided that hedging was just cowardly, and said, "He has to serve thirty days because he left Oklahoma when he wasn't supposed to leave the state, when he came up here to work. But when he's out he'll come back home with me, to live with us. You guys are still okay with that, right?"

Ruthie shrugged. "Sure. It's weird not having him around in the kitchen. And you love him?"

"I do," I told her, quietly. "I really do."

"Daddy asked me and Tish if you did," Ruthann continued, and my steps faltered.

"What?" I asked.

She shrugged again, this time appearing slightly uncomfortable, eyebrows quirking. But she said, "He asked us if you were going to marry Blythe. But Daddy called Blythe 'that criminal.'"

Jackie. Damn you. It's not a word of your business.

"What did you guys tell him?" I asked.

"Well, Tish said that you told us you fell in love with him. Daddy was quiet for a while after that, but then Tish was like, 'Didn't you fall in love, too, Dad, with that woman you work with?' and Daddy said that he was sorry that any of this happened. I felt so bad for him, Mom, he looked so sad. I think he's really sorry."

And there was the lame horse crossing the finish line. What Jackie couldn't do directly to me he was doing to the girls. Oh, no doubt he was sad…because he was jealous that I'd found someone, no other reason. What a lowdown tactic. I should have seen this coming. Dammit, and Ruthie was moved by him. Well, I reasoned, they did love their dad and I wouldn't begrudge that. Although I suddenly possessed a renewed interest in taking a baseball bat to Jackie's handsome, manipulative head.

Tish bounded down the porch steps and I hugged her, too. Her blue eyes sparkled like firecrackers as she said, "Mom, Dad says he's taking us tubing today!"

"Where? Washout?" I asked, feathering back a loose strand of her hair. She was practically jumping with excitement.

Tish nodded. "He's bringing me, Clint, and Ruthie. You should come with, Mom!"

"Oh, you guys have a good time," I said, not about to be roped into Jackie's machinations. "I'm not up for it today, love."

"So Blythe is back in jail, huh?" she asked, following me up the porch steps.

I turned and said, "Just for a month, and then he'll be out."

Clint burst out of the cafe, banging the door open and grabbing me around the waist for a hug.

"Hi, Aunt Joey!" he said. "Are you coming tubing at Washout with us today?"

"No, not today, honey," I told my nephew. "But you guys have fun, okay?"

"Kids, I packed a lunch," Aunt Ellen said, coming out the door to give me a squeeze. There was nothing like being gone a few nights to get a month's worth of hugs in one dose. But it made me happy to be home. Ellen added, "Coffee's on, honey."

"Thanks, Ell," I said, and headed inside. Behind me I heard the girls start yelling, "Hi, Dad!" and didn't have to look to know that Jackie was pulling into the lot.

I poured a cup and drank it at the counter, wondering where Jilly and Gran were. Mom appeared in the ticket window and said, "I'm glad you're back, honey."

"Hey, Mom," I said, before swiveling on the stool to peer out the window. Jackie caught the girls in a hug, one in each arm. He was wearing his swim trunks and a sun visor, grinning at whatever Tish was chattering about; I couldn't make out all the words even with the open windows. Ruthie danced ahead and clacked through the porch door, Jackie, Clint, and Tish not far behind.

I eyed Jackie, wondering just how much of his precious vacation time he intended to spend here. Or for that matter, how many days before Lanny got suspicious about his absence and decided to drive up to Minnesota to collect him. I pictured her clearly, gliding through the screen door on her ultra-long legs with a look of distaste at what she would consider the tackiest of surroundings, staring down her perfect nose, artificially full lips drawn up like an old-fashioned purse string. I almost giggled, imagining offering her a bottled beer and a plate of fried fish. *Ha.* In some ways it struck me as odd that Jackie would be drawn to someone so snobbishly sophisticated, so *Chicago.* He'd adapted to fit the big-city part in certain ways, but I knew the real him.

Or at least I'd thought I did, once upon a time.

"Good morning, Jo," he said, ridiculously polite. And then, "Tish, sweet pea, will you grab me a cup before we go?"

"I'm getting the cooler!" Tish responded, heading for the kitchen, Clint on her heels.

"I'll get it, Jackie," Mom said easily. I just barely refrained from rolling my eyes.

"Thanks, Joan," he said, taking a sip as he claimed a stool near mine, conspicuously keeping one between us. Tish and Clint chattered with Mom back in the kitchen, seemingly oblivious to any strain that I might be feeling. Ellen set a second tray of blueberry-crumble muffins on the counter. I studied the ticket window and imagined how amazing it would be if Blythe were to magically appear there, conjured by the intensity of my longing.

I sighed and finally relented, asking my husband, "So, where are you guys going today?"

"Washout, I was thinking," Jackie said, eating a muffin in two bites, referring to a stretch of river that flowed between Landon and Rose Lake, then out to Fairfield. In high school we'd gone tubing there many a time and dubbed it 'Wipeout.' And then, oh so casually, he offered, "You'd be welcome to join us."

"Yeah, Mom! Come on," Tish said. "It'll be so much fun!"

"I have a lot to do today," I said firmly. "Thanks, though."

Jackie shrugged. I really hated his power to make me uncomfortable in my own home. I also hated that, by contrast, he seemed so damn composed. And I couldn't even be justifiably rude to him, because our children were in the room.

"Be careful," I told Ruthann, who was spinning on the stool between Jackie and me. "And don't forget the sunscreen. And lots of water."

"Got it," Tish said, appearing with a cooler hefted in her arms, Clint with a second.

"Jackie, good to see you, boy!" Dodge boomed, coming in the screen door, aviator sunglasses pushed back on his head. So everyone was turning traitor on me. Jackie was just too familiar around here for anyone to truly shun him.

Except Gran. Good old Gran.

"Hey, Dodge!" Jackie replied with fondness, finishing his coffee and rising to shake the older man's hand. "You want to join us on the inner tubes today?"

Dodge laughed and his barrel-shaped torso quivered. "Are you shitting me? You kids have fun."

And a minute later Jackie loaded them into the station wagon, which Mom was gracious enough to lend him. I bit down the resentful comments I wanted to make to my mother, and instead found a notebook and a pen. I slid into a booth, all the way over to the window, and flipped past random notes and scribbles, a grocery list that was probably two years old, to a blank page. Twenty minutes later I was so absorbed writing a letter that I jumped when Camille asked at my elbow, "Whatcha doing, Mom? Homework?"

Without thinking, I moved a forearm to cover my words, as if I sat here doing something indecent. Immediately I dropped the pose, sitting back and sweeping the notebook closed with what I hoped was a businesslike air. I said, "Well, school does start in a few weeks."

Camille slid opposite me and stacked her hands atop one another, studying me from three feet away, trying to puzzle out my expression. Her eyes were the soft golden-green so particular to the women in our family. I studied her lovely face as though I hadn't seen it in months; maybe that was part of the reason she'd gotten pregnant; a mother whose own problems so occupied her thoughts that her daughter turned into a woman overnight, unnoticed.

Camille's long hair fell over her shoulders, dark and wavy, just like Jackie's. Her cheekbones were sprinkled with freckles from the summer sun; her breasts appeared nearly twice as large as they had a month ago. I remembered well that swelling ache of early pregnancy, especially the first time through, when your breasts outpaced your belly in growth and would for a few months, at least. Her long dark lashes, another gift from Jackie, swept to her cheeks as she considered her words; she wanted to tell me something. I recognized that she would be irritated if I attempted to guess, or suddenly turned sentimental.

Then her mouth twisted slightly and she said, "About that."

"About what?" I asked.

"School," she said in a tone that suggested I needed to keep up with the conversation. "I don't want to go, Mom. It would suck worse than I could possibly imagine. None of the girls I made friends with this summer have even called me since word got out that I'm having Noah's baby. It's like I have the plague, like I'm this dumb, rotten slut who got him in trouble."

Oh no. Shit, shit, shit.

Before I said anything that might be the wrong thing in this moment, I reached and caught her rather unwilling hands in both of mine, gently squeezing.

She allowed my touch, speaking on in a rush. "It's like I'm a prisoner out here. I mean, I love it at Shore Leave, and I love being here, but I can't *do* anything anymore. I'm so tired, and Dad won't let me go tubing with them. Last night I tried calling Cara back in Chicago, to tell her the news. But she's in Florida with her grandparents, having fun. She couldn't talk long, and in the end I didn't even tell her about the baby." Tears spangled her lashes now, and my heart ached for her. I parted my lips to speak, but she continued before I could make a sound. "Mom, seriously, I can't deal with this." She looked searchingly into my eyes and the question she wanted to ask, but didn't, hovered like something tangible in the air between our heads.

How did you deal with this?

"Camille, I'm sorry we haven't had a better talk yet," I said quietly. "That's my fault. Everything that's happened this summer has caught me off guard a little bit here. But I can tell you this, sweetie, you can't deal with it all at once. You'll go crazy. Just take things a day at a time. You're not a slut, and anyone who says that is ignorant and mean. You'll love your baby, and he or she will be the best part of your world."

"She," Camille whispered, and her eyes softened a little, as though looking inward.

"A girl, then?" I asked, smiling at her.

"Aunt Jilly says so," she responded with total certainty.

I let that sink in, pausing for a beat. Obviously she accepted this as a given. Finally I said, "I'm glad. I hoped for daughters when I was pregnant with all of you. Great-Aunt Minnie used to tell us it was like being linked to a chain of mothers since the beginning of time, or something like that. She was fairly poetic." I laughed a little at the memory, with affection. I wished my girls could have known Minnie. I glanced in the direction of the counter, almost certain I would see my great-aunt there, tall and angular, her golden hair in a twist, a number-two order pencil behind her ear, horn-rimmed glasses dangling against her breasts on their fancy turquoise chain. No one got away with a damn thing in Minnie's presence.

"But Mom, please don't let Dad go talk to Noah, please, Mom. I would die of shame," she said, withdrawing her hands from mine and slipping them beneath her thighs on the vinyl seat. Her eyes implored me, bordering on desperation.

Again I chose my words with great care. "Love, Dad is just worried about you. You know that it's wrong for Noah to just go back to school as though nothing happened. It's way worse than wrong, Milla, it's downright cowardly."

She swallowed hard and closed her eyes. She whispered, "I know that. But he's going to pay me child support. He said so. He's just in shock over all of this."

"No more than you are!" I told her.

Her lips trembled a little, but she bit down rather savagely on the lower and then asked, "So, how long does it take to fall *out* of love with someone?"

No one can explain how very much your children's suffering affects you, a sensation like a hard-knuckled punch to the gut. I said, "Oh, sweetie. He's not worth your love, I hope you know that. I'm so sorry."

She insisted, "But how long? How long did it take you to fall out of love with Dad?"

Ouch. Fuck. There was a subtle undercurrent of something negative in her tone. Resentment, maybe. Accusation. Anger. I finally said, "Camille, when I was younger, when you guys were all born, I loved your dad very much. Don't ever think I didn't. But we got married way too young. Before we knew what we really wanted out of life. And—"

"Because of me," my daughter interrupted, not pulling any punches now. "Because of *me* you got married."

No use acting otherwise. I said, "That may be partly true, but we loved each other, too. It wasn't just because we were going to have a baby. Sweetie, you and your sisters are the best thing that happened between your dad and me. You three make everything worth it. Did you think for a second that I would feel differently? Your dad loves you guys so much." She opened her mouth but I gave her a look and continued, determined, "You girls are getting older. You'll move out, leave us for your own lives. Don't you think Dad and I deserve to have lives that make us happy, too?"

Stubbornly, she remained silent.

"Camille?" I pressed. The day brightened around us as we'd been absorbed in conversation. The air in the cafe glowed with morning sun, the lake sparkling to life under its golden rays, the whine of outboard motors meeting our ears now through the open windows. Mom and Ellen were chatting with the new cook, a friend of Rich's hired to fill in for Blythe. Gran and Jilly came in at some point; Jilly was on the phone by the register, Gran making a fresh pot of coffee. A big restaurant supply truck rumbled into the parking lot.

Finally, her voice carrying a tentative wobble, she asked, "Mom, aren't you…aren't you sort of embarrassed that Blythe is in jail? That he's a criminal?"

My spine straightened almost inadvertently. Working hard to keep a defensive edge from my tone, I said, "First of all, he's not a criminal. If you knew the whole story you wouldn't think that at all. And second, he is one of the kindest people I've ever met."

She stared into my eyes as though attempting to pluck answers directly from my brain. She asked, "You really love him, don't you?"

"I do, Camille. I wasn't expecting it, but I do. And when you find the right someone for you, you'll understand. I promise."

She glared at these words, clearly unwilling to believe them; at last she sighed with an air of long-suffering and said, "All right, Mom. I trust you."

"Good," I said decisively, catching up the notebook containing my letter to Blythe. "And by the way, you are going to school this fall."

I headed for the kitchen before she could reply, hoping to find my apron and get the day started.

Chapter Ten

Jackie brought the kids home around supper time, all of them covered in dried mud, scrapes, and bug bites, smelling of lake water and sunscreen. The cafe was busy with the usual Wednesday night crowd, and I stood on the porch taking an order as the station wagon chugged into the lot. I watched as the kids piled out, laughing, and Jackie called after them to help him unload. He wore his Bears cap again, swim trunks but no shirt. His sporty sunglasses hung on a cord around his neck, bumping against his muscular chest; still a show-off, I couldn't help but think. As he followed the kids, headed for the cafe, he shrugged into a t-shirt in the one-armed way he'd always had. I turned back to the table and finished up their drink order, ducking conveniently back inside.

I busied myself at the bar so I wouldn't have to talk to him. The girls and Clint immediately zeroed in on the counter in the dining room, where Mom made sure they received plates of fried fish. I could hear the girls babbling with excitement even over the din of chatter in the two rooms. Jackie joined them, straddling a stool and gracing Mom with his toothy grin. She settled a plate of fried fish in front of him before you could say *hoodwinked*.

On my way back through the cafe, Ruthie called, "Hey, Mom! We had fun!"

"Good!" I responded, pretending to be too busy to join them. Jackie, his mouth full of food, shot me a speculative look that I ignored.

Minutes later, Camille joined them at the counter for supper; I was relieved to see her appetite slowly returning. I kept legitimately busy as the four of them, plus Clint, consumed plates of fish and fries; something about being on the water all day makes you ten times hungrier when you actually sit down to eat. And to my relief Jackie didn't linger after dinner. I remained on the porch, clearing a table as he left. He took a moment to drag the inner tubes from the edge of the parking lot where the kids dumped them, pulling them up to the far side of the building. He didn't look back as he got into his car and drove away.

The next couple of days passed with the comfort of routine working on me like an anesthetic. I picked up shifts in the cafe, registered the girls for school, and took a few drives with Jilly to check out houses for rent in the greater Landon area. The population of Landon was relatively small, less than four hundred, and most people lived within miles of downtown, in older neighborhoods decorated by overgrown maples, cedars, and sunburst locusts. The more expensive homes ringed Flickertail Lake, and I couldn't imagine being able to afford renting one of those, even with the child support that Jackie would pay as soon as the details of our divorce were hammered out. I hadn't talked to Jackie since Wednesday, but planned to make it a point next time he stopped out at Shore Leave. He hadn't mentioned the divorce papers he'd supposedly dragged with him from Chicago, but it was high time I signed them, or at least sat down and read them. I wondered, ironically, if I'd need a lawyer, despite the fact that my husband was one.

Rich called Thursday evening to say that he and Christy had been to visit Blythe, that he was doing all right in jail, and that Blythe told them to tell me he'd call Saturday evening, sometime between six and eight. I jittered with anticipation all that afternoon, studying the phone as though *willing* it to ring. I craved hearing his voice. I craved *him*, but I would take the sound of his voice right now. Rich told me Blythe would have to call the cafe since it would be collect, and so I hovered around the phone like an electron. It was busy as hell and everyone was annoyed with me for constantly reminding them to answer if I wasn't near. Gran finally made a show of dragging a stool near the register and taking a seat, with a theatrical sigh. I kissed her cheek before scurrying back outside to grab a drink order from a new two-top.

By quarter to eight, Blythe hadn't called yet, and a desperate, empty feeling began to take up residence in my stomach. I reminded myself that there were any number of reasons for this fact; maybe he wasn't even able to use the phone tonight, and of course I'd have no way of knowing. I agonized that I should have stayed in Oklahoma for another few days, so I could have gone to visit him at least once before driving home. Gran abandoned her post and sat chatting with an older couple in one of the booths. My tables closed out for the evening, I was about to take a seat on the stool near the phone when Tish came through the cafe for a refill and told me, "Dad's outside on the porch. He wanted me to ask you if you had a second to talk with him."

"Tell him I'm busy," I said distractedly, craning my neck to look outside; I hadn't realized he'd shown up. But sure enough, there was Jackie leaning on his elbows, beer in one hand, chatting with Dodge, who'd taken a seat across from him. Dodge brought his daughter Liz's kids, the triplets, out to see Ruthie, the four of them scampering down by the water's edge, playing fetch with Chester and Chief.

Tish shrugged, clapping her red plastic cup against the pour spout for the root beer and filling it to the brim. She said, "Okay. Hey, do you care if we have a fire tonight?"

"Ask Dodge," I told her, turning back to the phone.

Less than a minute later Jackie himself appeared before me. I was in the process of writing Blythe another letter in my notebook, leaning over the waist-high counter where the register and the phone both sat, one palm braced against the side of my face as I wrote. I'd mailed him the first a few days ago, kissing it before slipping it into the envelope, like a middle-school girl. The pen was flowing across the paper with the floodgate of my words when I realized I was being studied and looked up to see Jackie gazing at me with an expression of wry amusement.

"Homework?" he questioned.

I slapped the notebook closed and straightened.

"Hey," I said, and my cheeks felt hot.

"You have a second?" he asked.

"So how much time off did they give you?" I asked in response, trying and failing to keep a note of irritability from my voice. "How do Rocky and Bullwinkle get by without you?"

Jackie snorted and then laughed a little, rocking back on his heels. He used to hate how I'd nicknamed his partners, whose actual surnames were Rockford and Bunnickle.

"They gave me August. They know I've been going through some stuff," he replied easily.

Stuff. Trust Jackie to use such a flippant word for his failing marriage and pending divorce.

"And what about Lanny? She's all right with you being gone so long?" I asked, scrutinizing his familiar face for telltale signs of discomfort.

"She knows where I am," he said, though somewhat stiffly.

"Is she in the townhouse?" I asked, anger swelling in my stomach. But I let it go; no point.

Jackie's eyes narrowed a little. A definite bite in his tone, he said, "No, she's got her own place. Why? Jealous?"

I was about to turn away, not about to put up with this shit, when the phone rang. I snatched it up and demanded, "Hello?"

My heart thrust so vigorously it seemed to be lodged in my throat instead of behind my ribs.

"Hi, how late are you open?" asked a woman I didn't know.

"We're *closed,*" I snapped, slamming the receiver back into its cradle with so much force the bell inside the phone rang a little; my pen rolled to the floor and I bent to retrieve it.

"What in the hell?" Jackie asked. I straightened to observe his dark eyebrows knitted with indignation.

"What?" I demanded, tapping my pen furiously against the counter-top.

"Where'd you get that shirt?" he blustered, gesturing in the direction of my breasts.

Bewildered by this question, I glanced down; I wore Blythe's old sweatshirt…the one with his last name written across the back. Clearly Jackie had noticed this as I leaned down to grab the pen; my hair was tugged into a messy ponytail rather than hanging loose, allowing for a clear glimpse of the word TILSON framed between my shoulder blades.

"Jesus, Jo, you have to flaunt this…*this*…" Never without the right words, Jackie nonetheless stuttered to a halt. His face appeared hot, flustered blood gathering in his cheeks. And Jackie never allowed the indignity of appearing flustered.

"This what?" I challenged.

"This *relationship* with a goddamn criminal, that's *what*," Jackie all but spit out, leaning closer to me, eyes snapping. "Don't you care what our girls think? Don't you care what you're exposing them to?" He lowered his voice to hiss, "Are you wearing this guy's underwear, too?"

Fury momentarily rendered me blind; truly, for a split second, Jackie and the cafe disappeared behind a fog of swirling redness. But I was not about to let anger get the better of me, not when there was scarcely five minutes left before eight, the window narrowing on my chance to talk to Blythe tonight. I looked hard into Jackie's eyes, refusing to back down or appear shameful. And where in the hell did he get off, talking to me that way?

Slow and dead-serious, I said, "Leave me alone, Jackie."

He changed tone and tactics at once; all reasonability now, he insisted, "I just want to talk with you. Can we go sit on the dock for a sec?"

"No," I said shortly, and wished I *was* wearing Blythe's underwear, just because.

Jackie stared at me as though judging the wisdom of pressing further. I glared at him until he finally backed off, agreeing, "Tomorrow, then."

I needed to go to the bathroom shortly after, and again intercepted my middle child on her way to get a refill.

"Accept the collect call if it comes. I'll be right back!" I said, and Tish rolled her eyes but humored me willingly enough. And sure thing, as I returned to the dining room Tish wiggled the receiver urgently in my direction. I sprinted to it.

"I just accepted the charges," she said, before heading back outside. I brought the phone to my ear and my heart throbbed as though I'd just swum across the lake to take this call.

"Hello?" I all but demanded.

"Joelle," Blythe said gladly, so warm and immediate it was as though he was just around the corner in the bar, where he'd been the first night I met him, back in May. *If only.* My heart thrust with undiluted joy to hear his voice. I seemed weeks had passed since we'd spoken, rather than days. His voice was husky with longing as he said, "It's so good to hear you, baby."

"Blythe," I said, and longing saturated my voice, too. "Oh God, I miss you. How are you? I've hardly been able to think of anything else, I've been so worried about you. Are you all right?" My words gushed on top of one another. I clutched the phone as though it was a part of him.

"I promise I'm fine, baby, just crazy with missing you," he said. "I got your letter. I keep it in my pocket and sleep with it at night. Just so you know."

I laughed, but it emerged sounding more like a sob. I said, "Just three more weeks. I can hardly wait. Are you sure you're all right, not just saying that so I won't worry? I can't tell you how much I miss you. I think about you every second."

"Aw, Joelle, I miss you so fucking much. And when I saw what you wrote…you can read me pretty well, can't you?"

"I would hope so," I said. "I love you. You're mine, mister, so you better get used to it."

"I love you, too, baby. This reminds me of the first night I called your phone," he added, his voice so deep and familiar, and I was heartened to hear a hint of his usual good humor. "It was too late to call that night, but I just wanted to hear your voice before I went to sleep."

"After you kissed me for the first time," I murmured, leaning over the counter, my voice soft with remembrance. "I dreamed about that kiss for weeks before it happened, you know."

"Same here, you don't even know," he said. And then, "Joelle, I only have a minute left. Literally, a minute. They time us. But I'll call next week, same time, okay?"

"I'll be here," I whispered. "Has your mom been to see you again?"

"She was here with Rich once already," he said. "She told me about how you cried that afternoon. I can't bear to think about you hurting, baby, especially when I'm not there to hold you. So give the girls a hug and go sit on the dock, okay? And don't worry about me, I'm just fine here. I promise you."

"Okay," I whispered again, clutching the phone. "Just know how much I'm thinking of you. I can't wait to get my arms around you, sweetheart."

"I'm counting the hours," he said, and then in a rush, "I gotta go. I love you, Joelle."

"I love you," I told him, but the phone was hung up with an abrupt clunk, as though someone on the other end grabbed it from his hands. I held the receiver for a long time, just cradling it, until I realized I should take his advice and go find the girls, hug them, and then sit on the dock and appreciate the night.

One week down.

Chapter Eleven

The girls were having a pajama party when I found them later, after sitting for a half an hour on the dock, watching as an indigo evening seeped across the sky and permeated the glowing western horizon. I smoked the last two cigarettes from the pack on the porch as the setting sun backlit the trees ringing the lakeshore in a molten yellow, totally dazzling, though my thoughts were a thousand miles away. I played over our conversation, savoring Blythe's words, so grateful to hear his humor, if just for an instant; even with the distance between us his voice resounded in the depths of me, places untouched before him. I loved my girls unequivocally, and my family, but a powerful force connected Blythe and me; something I hadn't realized I needed until finding him. How was it that I felt I'd known him, loved him, long before this summer? Long before this life, maybe.

I wrapped into my own arms, a sorry substitute for the arms I wanted. I closed my eyes against the tail end of the sunset, letting it bathe my eyelids with the last of the day, picturing Blythe and his teasing, half-bashful grin, the love in his smoky eyes. I squeezed myself even more tightly, shuddering with the remembrance of his embrace. Earlier in the summer I'd been with him often enough that his scent would cling to my wrists, my hands and hair. I drew the neck of his old sweatshirt over my nose, wishing it smelled like him. Just wearing it comforted me to an extent, the soft material that once encased his shoulders, his chest. And his last name across the back filled me with sweetness.

Blythe Edward Tilson, I love you. I will wait for you.

It was times like this that the force of my need for him stunned me as would a physical blow; thinking of his words about not worrying, I scolded, *Enough of this for tonight. You talked to him and he's all right. It's not much longer. And your daughters need you. You can't sit out here all night.*

And so I rose from the glider and made my way through the gloaming, across the dewy grass to Jilly's apartment. I jogged up the wooden staircase that climbed the outside of the garage to Jilly's, one floor up. Dodge kept the stairs sturdy, although I always hated using them in the winter. My spirits lifted as I heard the radio atop my sister's fridge blaring; her outer light shone in welcome for me, and I pushed through the screen door into the sound of Cyndi Lauper's "Good Enough." The little kitchen was bright and cheerful, if slightly too warm for the heat of the evening, Tish and Ruthann busy popping corn and melting caramel, respectively, both swaying in time to the beat; Tish sang along in her painfully off-key alto.

"Hi, Mom!" Ruthie said over her shoulder, stationed at the stovetop, whisking melting caramels. She was barefoot, wearing white terrycloth pants and an oversized gray t-shirt, her long curls held up by a green scrunchy that had surely been in Jilly's possession since the 1980s. Tish, whose curls fell almost to her shoulders these days, was clad in an ancient Van Halen t-shirt and black cotton shorts covered with tiny purple horses; my tallest, curviest daughter, Tish remained singularly unappreciative of these things, which secretly amused me. She was also clad in the bunny slippers I'd given Jilly for Christmas one year in middle school.

"Hi, guys," I said, leaning to give each of them a kiss on the cheek. "I can't believe those are still intact," I added, indicating the fuzzy slippers with their ridiculous googly eyes and floppy pink ears.

Tish kicked out one foot to admire them. "Aunt Jilly said I could keep them if I wanted."

"Mmmm, it smells good in here," I said. "What else are you guys making?"

"Brownies with chocolate chips," Tish said. And then, as the chorus rang out, sang at the top of her lungs.

"Caramel corn'll be ready in five minutes," Ruthie explained.

Jilly bolted around the corner, yelling, "Pregnant lady needs a drink, outta the way, people!"

I giggled at her as she made a show of searching the fridge, jamming along to the song with the girls.

"Where's Clinty?" I asked, helping myself to a can of beer, reaching into the open fridge around Jilly. She was in her pajamas, a white tank and matching shorts printed with multi-colored ladybugs. Her toenails were painted a vibrant neon-yellow. She smelled good, like coconut oil and possibly a margarita.

"We kicked him out, didn't we, girls?" she said, as Cyndi switched to "Time After Time" and we all started singing along, inescapably.

"Remember how many hours we spent in front of the mirror, singing with our curling irons as microphones?" I groaned.

My sister giggled and then yelled in the direction of the living room, "Milla, what do you want?"

"Cola, if you've got any," my oldest called back, and Jilly passed a can to me.

"Here, sweetie," I said, heading around the half-wall that separated the two spaces. Only a small lamp glowed in here, and the television was on even though it could hardly be heard over the radio. I recognized the movie *The Great Outdoors*, which we'd seen enough to make sound superfluous anyway. Camille curled rather pitifully on the recliner, her hair arranged in a braid that fell over one shoulder, reminiscent of her elementary school years. She looked sweaty.

"Thanks, Mom," she murmured, holding the icy can to her neck.

My heart bumped with a moment of nostalgia, remembering those childhood days when her face was round and plump and dimpled, and she'd climbed aboard the bus like a big girl to become a part of the wider world. I perched on the arm of the chair as she cracked open the soda, and then smoothed a stray hair from her forehead, my baby who was having a baby. I asked, "How are you?"

"I'm so hot," she groaned. "I wish it was winter, seriously."

"Here, for heaven's sake," I said, leaning to redirect the oscillating fan.

I clicked it down to a less forceful flow and aimed it on her. It was humid as a sauna in here.

"How's Blythe?" she asked, closing her eyes in relief as the cool air rushed over her face.

"He's all right, just missing all of us. It was good to hear his voice."

Her eyes opened and flashed to mine, clearly hearing something unfamiliar in my tone. "That's good. I know you miss him."

If only she knew. My girls would be shocked at half of my thoughts these days, but that was beside the point. I was slowly realizing that beneath the mother-cloak I'd worn for nearly two decades there was still a woman. And that it was all right to let her out. Camille redirected her gaze at the movie and I commented, "Remember how much of a crush you used to have on the oldest brother?"

Camille laughed a little, shifting position and taking a long drink of the soda. "Buck. Yeah, of course."

"He is a cutie," I said speculatively.

"Ugh, he looks like Noah," she said, and my gaze snapped back to her.

"Have you talked to him lately?" I asked, proceeding with caution.

She shook her head without a word and so I didn't press the issue. Instead I said, "Hey, the Carters were out at Shore Leave today, did you talk to them? Bull said the homestead cabin over at White Oaks is just waiting for you to see it."

Camille's lips tipped into a half-wistful smile; she glanced upward, as though searching for a memory, biting the insides of her cheeks before finally saying, "Maybe sometime. I just don't feel up to it right now."

"Well it's not going anywhere," I assured her. "It's been there for over a hundred years, according to Bull. Diana told me that their son, Mathias, used to sleep out in that cabin when he was a teenager and that she worried he would get bit by—"

"Jo! You want a beer-ita or what?" my sister called, effectively interrupting me. She leaned around from the kitchen with eyebrows raised.

"A what?" I asked, perplexed.

"It's my own concoction, a beer mixed with tequila, lemonade, and lime juice. And ice," she added, as though just recalling.

"Are you already wasted?" I teased. "That sounds awful. And I'm good with this," I added, holding my can aloft.

Ruthie appeared, bearing a tray loaded with brownies and plastic bowls of caramel corn. And at that moment, probably sensing the goodies, there was intense thumping on the steps outside, as though a SWAT team ascended them. The screen door opened with a loud whack and Clint and his best friend Liam barged into the kitchen.

"No!" Tish yelped. "You guys are banished outside, remember!"

"She's right," Jilly agreed. "Boys in tents only tonight."

"Aw, Mom, we just need food," Clint wheedled. He stuck his head into the living room and said, "Hi, Aunt Joey!"

God, I loved my nephew. I grinned at him and said, "Hi, honey, you guys camping out by the fire?"

"Yeah, but we need supplies. We're starving! Hey, how's Bly? Mom said you talked to him."

"He misses all of us," I said. "But he'll be here soon."

"Great!" Clint took things in stride, without fail. He offered to Ruthie, "How about I carry that tray for you? It looks heavy."

And my sweet Ruthann paused to let Clint peruse the snacks.

Tish, not about to be conned in this fashion, shouldered between the two of them, snapping, "No way, Clint, we just made all of this! The marshmallows are for you guys!"

"Ruthie, bring me a brownie before they're gone," Camille requested. "Oh, and maybe a napkin."

"I'll get it," I said, and made my way to the kitchen to tear off a couple of paper towels. Jilly stood at the counter, pouring lemonade from a two-liter bottle into the blender.

"We'll take some of that, too," Liam teased, and Jilly slapped at his hand.

"Your mother would have my hide," she said.

"Not before me," said a new voice, full of teasing, and Justin was in the doorway next, backlit by the yellow glow of the outside light, grinning at Jilly.

Jilly made a face at him and ordered, "You get out of here! It's girls *only* tonight."

"We'll see about that," Justin murmured to her, and then added, "Hi, girls. Hi, Jo." He did manage to collect Clint and Liam, in addition to half the pan of brownies and a twelve-pack of soda. After the boys thundered back down the steps, Jilly sent Justin a little look over her shoulder and he dared to enter the kitchen, wrapping an arm around my sister's waist and commandeering her for a quick kiss. I watched with amusement as she struggled playfully before relenting and kissing him back, but chastely, just barely brushing her lips over his.

"That'll have to tide you over," she said to him.

"You know where I'll be," he said, squeezing her waist, then told the girls, "Thanks for cooking, ladies, this looks great."

"You're welcome," said Ruthann, pleased and beaming, while Tish glared at him and remarked, "You guys took almost all of it and we weren't cooking, we were *baking*."

Justin grinned in amusement and winked at her before heading back outside.

"Ugh, I'm *never* falling in love," Tish grumbled.

Two hours later Jilly and I leaned on our elbows on the small round table in her kitchen. Camille dozed in the recliner, snoring lightly, while Tish and Ruthann watched *Mystic Pizza* with rapt attention, both sprawled on their stomachs in front of the television, the last of the caramel corn between them. The kitchen radio still played, but softly now, tuned to the local country station out of Bemidji. Every other song reminded me of Blythe.

"So how's everything with you and Justin?" I asked Jilly in an attempt to redirect my attention. Three empty cans sat on the table near me while I worked on a fourth, past the giddiness and into the sentimental-bordering-on-melancholy phase of beer drinking.

Her lips curved into a sweet, joyous smile, answering my question better than any words.

"He is one smitten kitten," I said, using a phrase from our high school lexicon. "Tail over teakettle, as Gran would say."

"Jo, I am so in love with him," my little sister said then, and I looked hard at her. We'd talked about this, but the depth of her sincerity plucked at my heart; I tended to get so involved in my own concerns that I downplayed hers, and leaned over the table to listen. She continued, "I mean, we've known each other our entire lives. Dodge always brought him and Liz out here to play when we were little. And I remember when you'd drag me to football games to watch Jackie, Justin was always playing, too. And for so long he had Aubrey, and I had Chris. But now, it's like I've been waiting my whole life for Justin, and I just realized it."

"Jilly," I whispered. "Oh God, I remember that day we sat at your old kitchen table and you vowed to never love again. I didn't dare say anything. But I'm so glad you were wrong."

Her blue eyes poured into mine. "Back then I thought that was it for me, Jo, you know I did."

"We were all so worried about you. Jilly, seriously, I know you loved Chris. We all loved him. He was just like Clinty is today."

Jilly's eyes welled with bright tears, but they weren't the type that led to broken-down weeping. Instead they gleamed like tiny crystals, the kind of tears that spring almost unbidden to a mother's eyes when she thinks about her children in any capacity. Oddly, Jilly hardly ever cried otherwise, though I never doubted the depth of her anguish over Christopher's death. It just wasn't in her physical and emotional make-up to show overt sadness. It ran like a river underneath the surface, though, which very few people knew. She was too good at displaying only the bright, effervescent parts of herself. But I knew her better.

She sighed a little and then said, "God, I know. Sometimes when Clint says something and I'm not looking at him, I'll think for a split second that it's Chris. He even sits at table three, like Chris always did. I never told him that's where his dad always sat."

"I noticed that, too," I told her.

"Clinty gets along really well with Justin," she said, pressing her pinkies into the outer corners of her eyes, banishing the last of the tears.

"Clinty gets along with everyone," I teased. "But he does seem to genuinely like Justin."

"What's not to like?" Jilly asked, sounding more like herself. A new gleam appeared in her gorgeous eyes now, and I smiled to see it. She whispered, "Jo, he is so incredible. Oh God, he's so passionate, I can't even tell you."

"You can tell me," I assured her.

Jilly continued as though I hadn't spoken, her eyes a brilliant flame-blue. "When he kisses me it's like I've never been kissed before. I crave him, down to my *bones* crave him. I can't get enough of him. It almost scares me."

I reached and slipped my hand into hers. I said, "Don't be scared. He loves you, you know it. It's as plain as day all over his face every time he looks at you. What have you got to lose?"

She snatched her hand away. "Bite your tongue! Jesus, you know I hate those kinds of statements! Quick, knock on wood."

"Jills, the curse on our family isn't real," I said with more conviction than I felt; my spine felt oddly cold.

"So where are all the men then?" she asked point-blank.

"Justin's here," I said, determined not to squirm under her gaze. "And Blythe will be."

"Oh my God, knock on wood!" she ordered again, not satisfied until I did so, on the tabletop. She added, "Look at Mom, Ellen, Gran…shit, even Camille."

I winced at that, and Jilly said quickly, "I'm sorry. Don't listen to me."

"No, I'm not fooling myself with that one," I muttered. "At least Jackie stuck by me for a long time."

Jilly's expression changed. I could tell she was debating whether to tell me something, though she was usually free with her opinions. Finally I prompted, "What?"

"I'm worried about Jackie," she said.

My eyebrows lifted in surprise. "Worried?"

Jilly waved her hands, palms facing me, and shook her head in the manner of someone who has just confused the shit out of you and is attempting to reverse it. She said, "No, no. I mean, I'm worried about how he's acting, not *for* him. He's questioning the divorce. He's said as much to Justin."

"No," I said immediately. "He's just jealous because of Blythe. It'll blow over. He's jealous that I dared to find someone new."

"And the 'someone new' is smokin' hot and managed to beat the teeth from Jackie's mouth, which doesn't help much," Jilly said, with unmistakable glee, waggling the tip of her tongue at me.

I rolled my eyes. "Dammit, that isn't funny."

"It was satisfying though, admit it!"

"Okay, yeah, maybe a little. But it was part of what landed Blythe back in jail."

"Aw, Jo, don't go getting all sad on me right now," my sister ordered. "He'll be out soon. But I'm just warning you about Jackie. He's been getting more determined every day."

I shrugged, my thoughts centered on Blythe. I said, "I talked to Blythe tonight, and it was so good to hear his voice. Fuck, I miss him."

"I forgot he called. He's doing all right?"

I nodded, my throat tight.

"Jo, he's not in danger. Wipe that expression off your face," Jilly said, though not unkindly. "Write him another letter tomorrow and you'll feel better."

"Mom!" Tish called from the living room. "Can you bring us more lemonade?"

"Sure," I called back. And then to Jilly, "He said he carries my letter with him and sleeps with it at night."

"That's sweet," she said. "And that big stud will be here before you know it."

I rose and poured two lemonades for the girls, picking up the earlier thread of our conversation, saying over my shoulder in a stage whisper, "And what about Lanny? What in the hell? Jackie told me he's going to marry her. He brought fucking divorce papers up here, for Christ's sake!" And then I swallowed the edge in my tone and called, "Tish, come get these!"

Jilly said quietly, "I don't know what he's playing at, but I don't like it."

"Me, neither," I told her, and handed off the drinks to Tish, before opening the fridge. "What else do you have to eat in here?"

"I don't know, look," she said, brandishing her beer-ita at the fridge and cupboards in general.

"I'm hungry for Italian food," I said and for just an instant missed the take-out convenience of Chicago. "Or Greek."

"We could drive into Bemidji tomorrow," Jillian suggested. "Just me and you." Her cell phone suddenly chirped and Jilly snagged it from the counter, read the text message, and then giggled.

"Look," she said, angling the screen so I could see. "It's from Justin."

What are you wearing? it read, with a little smiling-devil emoticon.

"Wow, that's original. Text back 'a big old quilted robe that covers every inch of skin,'" I teased. "And oversized carpet slippers." I giggled, a little drunk, adding, "And baggy granny-panties."

Jilly laughed, her fingers flying as she replied to his message. She said, "As if that would deter him. The man has a sex drive that knows no boundaries. And I'm happy to help him with that."

"Well, that's good. It's probably been a while for both of you."

She sent the message and then sighed, running a hand through her short golden hair. "You can say that again. It's funny how you don't realize how much you missed making love until you have it again. I think it must be a survival thing."

Her phone chirped almost instantly, and she snorted and then actually flushed. I grabbed for it, but she dodged to her feet to evade me and yelped, "No way, you can't see this one!"

She tried to get away but I caught her around the waist, laughing as we tumbled into the living room. The girls looked over in surprise. Jilly tossed the phone across the carpet, then realized what she'd done and cried desperately, "Wait! Give that back, Tisha!"

"No, throw it here!" I ordered, laughing as Jilly tried to block me.

Camille opened one eye and groaned, "I'm trying to sleep."

There was a sudden pounding on the door and someone called in a low-pitched, serial-killer kind of voice, "We know you're in there!"

Ruthann and Tish shrieked.

"We know you have food!" another voice growled.

"Tish, phone!" Jilly demanded.

Tish slid the phone back to her aunt before racing around the corner to stop Clint and Liam from making off with the rest of the food in the house. I grabbed for it, but Jilly was faster. She stuffed the phone into her pajama shorts and shouted, "Ha!"

"Justin's the only one who can go after it there," I teased her.

"Mom, we're gonna go sit around the fire for a while!" Tish said, disappearing out the door. Ruthie grabbed a bag of marshmallows and ran after them.

"I think I will, too," Jilly said, slipping her feet into a pair of red flip-flops and grabbing her hoodie from the hook by the door.

"*Jilly,*" I complained, wanting to keep talking in private. "Darn that Justin. What in the hell did he text?"

Her answering grin made me roll my eyes. She disappeared out the door, calling, "You coming or what?"

"Sure, why not? Milla, you coming?"

"No, I'll go to sleep again now that you guys are leaving," she grumbled, rolling to her other side. I moved to cover her to the hips with the afghan from the back of the couch and she muttered, "Thanks, Mom," before her eyelids drifted shut.

Outside, under the midnight sky, Jilly and I linked arms and made our way over the lake path, sharing a quick smoke on the walk. The lawn chairs around the fire were occupied by Dodge, Aunt Ellen, Justin, Clint, Liam, and the girls. I was relieved to see that Jackie was nowhere in sight. Dodge was telling some story that had Ellen laughing; both of them clutched bottles of beer. Ruthie passed out marshmallows while Clint and Liam staged a swordfight with their marshmallow roaster sticks, and Justin, directly opposite us, caught sight of Jillian, pinned her with his dark eyes and gave her such a knowing, sexy, lascivious grin that she flushed again. I could tell even in the darkness. Her whole body probably turned red. I was happy for them, but damn. Their flirting just made my ache for Blythe intensify. I snagged a seat near Ruthie and accepted a stick from her, then skewered two marshmallows.

"Love you, Mom," she said, resting her head briefly on my shoulder, and I reflected how my girls made everything better already.

Sunday morning dawned gray and cheerless, much like my mood. I was so grateful to have talked to Blythe yesterday, but the week stretched ahead like an expanse of empty desert; I would have to wade through all that featureless dryness until next Saturday to hear his voice again. *Joelle*, I scolded. I ground my knuckles against my eyes and sat up to see the window streaked with long silvery trails of rain. Better to get up and face it than stay in bed and be depressed. And so I did.

Late in the day, after lunch, the rain ceased, the clouds slowly shredding apart, like pieces of torn cotton candy. As I stepped out of the cafe, ready to head for the house, I saw Jackie just getting out of his car; my feet stalled. He caught sight of me and waved, calling, "You have a second now?"

"Yeah," I half-sighed. "Come on." And I indicated he join me with a tilt of my head.

"Do you mind if we walk instead?"

A rogue beam of sunlight struck the ground just behind him, flooding that part of the blacktop with golden light, angelically backlighting his curls. Suddenly I didn't want to hear anything he felt compelled to say, but if I kept avoiding him he would grow all the more determined, not to mention continue showing up unannounced. Typical Jackie.

"Sure," I said, casting a glance over my shoulder at the front windows of the cafe, reflecting the sky as it brightened blue again, hiding the curious faces that were most certainly observing as Jackie and I turned to the lake path that wound back to Landon. At first there was enough distance between us for a car to drive through, but as we walked he eased closer, ever so casually. I kept stubbornly silent until we reached the spot on the road where I first climbed into Blythe's truck, back in June, the night he'd kissed me for the first time. I was still wearing Blythe's sweatshirt; I'd slept in it last night.

"Listen, Jo," Jackie was saying, on my left.

"Do I need a lawyer?" I asked abruptly, ready to expedite this whole process. "In your professional opinion?"

He seemed caught off guard, pausing to turn and look at me. The clouds played cat and mouse with the sun, casting shadows and throwing light in random patches, as though we were facing off beneath a natural disco ball. We left the cafe behind; only the birds were witness to our words now. As if he hadn't heard correctly, he repeated, "A lawyer?"

"Well, I don't know. What about the papers you brought? Should I have someone look them over?" I really wanted to know. "What about the townhouse? And I know Lanny's living there, so don't bullshit me, seriously. When I called there last week she answered, even though you were on your way to Minnesota."

Again his eyes narrowed at my mention of his alleged fiancée. For the first time, I noticed a few silver threads in the thick hair around his temples. Apparently I hadn't looked at him, *really* looked at him, for a long time either. Finally he sighed, cupping his nape in an old gesture of defeat, admitting, "She does have her own place, but she's at the townhouse most of the time, yes."

"So will the two of you live there?"

Jackie frowned deeply, his dark eyebrows drawing together. He said, "You're really set on staying up here? Putting the girls in school at the senior high? I thought you'd get over this, Joelle. Move them back to Chicago, at least. All of their friends are there, their schools. Why stay in Landon?"

"Why not?" I asked brusquely, folding my arms. "I love it here. My family is here. And the girls love it, too, just ask them."

"What about everything you left behind in the townhouse?"

"I'll have to come and get it eventually, I guess. Or you could ship it to me when you get home. Are you and Lanny going to live there or sell it?"

He kicked at a pebble and studied the ground, at last admitting, "She loves the townhouse. We would buy your half."

"What about child support?"

"It's all in the agreement, if you agree, that is," he said. "Exact percentages according to Illinois state law. Jesus, as though I wouldn't be fair about it, Jo."

"I never said that," I told him honestly. "I trust that if you prepared it, it's fair. Did you bring it to sign? Is it in the car?" I had no idea how this worked and studied him searchingly. "Do we need a notary to witness?"

Jackie studied me in absolute silence.

"I'll sign it so you can go," I insisted, impatient and jittery, as though I'd binged on coffee. "The girls can come and visit over Thanksgiving break."

He suddenly asked, "Why is he in jail?"

Now it was my turn to stare mutely at him.

He insisted, "Tell me, Joelle. What are you doing with this Tilson guy besides fucking around?"

With effort, I kept my cool and said, "You don't know anything. He's not a criminal, not the way you're thinking."

"Don't give me that bullshit," Jackie snapped, insulted. "You're getting back at me with a fucking convict. What does that say to our children?"

"What does that say?" I repeated, the redness of fury infusing my face. "Funny you never seemed to consider that question when you were bending your assistant over your desk! What does it say to them that their father chose to step outside of his marriage for *the last five years*?!"

"They didn't know!" he yelped.

"Well they know now!"

"And they also know that their mother is busy getting laid by a criminal with a ponytail!"

"How *dare* you –"

"That's fucking great, Jo, *not at all* like a whore."

Though never one prone to violence, I shoved him in the chest with both hands. He quick-stepped back, then lunged forward and caught me by the upper arms. His breath came fast and I expected him to shake me, or maybe shove me back, but he did neither. Instead he leaned in and kissed me, roughly. For just a second I kissed him back, bowled over by the suddenness and familiarity of his lips.

But then I made a sound of enraged protest, struggling against him, and he ended the kiss as abruptly as he'd begun it, freeing my arms and blinking at me in what appeared to be stun, as though he couldn't believe he'd just acted that way either.

"Don't ever touch me again," I ordered through my teeth. I imagined for a moment what Blythe would do if he were here, and the thought strengthened me.

"Dammit, Jo," Jackie said, and he sounded shaken. His voice trembled, but I wasn't in the mood to sympathize.

I turned to walk away; despite what I'd just said he grabbed my upper arm, halting my retreat.

"I'm so confused," he said. His grip was firm but not painful, though when I shrugged out of it he didn't stop me. I crossed my arms, staying momentarily put, somber as I regarded his face. To be fair, he did appear incredibly agonized.

"What do you want me to do about it?" I asked quietly.

"I don't know. I don't fucking know," he said. He plunged both hands through his hair and then braced eight fingers on his forehead. "It's this place. I have so many memories of us here. All the things we used to do, how we used to make love. I feel like I'm going crazy."

I understood what he meant; it was how I'd felt when the girls and I first arrived, back in May.

"Jackie…" I said tentatively, but he dropped his hands from his face and glared at me, as though to blame me for everything. And without another word he spun and walked briskly the way we'd come.

"I'll leave the papers for you," he said without looking back.

I stood there watching as he retreated. I waited until he was out of sight, then drew a deep breath and headed in the same direction.

In Jilly's kitchen that night, this time with no kids around, I told her the whole story.

"I knew he'd make a move," Jilly said. "He actually kissed you?"

"With tongue and everything," I said, anger seeping again into my belly. With grim satisfaction I added, "Blythe would kill him. But he'll never know. I'm not risking that."

"I knew Jackie was wavering," she said. "I knew he was reconsidering. Well, don't buy it."

"Please," I said, rolling my eyes at her. "Do you really think—"

"No," she assured me, and then indicated the gray folder on the table, emblazoned with the words *Rockford, Gordon & Bunnickle, Associates at Law*. When Jackie was first made partner, I'd been so thrilled to see our name on the stone building. It seemed so permanent, afforded our family so much security. Now I could hardly wait to shed it, detach it from my first name. I found myself doodling 'Joelle Anne Tilson' all over my notebook, then surrounding those curlicue words with interlocking hearts. Jilly continued, "Have you read through everything?"

"Not all of it," I admitted. "I trust that Jackie won't try anything sneaky when it comes to this."

"Yeah, I suppose. Not when it concerns the girls," she added. "Anyway, who cares if he and his home-wrecking whore get the townhouse? I remember it being big and echo-y and cold. Besides, you get Blythe."

I grinned at her, feeling a welcome rush of gratitude. "That's a damn good trade," I agreed. "And thank God that Lanny wrecked our home. I would never have known, Jilly. I would never have come back here."

"Yeah, let's call her and tell her thanks," Jilly teased, and lifted her glass of beer-ita to toast mine.

Chapter Twelve

On Tuesday Justin's little sister, Liz, who also worked as a realtor, called to say that she found a place I might like, just a few streets off of Fisherman's, and came to pick up Jilly and me in the late afternoon.

"And it's fine for Ruthie to sleep over tonight?" Liz asked as she drove around the lake road and turned back into Landon.

"For sure," I told her. "Thanks for the invite. She's excited."

"Jills," Liz said, catching my sister's eye in the rearview mirror. "I just want you to know how happy my brother is every time I see him. I'm so glad you guys are dating."

Jilly leaned forward and for once didn't tease; she said softly, "Me, too, you don't even know."

"Well, I couldn't be happier," Liz said. "And hey, you two having a big birthday bash this month?"

I turned in the passenger seat to look at Jillian. Our birthdays, one day apart in just a few weeks, were the furthest thing from my mind. My birthday was the thirtieth and Jilly's the thirty-first, and as kids we'd always been allowed a huge, mutual celebration as a sort of last hoorah to summer.

Jilly said, "We should renew our old tradition and have a kick-ass party."

"Sure," I said. "That would be fun." And maybe, since Blythe would be out of jail a couple of days after that weekend, I would actually feel like celebrating.

"Here, Jo, it's just off Second," Liz said, taking a right. All the streets in Landon were familiar to me, though we'd never lived anywhere but Shore Leave. This particular one, two blocks and one right turn from downtown, was lined with ancient maples whose branches stretched across the street to touch fingertips. The houses were circa 1950, square and squatty, with dormer windows, enclosed porches and single-car garages. Liz parked at the curb of a small, neat, dark-blue place with white shutters and a white front porch, no enclosure.

"This one just came up for rent," Liz explained, hopping out.

I hung back, lingering, truly attempting to imagine my family in this place. I felt as though I should experience a chill, a bone-deep *knowing*, that this was the right place; I liked it, but I wanted to feel more certainty. I'd spent a few days looking at places with Liz before I left for Oklahoma, but given the size of Landon, there wasn't much available. And I needed to choose something, unless I planned to continue living in my childhood home with my daughters, mother, aunt, grandmother, and lover.

Would the girls like this place? Would Blythe? Would he want to move in with us right away? I truly hoped so, but we hadn't talked about it. I would ask him this Saturday. No, I'd write a letter. He'd mailed one back to me; I'd received it yesterday, and it was currently pressed against my chest, tucked safely in my bra. Though slightly uncomfortable, I couldn't bear to part with his words for even a moment, though I didn't share that with anyone, least of all Jillian. There was a limit to even her patience with me. Jilly climbed the porch steps and leaned over the rail, examining the Russian sage bushes blooming in a mass of pale purple. I stopped and rubbed a stalk between my fingers and then inhaled; not much smelled better this time of year.

"Look, a swing," Jilly said with delight.

I climbed the steps in her wake and joined her on the wooden swing suspended from the overhanging roof. The porch ran the length of the front of the little house, old and slightly creaky, but pleasant. The floorboards were worn a dull gray, but the potted petunias that seemed to be everywhere lent it color and cheer.

"Who takes care of the flowers?" I asked Liz, who was attempting to unlock the front door.

"Oh, the neighbors," she explained, gesturing at the house next door. Referring to her husband, Mark Worden—who most people in Landon knew as 'Wordo'—she said, "Mark's step-sister lives there, so her son is technically our nephew. I told him I'd pay him to take care of the plants. He was kind enough not only to agree, but won't take money."

"That's nice," I said.

"Oh, Jake's a good kid," Liz agreed. "Here, I finally got the door open."

We followed her into the front room. It was almost a perfect square, empty of any furnishings, with a gleaming wooden floor; an archway straight across led through to the kitchen. A set of wooden steps climbed the wall to the right, turning a corner at a small landing. There were built-in shelves in the walls, painted a buttery yellow.

"The kitchen is pretty big," Jilly called, ahead of us. I followed her while Liz struggled to open a few windows.

"It's a little stuffy in here," she explained.

The appliances were harvest gold; someone had remodeled the space, but I would guess that was around 1975. The floor in here was a continuation of the wide, walnut-brown planks from the living room. There was a nice center island between the kitchen and a tiny dining room, where a buffet server remained pushed against the far wall. There was no other furniture, at least in view. A sliding glass door led to a small deck in a fenced backyard. I peered out and caught sight of a brick patio where you would step down into the yard from the deck.

Jilly turned the sink on and off, opened the cupboards and the fridge, exclaiming under her breath.

"There's a nice pantry, too," Liz added. "And three bedrooms, two up, one down."

"Well, Tish and Ruthie would have to share," I mused. "But that's all right."

We checked out the second-floor bedrooms, which were teacups, but also wood-floored and painted in pale, pastel shades, one peach, one green. Almost Easter-egg-like. There was a bathroom between them with fixtures from the build date, I was certain. The tub was a claw foot, with no shower.

"Oooh, that is so pretty," Jilly observed, standing on tiptoe and sticking her head over my shoulder. "I love those old tubs. Justin has one."

"But is there a shower anywhere?" I asked.

Liz called from one of the bedrooms, "Yeah, downstairs in the three-quarter bath."

"You could always get a shower head in here, too," Jilly added. "I like this place. It has a good vibe."

I agreed with her, though it might have been inspired simply by the peaceful, mellow sunlight slanting in through the windows. We examined the basement last, which was the first carpeted space in the house. This could be the TV room, I decided. And the bedroom down here would be mine and Blythe's.

Don't count your chickens before they hatch, I suddenly found myself thinking, and shivered a little. Dammit, I hadn't slept enough in the past week, and it was aggravating my superstitious side. I peeked into the bedroom space, which was also carpeted in a neutral cream. There were two tiny windows, up high near the ceiling, where the ground gave way. The closet was a joke, but again, this place would be a rental, and just temporary.

Until what? Until you get a better job? Until you and Blythe go back to school and earn more money? Your savings will barely get you into the place, let alone sustain you here.

And then, far worse, far more deeply terrifying, the old story of the family curse scraped at the back of my mind. Women in this family lost their men—whether we liked it or not.

No, I thought fiercely. *Not this time. I don't believe in that—it's not real. I will not lose my man this time.*

I willed away those thoughts and pressed my fingertips to the crackle of paper under my shirt, Blythe's letter to me, seeking reassurance. His words of love were still there, tucked close to my skin.

"I like it," I told Liz. "How soon should I let you know?"

"Well, the sooner the better," she said as she locked the front door.

I debated for about five minutes; just as Liz pulled into the parking lot at Shore Leave, I said, "Okay, I'll take it."

"Girls, I found us a place to live in town," I told them at dinner that evening, as they sat on the porch sipping root beers and eating tuna sandwiches.

"You did? But I *love* it here," Tish complained, as fond of speaking in italics as any fifteen-year-old. "I don't want to leave the cafe."

This from my child who complained on a daily basis about being crammed into a single bedroom with her two sisters.

"What about being so crowded up in that loft?" I reminded her.

"Well, I wouldn't *be* crowded if I was here by myself," she said, watching carefully for my reaction.

"And not live with us?" Ruthie gaped at her.

"It's not like I wouldn't see you guys every day," Tish insisted. "Mom, listen—"

"Sweetie," I interrupted, but then Camille cleared her throat, in a way that suggested she was ill at ease.

She said quietly, "Mom, I've really been thinking about something," and effectively cut off both mine and Tish's words; we all looked questioningly at her. Camille gathered her long hair at the nape of her neck and held it there with both hands, another nonverbal sign of anxiety, simultaneously fixing her sincere, golden-green eyes upon me. She said, "I talked to Grandma about it, and she said it was fine as long as you agreed, Mom."

"Agreed with what?" I asked, thinking, *Thanks, Mother.*

"Well, I thought I might just stay here and have the loft all to myself," she said in a rush, releasing her curls. She leaned forward earnestly. "I could get it ready as a nursery, and Grandma and Auntie Ellen will help me. And I like being here on the lake. I don't want to move into Landon, Mom, for real." At last, with a slight tremble in her voice, "What would you think?"

A sharp pang struck at the notion of my oldest daughter living under a separate roof. I bit my bottom lip and simply studied her, caught off guard even as my mind raced ahead and understood that what she asked was not only reasonable, but perhaps the best idea for everyone involved. She could have privacy. And there weren't two more doting caretakers than Mom and Aunt Ellen; perfect for a pregnant girl who needed a little pampering.

But it meant I was already losing one of my girls to her adult life, like it or not. I had not been ready for this, not yet.

All three of them studied me for a reaction, as they might nervously watch a couple of bats roosting near a door they needed to enter. I sighed and said, "I'll have to talk with Grandma," thinking, *Will I ever.*

Camille said, "All right. But it's a good idea, if you think about it."

"But *I* wanted the loft," Tish complained, her shoulders sagging.

"Are *you* having a baby?" Camille snapped at her, and Tish's posture became immediately offensive.

"So you get first dibs on everything?" Tish fired right back. "Like that's real fair!"

Tears instantly filled Camille's eyes, as they were prone to do of late. Tish released an angry breath but bit back any additional words, while Camille swiped with angry motions at the moisture seeping over her cheeks. Ruthie moved around the table so that she could pat her oldest sister's back; my sweet Ruthann.

I said to the table at large, "We could all be a little more patient with each other's feelings, all right?"

Tish huffed a little and I shot her a warning look.

"What about the house you found today, Mama?" Ruthie asked, neatly changing the subject. "Is it nice?"

Tish and Camille continued to glare at one another, but were thankfully silent, and I focused gratefully on Ruthann. I said, "Let me tell you," and then proceeded to fill them in on my afternoon.

It was well after dark before I managed to snag my mother alone. She stood behind the bar, wiping down its gleaming length, humming softly to herself, a second bar towel slung over one shoulder. Her long, gray-streaked golden hair was caught up in a tortoiseshell comb and she sported a pair of the feathered earrings Aunt Ellen made, peacock-style.

I sat at the empty bar and leaned over it, stretching my hands palms-down across the bar, a gesture communicating that I wanted her attention. She looked up and smiled, but then caught sight of my expression and heaved a sigh.

"I'll bet," I said, but not as meanly as the words implied.

Mom moved opposite me and studied my face, without apology. She asked, "Did Milla chat with you about staying out here?"

I nodded, admitting, "I've actually been considering it all evening. It's not a terrible idea, although I hate the thought of her not living with me. But Mom, what I really hate is how you bypassed me in the whole decision. You could have talked to me first, *then* your granddaughter."

"It was Camille's idea in the first place, Joelle, not mine. But I think it's a good one. If you're not going to move home to Chicago, it's reasonable that she and the baby have their own space."

"You know we're not planning to move back to Chicago," I said.

Mom was silent for a moment; finally she said, "Jo, I love having you up here, so close. But have you really thought this through?"

I felt a creepy little ripple start in my stomach, edging upward and outward.

Mom continued as though not noticing my expression. She implored, "Jackie has been trying so hard. Haven't you realized?"

"Meaning what, exactly?" I asked, keeping my voice light with effort.

Mom pinned me with her eyes. "You know exactly what I mean. I had my doubts about him earlier this summer, but he's proving himself. He wants to be in your life again. He wants you to move home. He's realizing what a terrible mistake he's made."

"So you've chatted with him about this?" I asked, my face growing ever hotter.

"A little," she admitted, and my chest felt tight. "He is sorry for a great many things. Would you really throw away your marriage and everything the two of you have built together to stay in a little rental house in Landon?"

I swallowed down the bitter anger trickling into my throat. I knew, *I knew*, she was just trying to be reasonable. I knew she believed what she was saying. But she didn't truly *know*. She'd never looked into Blythe Tilson's eyes and seen his incredible love. I inhaled slowly, missing him with a palpable ache that settled behind my breastbone, like lead. There were many things I might have said, but out of nowhere I heard myself ask, "When was the last time you saw Mick Douglas?"

Mom's eyebrows lifted and her spine straightened a little. She seemed to be considering, almost cautiously, where I was going with this particular question that concerned my father, though I truly didn't know; I'd asked it completely out of the blue. Finally she said, "You know, he called us once when Jilly was about five or so. He was near, in Minneapolis, and he wanted to know how the three of us were doing."

"Why? What was it to him at that point?" I demanded.

Mom shrugged. "Aw, Jo, your dad wasn't a bad guy. Just an immature one. But I did love him. After all, he gave me you and your sister. But I honestly can't imagine how my life would have been with Mick here all these years. I'm so happy taking care of this place with Ellen. We do better than any menfolk, I think."

"But don't you get lonely?" I pressed. "What about Rich? Have the two of you ever thought about…you know…"

Mom actually laughed, bending back and wrapping one arm around her ample waist. She said, "I'll have to let him know you asked."

"But you've never…"

"Heavens no, Joelle. What a question. Rich is one of the kindest men I've ever had the privilege of knowing. He's one of my dearest friends. But you know how much he loved Pamela. She was the love of his life, which is why he's so good to Christy and…Blythe."

Just hearing his name sent my pulse wildly thrumming.

Mom continued, determined to exhaust all of her points, "I like Blythe very much, Joelle. I know you say you love him, but I remember how much you loved Jackie, once upon a time. And Jackie is your children's father. He has a good job and the two of you have made a beautiful home in Chicago. I just don't want you to throw that away. You know what Ruthie said the other day?" When I didn't immediately respond, she answered herself. "She said how happy she was to see you and her dad talking. The girls need the two of you to be together, to try again. You know it, Joelle." And then she leaned back, content that she'd spoken her piece.

I knew if I opened my mouth I would say something I would come to regret later. Something like, *Are you fucking blind? Is my own happiness worth nothing at all?* Or, *How dare you bring* my *children into this?* But in the end I remained silent, though I felt as if I just might detonate and spatter all over the bar.

"Life can't just be about you," Mom said into the silent void surrounding us, as if I didn't have that knowledge rammed down my throat on a daily basis. To her credit, her golden-green eyes were full of compassion. She added, "Not now. Not with Camille having a child. The girls need a stable home. They need you and their father under one roof."

"Good-night," I told her, my voice strangled. And before I could say another word, I removed myself from the cafe.

I walked briskly into the night air, wanting (but not giving in to the urge) to the slam the screen door with the full force of my mood. Restless clouds rolled across the sky, randomly blotting out the stars and chasing across the enormous silver-dollar face of the full moon. I couldn't sit on the dock in my current emotional state, and so I set out around the lake road, wishing, longing, fantasizing, that somehow Blythe would pull up in his truck like the first night we'd kissed. I played that moment over and over in my mind, hugging myself, as though to hold those memories inside where they would remain safe. We would make it work. We would, and Mom would just have to accept that. I knew she wanted me to be happy; that just got tangled up in what she thought was right. I knew she loved me and had no desire to hurt me. But she didn't know Blythe like I did; she didn't understand what we had. I was so agitated that I made it all the way to Fisherman's Street in no time flat.

Might as well keep going, I thought. *Check out my new house.*

I slowed my pace as I stepped onto the sidewalk of Broom Street, where the little blue house we'd looked at this afternoon waited quietly. There was one streetlight just across from it, projecting a white phosphorescent glow, and a handful of porch lights glimmering here and there. The street itself was otherwise dark and calm; not even a breath of wind moved through my loose hair. The clouds almost totally obliterated the moon, though I could see its faint sheen behind the not-quite-opaque gray of the sky, as though it was shining behind a smoked-glass window. I figured I would sit on the swing for a moment, chill out and collect myself, before heading back to Shore Leave. I wished that I could call Blythe and tell him I found us a place; I'd written today, but I hated the delay. I climbed the porch steps and settled onto the hanging swing, setting it into gentle motion with my foot.

I decided I quite liked the little porch at night. Of course, I couldn't see Flickertail Lake. I couldn't smell the scent of the lakeshore, but it was peaceful and homey, nonetheless. The chains issued a faint chiming with each backswing. I reached into my shirt and pulled out Blythe's letter, and caressed it as I imagined caressing every inch of his skin when he was in my arms again. I tilted his words into the faint shine from the streetlight, reading them again, though I'd almost memorized the letter by now.

Joelle, he'd written. *I close my eyes and see yours as I lay here at night trying to sleep. Your eyes are so insanely beautiful, green and gold at the same time. God, I wish I could write this better and really let you know how I feel because it's like I'm dying inside without you. My heart is yours forever. I can see you so perfectly, and feel you against me, where I want to hold you always. I will never stop loving you and never stop wanting you. I see your soft sweet mouth, baby, your lips that taste like—*

"Hey, that's private property!" someone called, sounding as though he was on the porch with me.

I jumped and looked wildly around, then realized that a kid stood on the porch next door, leaning way over the railing and peering into the darkness as though trying to decide how much a threat I posed and if he should call the cops or not. And Landon's go-to law officer, Charlie Evans, was the last person I wanted to see at the moment.

"No, no!" I said, getting to my feet in a hurry and moving immediately to the railing nearest him. "It's okay! I am going to be renting this place. Your aunt, Liz Worden—"

"Oh," he said, and his voice held a cease-and-desist tone. "Yeah, she mentioned. Sorry. It's just late and I didn't think anyone should be over there."

"No, that's actually really nice that you worried about it," I said. In the darkness I couldn't tell much about him, other than he seemed to be somewhere in the mid-teens. I decided introductions were in order, and said, "I'm Joelle Gordon."

"Jake McCall," he said politely. "We've lived here since I was little."

"Well, nice to meet you," I told him. "My girls are probably about your age."

"I'll be a senior this year," he said. "How about your girls?"

"I have three, and they're seventeen, fifteen, and twelve. Do you have any sisters?"

"Nah, just me and Mom."

"Well, hey, thanks for keeping an eye on the place," I said. "And for taking care of the flowers."

"No problem. Good to meet you, too. G'night." And he retreated inside his house.

I refolded Blythe's letter, kissing his signature before tucking it gently back into my bra, and smiled into the darkness. I debated calling Jilly for a ride as I walked slowly back around the lake. I was wearing tennis shoes without socks and my right heel was rubbed raw. I reached for my cell phone just as it buzzed with an incoming call and Jilly's name flashed onto the screen. Of course she'd sensed that I needed her.

"Where are you?" she asked immediately.

"On Flicker Trail," I said. "I just went to sit on my porch swing for a while."

"You did? At this time of night?"

"Mom and I had…some words," I admitted. Poor Jilly always took the same role that Ruthann did now, as peacemaker, hating when Mom and I fought.

"She said," Jilly affirmed. "She told Ellen and me what she told you, and I was all like, 'Are you fucking kidding me?'"

"You didn't say that."

"Noooo…but I thought it. Jo, don't listen to Mom. I mean, I know she loves us, but she's so easily manipulated. She lets Jackie bulldoze her."

I sighed and stopped walking, my heel burning.

"I'm on the way," my sister said at once.

Twenty minutes later I sat at her kitchen table; Clint and my girls remained over at Mom's house playing a high-stakes game of Monopoly they'd apparently started before lunch. It was currently half past midnight.

"You want a rum and coke?" Jilly asked, peering into her fridge as I slumped at the table. I wanted to pull out Blythe's letter and reread it, but Jilly would be irritated with me. Her nose in the fridge she asked, "How about a wine cooler?"

I giggled a little at this option, asking, "Is this eighth grade?"

She snorted a laugh. "Right? They were on sale and looked good. Kiwi-strawberry, I think."

"So where's Justin tonight?"

"He's out with Jackie. The two of them drove into town and are probably at Eddie's. I guess Jackie told Justin about what he said to you on Sunday."

"Ugh, what did Justin say?"

"He told Jackie he was out of line, but he also believes that Jackie is sorry for what he's done," Jilly said. "He's buying into to it, too."

"Well, maybe Jackie *is* sorry," I allowed. "Mom sure as hell seems to think so. And I suppose if I'm really honest, there is a certain amount of satisfaction in knowing he's sorry." I chewed my lower lip. "But it doesn't mean much anymore."

"Well, don't let Mom get you upset," Jilly said. "Besides, she's excited at the thought of Camille living here with the baby. She's helping her plan the nursery. And Ellen was talking about finding Clint's old crib in the attic. Dodge said he'd fix it up."

"You know, I've been thinking about that all afternoon. Maybe Milla would be better off here. At least she'd have a little more privacy, and then Tish and Ruthie could each have their own rooms at our house. And under other circumstances she might be moving in with Noah. " I buried my face in both hands, whispering, "God, I can't imagine my baby is that old."

Jilly turned to look at me, her blue eyes overflowing with sincerity. She said, "Jo, don't let Mom influence you in any way over this. I'm so happy you're staying around here. I don't care if you moved in with me for good."

"Aw, Jills," I said, tears brimming. "Thank you. I've missed you so much. I don't know how I would have gotten through this summer without you. This life, actually."

"Same here," she said, and reached for my hand.

By Saturday evening I'd grown edgy, irritable with everyone. My daughters took to avoiding me, and I knew I was being ridiculous. I was just so tired. At night I alternately rolled to the other side or punched up my pillow in an attempt to make it fit better under my aching head. Last night Gran complained, "Joelle, I can hear you thinking all the way over here."

Blythe's letter looked like a relic from another century, the way I clutched it at night and wore it next to my skin all day. I'd mailed a third just today and received another from him, which I carried out to the dock to read after lunch rush. It only served to make me miss him all the more, and was hardly a substitute for hearing his voice, let alone seeing him, but I found I enjoyed communicating in this fashion; I couldn't remember the last time I'd actually held a handwritten letter. There was a particular intimacy about it that I'd never before considered. When I read his words, his voice spoke them in my mind; I pictured him bent over the paper with pencil in hand, shaping sentences to express his love. I knew him for a tender soul, but was delighted by the way he described things with precise detail, the words he chose just for me. Even the way he wrote *Joelle* made me smile, with an extra flourish on the Ls; sometimes he shaped the tail of the J into a heart.

I'd explained in my second letter, six pages, double-sided, about the rental house, and how I hoped he would move into it with us. I told him about Camille's wish to stay at Shore Leave for now, and about how upset I felt over the idea of her moving out. I wrote nothing of Mom's opinion, or her desire for me to reconsider Jackie's apology. I did, however, let Blythe know that Jackie remained in town, and that I was in possession of divorce papers. The letter from Blythe this morning was written after my second, because he responded to everything I'd mentioned. I traced my fingertips over one paragraph in particular, which read, *Writing to you this way reminds me of this book I read for school once, about a husband and wife writing to each other during World War II, and how the husband wrote that the thought of getting home, of being able to hold his wife close each night, was all that kept him going day to day, the thought of getting back to her, because she was his home. I know this rental place won't be where we settle for good, but I want you to know that the thought of getting home to you, my Joelle, is what keeps me going day to day.*

By the time I accepted the collect call charges, I needed so badly to hear his voice that my nerves were as frayed as pieces of old rope. I'd given him the house phone number in my second letter, so I could at least have privacy while everyone else was over at the cafe for dinner rush.

"It's me, I'm here," I babbled, curling around the phone; I swore that if I started to cry and wasted this phone call in tears, I would never forgive myself.

"Joelle," he said, the warmth of his deep voice in my ear at last.

"I miss you so much," I said. "It's so good to talk to you. I don't think you know how much I miss you."

"Believe me, baby, I do. Oh God, if I could just hear your voice every day. You sound so close."

"I got your letters. I wear them in my bra all day and sleep with them at night. Do you think the wife from the book you read did that sort of thing?"

He laughed and exhaled in a rush at the same time, and said in a slightly strangled voice, "I would surely hope so. Don't mention your bra, baby. I wish I was there taking it off of you. With my teeth. And my tongue...*oh God...*"

I shivered hard, his words eliciting from me a soft, inadvertent sound of pure longing. He groaned, "You just made one of your sexy little sounds. Jesus, I'm gonna die here..."

Still wrapped in his sweatshirt, I vowed, "I'll come to get you and we'll make up for all this time apart, I swear to you."

"I'm counting the seconds," he said hoarsely, and I pictured him leaning his forearm against the wall and resting his forehead upon it—he'd written that the phones were behind a locked door, lined up on a concrete wall, which was painted blue; to keep inmates calm while on the phone, he said, but which really just made everyone feel lower than shit. My heart clenched imagining him standing there and leaning against the wall, a posture which spoke of lonely pain.

I said, "I love reading what you wrote. I should have known you'd have a way with words." And I pleaded, "Don't be sad, sweetheart. You're hurting and I can't even touch you, and I hate it. Oh, Blythe..."

He said, "I'm all right, baby, I promise. I don't think a month has ever seemed so fucking long, though. What are you guys doing tonight? Bonfire? Midnight swim?"

"The girls want Jilly and me to give them manicures. Well, at least Ruthie and Milla do. Tish won't let us near her nails."

I sensed his smile as he said, "Sounds about right. Margaritas later?"

"Yes," I whispered, smiling now, too. "On the porch."

"Tell me what you're wearing so I can hang on 'til next Saturday," he requested softly.

"Your sweatshirt," I said. "I've hardly taken if off."

"I love you, woman," he said intensely.

"And nothing else," I added, heartened anew to feel the heat of his grin even across the miles separating us.

"On that soft skin of yours that I'm going to kiss every inch of the moment I see you, everyone else be damned?"

"Yes, yes, and yes."

"Shit, I just have a minute left. Write me another letter, I treasure them. And don't worry about me, truly. Gramps and Mom came to see me yesterday."

"They told me," I said, trying not to get panicky now that it would be another week before we talked again. "I'm so glad they're close to you. Rich said you looked all right and I know he wouldn't lie to me. Your mom was worried you'd be losing weight."

He laughed a little. "Mom thinks they serve bread and water and nothing else. Not that it's much better, but I'm all right."

"I plan to keep your sweatshirt on. I wish I had more of your clothes, I love snuggling into them."

He said, "Soon you'll have me." And then, in a hurry, "Bye, sweetheart. I'll call you next week, same time, okay?"

But before I could respond the phone call was abruptly cut off, and I sat alone with the dial tone. My chest hurt.

Two weeks down.

Chapter Thirteen

On Monday I met Liz at her little office on Fisherman's and signed the rental property and insurance papers. I opted up for a six-month stint; that way, if we found something better this fall or winter, it wouldn't be such a commitment to break. An hour later, after we'd eaten lunch at the Angler's Inn, where longtime owners Joe and Helen Thompson proceeded to sit with us for a spell, exclaiming how delighted they were that Jackie and I were moving home—I explained, patiently, that only the girls and I were relocating to Landon, and then fielded a dozen new questions—Liz turned over two sets of keys to me, along with a folder of information about the house itself.

"Small towns," Liz murmured as we parted ways in the parking lot, with a quick hug. She added, "I heard you met Jake."

I laughed at the memory. "Yeah, he's a neighborhood watch and security officer all rolled into one."

"He takes himself pretty seriously, but he's nice boy, takes good care of his mom," Liz said. "He's the one to call if you need help with anything before your hunky man gets back to town." And she grinned at me as she climbed into her car. "Or call us. I'll send Mark over if you need help with heavy lifting or something."

"Thanks, Liz," I told her, flushing a little. We'd discussed Blythe at length over lunch.

"See you later," she said, waving as she pulled away.

Leaning against my car, sun warm on my shoulders, I called the cafe and got Jilly, asking her, "Hey, is Camille around?"

"Yeah, she's having a strawberry shake," Jilly said, then leaned away from the phone to call, "Milla! Your mom's on the phone for you!"

"I just got the keys to the house," I told my daughter. "Why don't you round up the girls and drive them over. Just ask Grandma if you can use the station wagon."

"Sure," she said. The girls had seen the outside of the place yesterday, so I didn't need to give her directions. "We'll be there in a few."

At the house, I stood in the front yard and regarded the porch, the steeply-angled roofline with its two symmetrical windows popping up like afterthoughts through the shingles, the overall pleasant appearance of the little place. The siding looked relatively new, the blue of rain-heavy storm clouds. The afternoon sun shone brightly as I walked around the foundation, studying everything with a sense of wonderment and growing excitement. When compared to the luxurious, upscale property I'd left behind in Chicago, this house was a joke. But I loved it already, with a distinct sense of accomplishment. I'd taken a step away from role of the dependent wife I'd filled for way too long. On that note, I signed Jackie's papers last night; the gray folder from his law firm remained in the trunk of my car, just waiting until he showed up at Shore Leave to collect it. I dearly hoped that when I handed over the documents he would be on his way back to Illinois, and Lanny.

And Mom would just have to deal.

"Hey there," I said suddenly, pausing as I spied a lanky orange cat stretched out in the wilting ferns on the north side of the house. It had the look of a serious predator, crouched low in wait. As I watched, the cat regarded me with golden eyes and opened its mouth in a small mew. I saw a collar, so didn't worry, leaving it to its hunting. I opened the gate in the shoulder-high wooden fence, letting myself into the backyard. The grass here was browning, surrounding two decades-old cedars along the back fence, in addition to a row of healthy-looking lilacs; if we stayed until spring, they would be a treat. The backyard faced east, laden with welcome shade at this time of day. I climbed onto the deck, which was simple and sturdy, contemplating where I might put a grill, when I heard

Mom's station wagon chug into the driveway, followed by the excited voices of my girls.

I called, "I'm back here, guys!" and Tish and Ruthie ran into the backyard.

"Mom, this is so cool!" Tish said, and I grinned at her enthusiasm. "Can we go inside?"

"Here," I said, handing her a key. "Check out the bedrooms upstairs. Decide which one you want."

They raced back around the house, startling the cat; I followed more slowly, to spy Camille just climbing out of the car. She paused and studied the house with both hands curled around the top of the open driver's side door, the sun beating down on her head. I could almost hear her thoughts, no doubt equating this place to the one in which we'd lived in Chicago; it was almost impossible not to make comparisons. I opened my mouth to speak when I heard someone behind me say, "Hi, Joelle. You guys moving in today?"

I turned to see Jake approaching, pedaling an off-road bike. He cruised into our driveway and grinned politely at me, bracing the bike with one foot on the ground before turning his attention to Camille. She tossed her hair over one shoulder and regarded him with tepid detachment, barely offering a smile. I said hastily, "Milla, this is our neighbor, Jake McCall. Jake, this is my oldest, Camille."

He blinked once, as though in slow motion. In the daylight he was lean and lanky, all legs and elbows, though his height suggested that he'd fill out one day. He had shaggy, tangled brown hair (as though contained under a helmet for the duration of his ride), freckles over his tan, and eyelashes that would make Gran say he should have been a girl.

"Hi," he finally said, and immediately cleared his throat.

Camille managed a small, tight smile before heading silently into the house, leaving me groping for something to say that might smooth over her obvious rudeness.

"So, is that your orange cat?" I asked, and Jake refocused on me with effort, still staring at the screen door through which my oldest had just disappeared. My heart bumped in sympathy for him; if there was anyone off limits right now, it was Camille.

"Yeah," he said, looking over his shoulder at his own porch. "That's Taffeta. I know it's a dumb name, but we've had her for so long we can't change it now."

The dormer window to the right suddenly creaked in protest at being forced open and Tish appeared. She yelled down, "Mom, I'm taking this room!"

I asked immediately, "Does Ruthie like the other one?"

"Yeah, she wants the peachy-pink one."

"Your other girls?" Jake guessed.

I nodded. "That was Tish, and Ruthann is the youngest."

"Well, welcome to the neighborhood," Jake said, and waved as he glided to his own driveway.

I banged through my new screen door and called, "What do we need first in here, girls?"

"A radio!" Tish called from upstairs. Ruthie appeared on the landing and added, "A cat!"

"Oh, no," I said firmly. "Well, what do you guys think?"

"It smells funny," Tish said, pounding down the steps to join her sister on the landing.

"No, it's just stuffy. Remember, a woman Gran's age lived here alone and never opened the house up."

"Did she croak in here?" Tish wondered aloud, and I rolled my eyes in exasperation.

"No, my kind-hearted child. She went to live in the nursing home," I replied.

"Let's see the basement," Ruthie decided, and disappeared that way. I followed them but stopped in the kitchen as I saw Camille standing silently at the sliding glass doors, staring out into the backyard, both arms wrapped around her midsection. It was a pose I recognized, one of tension and vulnerability; I wanted more than anything to hug her close, but her posture and my sixth sense warned me not to attempt it just now. She was brittle as an antique tea cup these days, retreating into herself as a way to survive; how well I knew that feeling. At this stage of my first pregnancy, I was newly married and living basically alone in a tiny Chicago apartment, while Jackie attended college. The loneliness of those days was something I tried hard not to revisit; at least, I reflected, Camille was not alone in a strange new city.

"Mom," she said, noticing me. "Have you thought about what we talked about?"

I sensed a gulf forming between us, hating this notion but unsure exactly how to bridge it, or even paddle across it, at the moment. At last I said quietly, "Yeah. I have. I think it would work out pretty well. As long as that's what you want, sweetie."

She peered at me as if attempting to read my mind, as though because I'd agreed without an argument there must be a catch. I risked her annoyance and said, "I love you so much."

And to my relief, a genuine smile overtook her face. She whispered, "Thanks, Mom. I really do want to live there."

"Come give me a hug," I ordered, expecting her to roll her eyes, but she surprised me, moving into my arms without a word. I held her close, imagining the baby growing inside of her, the little girl who would become my first grandchild and the fifth generation of Davis women here in Landon. I pressed my face to her soft curls and rocked her side to side.

Downstairs and out of sight, Ruthie suddenly shrieked and Tish yelled, "There's a *huge* bug crawling on the carpet, Mom, hurry!"

Jilly and the girls, along with Clint and his best friend Liam, helped me the rest of the week. Mom and Ellen pitched in, boxing and loading our belongings. Mom gifted us with a bunch of cast-offs from the house, which I chose to interpret as a peace offering; we hadn't spoken beyond what was necessary since our conversation in the bar. I wanted an apology, but didn't press the issue; Mom was never one easily swayed from her opinions, and instead we simply chose to avoid the topic. By Friday evening the move was complete, I'd arranged for electricity and water in my new house, as well as a phone, and Jilly and I arrived back at Shore Leave, dusty and sweaty, ready to celebrate our hard work with a couple of beers and a dip into the lake.

"I'm just jumping in, fuck it," Jilly said, as I put my car in park.

I giggled, running both hands through my damp, wilted hair. "Thanks for helping all week."

"Oh shit. Don't give me that, like I'd just sit back and watch you work. Come on, let's get in the water!"

It was late enough that the dinner crowd had thinned out. Mom, Ellen, Gran, and Sue Kratz, who filled in on summer weekends, all sat rolling silverware and drinking coffee at a porch table.

"You girls hungry?" Ellen called down as Jilly and I made our way across the parking lot.

"Just hot," I responded.

"We're hitting the water," Jilly explained, and suddenly we were kids again, racing for the lake, pausing only to shed our shoes, laughing hysterically as the dock shuddered beneath our bare footfalls. We leaped at the same instant, lukewarm water closing momentarily over our heads; when we surfaced, I could hear the womenfolk laughing.

"Ahh, that's perfect," I rejoiced, ducking under again, smoothing hair from my forehead and then stretching out to float on my back, studying the expanse of familiar sky above Flickertail, tinted a mellow blue as the sun sank into a coppery spill of low-lying clouds. Jilly swam under me and blew bubbles; her head popped out near my stomach and she roughed up her short hair with both hands.

"Now if only we had a beer," she said, treading water, looking no older than the girls. I grinned at her, my stomach all at once buoyant; I'd rented a house, my girls were happy to be staying in Landon, I'd signed my divorce papers, and best of all, Blythe would be calling tomorrow. I'd written him enough letters by now that he'd have an album's worth when he got here.

Jilly caught sight of Clint and hollered, "Son! Get us something to drink!"

"You want to get us fined?" Mom called, standing on the porch holding a tub of rolled silverware, but I could tell she was smiling as she went back inside. Clint and Liam, who was ever-present these days as August drew to a close and the threat of school made the kids increasingly hedonistic, walked to the end of the dock to hand off two beers to Jilly and me.

Clint sat and kicked his bare toes in the water. He said, "Aunt Joey, it sucks that you guys aren't gonna be living here anymore."

"Aw, buddy, we'll be just over in town. And we'll be out here all the time, don't you worry." His face remained glum, his shoulders slumped. I added, "And Camille will still be living here."

"Yeah, but she's so grouchy all the time. She's no fun anymore," he said.

Jilly snapped, "Clint Daniel!"

Clint raised apologetic blue eyes to his mother. "Mom, I just mean she's not the same."

"It's okay, Clinty, I know what you mean," I told him. "She's moody these days."

Justin, with Liz's triplets in tow, suddenly appeared from the direction of the parking lot.

"Hi, sweetheart," Justin called down to Jillian and she grinned at him.

"Honey, go grab Justin a beer," she told Clint.

"Only if me and Liam can have one, too!" Clint said, his gloomy expression changing into one of teasing speculation. He grinned at Jilly and added, "That's the deal."

She splashed her son, ordering, "Get!"

Justin headed our way, sidestepping the boys as they ran up the incline to the cafe. At the end of the dock he latched both hands on his hips, grinning at Jilly as she asked, "Are you coming in?" He wore his usual faded jeans and a dirty work shirt undone past two buttons; he appeared sweaty, hands streaked with motor oil. He said, "Not in these clothes."

"Take 'em off then," she challenged.

I picked up the gauntlet, giggling as I said, "Oh, he wouldn't dare."

Justin's beautiful dark eyes, brown as fresh-shelled pecans, smoldered at Jillian, and I could tell he was considering. She waggled her tongue at him, adding, "Oh, he's way too conservative for that."

In response he began unbuttoning his work shirt, slow and deliberate, like a stripper. We shrieked and splashed at him, and I whistled shrilly as he tugged off his shirt, baring his muscular chest and lean belly. Our antics kept me from noticing that someone else walked down the hill from the parking lot, and by the time Justin shucked his jeans (I don't think he actually would have if not for wearing boxers) and cannon-balled into the lake with a huge splash, it was too late; Jackie already stood in the spot Justin had just vacated, sporting a much more lawyerly look this evening, complete with khakis, wingtips, and his gold Cartier watch.

Justin hauled Jilly into his arms and pitched her about three feet into the air. She surfaced and jumped on his back, laughing and struggling to dunk him under. I swam to the edge of the dock and stood on my tiptoes in the mushy, lake-weedy bottom, looking up at Jackie, who tilted his chin and returned my gaze, his expression amused but also wistful. I refrained from fidgeting and tried to pretend that Jackie was not studying me with what appeared to be a combination of regret and love.

"Hey," he said, and his voice was very soft.

"Hey," I said back.

"So, you left me a message," he added.

"Yeah, I signed all those papers. They're in my car if you give me a minute," I said, but he didn't seem inclined to move just yet.

"You found an acceptable place to rent, Liz was saying."

"Yes," I said, determined to keep this as brief as possible. But then I had to ask, "Did Mom tell you that Camille is going to be living with her and Ellen?"

He said, "I think that might be a good idea." He cleared his throat and added, "If you think it's best."

I nodded without comment.

"Well, I just came out to…" He drifted into silence as he continued staring at me.

Dammit, Jackie. Don't do this.

"Dad!" Ruthann called from the direction of the cafe and Jackie turned to greet her; I used this opportunity to hoist myself out of the water; I intended to hand over the divorce papers so Jackie could finally leave. I braced on my elbows but felt my water-logged jean shorts threatening to slip down. I made an inadvertent noise of alarm, and Jackie bent immediately to help me out of the lake. There was no choice but to allow him to haul me ungracefully out of the water. He lifted me without effort, but the sleeves of his dress shirt grew soaked.

"I'm sorry," I said, gesturing at the wet spots, nearly ill with unease as I scraped my hair over one shoulder and squeezed it out. Jackie's gaze slid down my front side as easily as water droplets; the outline of my breasts and belly was plainly visible, lake water dripping over my bare thighs. He returned his gaze almost instantly to my face, but the old heat burned in his eyes. He swallowed and turned to greet Ruthie as she scampered along the dock. I shouldered neatly around him and made my way back to the cafe, trying to pretend I didn't feel him watching me.

Rich called on Saturday afternoon.

"What do you mean, they all lost phone privileges?" I wailed. *No, no, no.* "Rich, I'm coming down there, I can't handle this anymore."

"His whole cell block is being punished for something, honey, not Blythe individually. He's all right, just missing you. When Christy and I saw him yesterday he looked a little rough. He's upset. He said he's not sleeping."

"Oh, Rich," I moaned, agonized. "I can't take this anymore. I have to see him. Tell him I'm coming down there."

"Now, Jo, I don't think that's necessary. He's out the week after next. And Joanie told me that you and Jillian are having a big birthday party next weekend."

"I don't even care about that," I said, chewing my thumbnail to bits. "Not if Blythe isn't here. Rich, I'm so glad you're down there. Thank you for being there. Is Christy all right?"

"She's fine, honey. Truly. And pretty soon this will all be behind you guys. Now, listen, Bly would want you to enjoy your birthday, you know it."

I sighed, curling up on Mom's couch; I'd been in the house when Rich called, gathering the last of my bathroom supplies. I whispered, "I know."

"He loves all those letters you've been writing," Rich went on. "He keeps them in the pocket of his jumpsuit."

Tears stung my eyes. I couldn't bear to picture Blythe behind the bulletproof glass, cradling a phone receiver as he talked to Rich during visiting hours, shoulders hunched forward, shadowy smudges under his eyes as there had been back in July when I'd broken up with him, thinking it was the only choice. Despite everything, I knew Blythe still worried that I would decide I didn't want to date, let alone marry, an ex-convict, that I'd be conspicuously absent when he was released, thereafter withdrawing from his life. All this time alone in jail destroyed his confidence, I knew. I would just have to show him that these doubts were unfounded. I whispered, "When will you see him again?"

"We'll get over there in this next week," Rich assured.

"Can you hug him for me? I don't suppose you can," I said bitterly.

"No, we can't touch him," Rich said. "He looks like he could use a hug, too."

I wanted to scream out my defiance at these rules.

"It'll be all right," Rich said again.

"I know," I whispered. "I'm just so damn tired. I miss him so much I can't sleep or eat. I'm a mess."

"Now, that's the last thing he'd want to hear," Rich admonished. "And I hear you have a nice new house?"

I pulled myself together. "Yes, it's over on Broom Street."

"That's a pretty little street," Rich said. "Now why don't you go and find your sister and have some fun this evening? No more moping, okay, doll?"

Good old Rich. I said, "I will, I promise. Please tell Blythe that I'm counting the hours."

"That's more like it," Rich said, with satisfaction.

Three weeks down.

Chapter Fourteen

GRAN SAT ON THE PORCH SIPPING FROM AN ICED GLASS when I drifted uselessly back that way, carrying a plastic basket of toiletries. Lunch rush was over, dinner rush not yet begun. She waved me over and I joined her, setting the basket on the chair to my right. I leaned and sniffed at her drink, then asked, "Gran, can I have a sip?"

Gran slid her vodka lemonade my way, demanding, "Why are your eyes red, girl?"

"I'm just so low," I whispered, taking a long, restorative drink from the skinny pink straw.

Her gaze sharpened beneath her floppy hat brim, reminding me of Jilly. She asked, "Are you pregnant?"

"No, I just had my period."

She appropriated her drink from my grasp anyway, saying, "Well, that's a relief. I don't know that your mother could handle both you and Camille in the family way."

I said recklessly, "I wish I was, Gran."

She pruned up her lips at me, observing, "Joelle, you've got it bad for that boy."

"Gran, Blythe is no boy," I argued, absolutely drained by defeat. My family seemed set against me.

"Oh, I know. He's more a man than any man I've ever seen," she said, grinning at me, hazel eyes with a naughty gleam. I managed a small smile, which she'd intended.

"I love him," I said simply, letting my head fall back a little, looking straight up at the sky.

"I know it," she said, all teasing vanished from her tone. "And I know that Jackie is sniffing around you again. You watch out for him." She rapped her drink on the table and added, "No matter what your mother says, all right?"

Grateful relief rose in my chest. I whispered, "Thank you, Gran." And then, "How about we get started with margarita night a little early?"

She grinned at me in a web of wrinkles, eyes still sparkling. She said with soft satisfaction, "Now that sounds more like the Joelle I know."

"One more!" Jilly ordered, launching wholeheartedly into the first verse of one of our old favorite songs, sending her voice up into the black-velvet and diamond-spangled sky.

I laughed and raised my green goblet in praise. Gran rocked side to side, her own margarita glass brandished high. Mom and Ellen collapsed against each other, laughing. I felt good, better in the company of my mother especially, than I had in weeks. I was also pretty drunk; though I'd promised myself I would quit setting a bad example for the girls, it seemed justified tonight, when I'd counted on hearing Blythe's voice and was now denied the privilege. Not only that, but it was a Davis women Saturday margarita night and summer was edging into fall. To opt out of drinking was just plain bad manners.

The kids, including Liam and two of the three triplets, were holed up in Jilly's apartment, supposedly watching movies and eating fudge. What they were really doing was anyone's guess; at their age, Jilly and me and our gang would have been swigging misappropriated wine or beer and enjoying a rollicking game of Truth or Dare. I took a moment to be thankful that my kids had never proven as wild as my sister and me (and their father, for that matter). Then again, my Camille was pregnant. Right now she was out with her dad; Jackie took her for a special father-daughter dinner in Bemidji, just the two of them. Though she'd tried to disguise it, I knew she was pleased.

I wobbled to my feet and joined Jilly in the final verse; the resultant noise was pretty pitiful and anyone on the streets of Landon, just across the lake, could surely hear. The last note warbled over the water and was answered by the sudden wailing of a loon. Another responded instantly from a different part of the dark lake.

"Oh, I love to hear them," Ellen said.

"I think they enjoyed our singing," Jilly said, then snorted and giggled.

"You girls ready for another round?" Gran asked, lofting the pewter pitcher reserved for this noble purpose since before the grand opening of Shore Leave, decades ago.

"One more," I said, though I shouldn't. I knew I would feel like shit in the morning, but since I didn't get to talk to Blythe tonight, I would feel like shit anyway. What was a headache on top of that?

Gran poured yellow-gold slush into my glass, and then Jilly's. I drank a long swallow and then ungracefully backhanded my mouth. Mom waved the pitcher away and Ellen said, "Ma, I'm full up."

"Here's to Joelle's new place," Gran said, grinning at me in the candle lantern's glow. "We're so happy for you, girl."

"Thanks, Gran," I said, chiming my glass lightly against hers on the second try. "I'm so happy, too."

"Same here," Jilly added, poking me with her toe, and Ellen echoed the sentiment and blew me a kiss.

Gran sent a look at Mom, who sat in silence, gazing reflectively over the lake. Mom seemed to come back to herself and said, "Of course, honey, I'm happy to have you here."

"But?" I asked belligerently.

Mom reeled in her gaze and looked into my eyes. Other than the stars, only the glimmer of one candle offered illumination. She said, "Joelle, I gave you my opinion. But it's in your hands now."

The need for combat rose swiftly into my mouth. I snapped, "Well, if that isn't the most passive-aggressive statement I've heard tonight."

Everyone's spine stiffened at my tone. I'd slurred over the words *passive-aggressive*, but I continued anyway, "But that's just so *like* you, Mom."

"Dammit, Joelle, don't talk to me like that," Mom said. "You know what I said was true. Your children miss their father. They shouldn't have to choose between the two of you."

"Joanie," Gran snapped. "That's not a fair statement."

"Ma, please," Mom implored Gran, though not without respect. Her aggravation, however, was apparent.

"You've been letting Jackie play you all month," I accused. My eyelids felt hooded and I knew I should shut the hell up, right now. But something in me kept pushing, setting free all of the resentment boiling under the surface of my skin. I insisted, "He's limping along to get your…sympathy. And you're falling for it…hook, sinker and line!"

Something about that hadn't sounded quite right, but Mom interpreted my meaning. Even in the meager light from the candle flame centered on the table, she appeared to flush with temper. She said, her voice tight, "You are throwing away a second chance with a good man. Your *husband*. Your children's *father*."

"Mom, he doesn't deserve her anymore," Jilly said quietly. She looked between Mom and me with her eyebrows quirked at half-mast, drink forgotten in her hand. She hated conflict of all kinds. Gran watched with her mouth set in a grim line.

"He made a mistake!" Mom said again. Jackie could not have paid her to be a better cheerleader for him. *Jesus.* She asked, "Doesn't he deserve a chance to show you he's sorry?"

"No, he doesn't," I managed to say past the ball of anger in my throat. I turned to Aunt Ellen, certain she'd be on my side. "Wha' do you think?"

Ellen sighed and said, "Joelle, it's not for me to say." She said anyway, "I know you love Blythe. But it wasn't that long ago you were still crying in the night for Jackie. I say, just think about this. Think it through."

"You, too?" I gasped. I was stunned.

At that moment the man we'd been discussing drove into the parking lot, Camille in tow.

"Screw this," I muttered, slapping my drink on the table; it sloshed over the side and onto my wrist, but that didn't slow my progress. I stomped down the steps and headed directly for my car. I wasn't thinking clearly and just wanted to leave. Obviously no one in the vicinity was going to allow that in my current inebriated state.

Camille climbed out of Jackie's car and regarded me with surprise as I breezed by her, en route to my purse, sitting innocently on the passenger seat. I opened the door and dug through it, spilling its contents to the floor of the car, at last locating my keys with a grunt of satisfaction. Behind me I could hear voices clucking in alarm. The next thing I knew Jilly was by my side, saying, "Come on, Jo, let's get you to bed."

"No," I snapped at her, shrugging off her gentle touch. "I wanna gome."

"You are home," she murmured in my ear. "Come on, please, Jo. You know you can't drive anywhere."

"Fucking *hell*," I muttered. I moved out of her grasp and stumbled around the hood. I felt tears on my face. I just wanted to talk to Blythe. Couldn't I just have that? I needed it so badly tonight. And he needed me.

A man's strong hands cupped my upper arms now, but not the ones I craved. Not the ones I wanted.

"Easy there, Jo," Jackie was saying, near my left ear, and amusement colored his words. He went on, easily, "Where do you think you're going?"

"Get away from me," I said, or at least that's what I intended to say. Ineffectually, I shoved at his chest with my left elbow.

"I'm sorry, I can't," he said, his mouth against my hair.

Even in my drunken state I sensed he intended to convey more than one meaning. His hands moved from my arms to my waist and the next thing I knew I was seeing everything upside-down, my head lolling back over his forearm as he lifted me up and carried me back to the porch, Jilly dogging his footsteps.

"No, take her to the house," I heard Mom direct. "Camille, come up here, love."

Jackie redirected his route into the darkness, Jilly still clinging to us.

I felt as though I was being rolled down a steep hill and managed to make a sound that alerted my sister. Not a moment too soon she yelped, "Jackie, she's gonna puke!"

He knelt and managed to get me around to my knees. I felt his hands gently gather my long hair before I retched, hating myself for acting this way, for being so vulnerable. Jilly patted my back, saying over and over, "It's all right, Jo, it's all right."

"God, this is just like high school," Jackie observed wryly from behind me. I felt his hand on my back, low on my spine. I would have bucked it off if not engulfed by another round of vomiting. The only person whose hand could touch me there was Blythe.

After a time I brought up everything in my appreciable body, muttering, "I'm sorry."

"It's all right," Jilly said one last time. "Come on, let's get you to bed."

Without asking permission, Jackie hoisted me into his arms again. "Where we headed, Jill?"

"Our old room," she said, and I watched from my disabling vantage point as Jilly opened the front door for him and clicked on the hall light; he followed her up the steps.

"This is where you've slept all summer?" Jackie asked in disbelief as I was deposited on the twin bed. God, the bed where we'd made love many a stolen time as teenagers. He remained sitting on the mattress beside me, his hand lingering on my hip.

I felt too miserable to continue looking at him and rolled to my other side, with a groan.

From out in the hall Jilly said, "See you in the morning, Jo. Come on, Jackie."

One of his hands stroked slowly over my ribcage, which I knew Jilly could sense if not see. His fingers reached the lower curve of my breast, then brushed over my nipple, and he leaned down to press his lips to my bare shoulder, saying, "I'll be down later."

"No," my sister said firmly, and I was so grateful to her that I tried to make a sound, but I was so depleted; Jackie tensed and I elbowed away his groping hand.

Jilly ordered, "Let's *go*."

And Jackie followed her out of the room.

I opened my eyes to late-morning light and winced, immediately squeezing them shut. Ball bearings seemed to chase each other around inside my skull, but I deserved every moment of it. I recalled what happened after Jackie put me on the bed, and was doubly glad for my sister's presence. Not that I'd have allowed him to do anything, but he would have tried. Trust my cheating husband to take advantage in such a way, waiting until I was drunk, conveniently shelving all thoughts of Lanny, his live-in lover and the woman with whom he planned to share the rest of his life. It made my stomach cramp with rage, even secondary rage for Lanny. What would she have to say if I called my old house in Chicago with this pitiful little anecdote? Further, if any of my daughters behaved the way I had last night, like a potential walking disaster, I'd lock them away for a month. I'd understand, but would still be unduly harsh with my punishment.

I also owed my mother an apology.

Later, I promised myself.

I slept again until late afternoon, waking with a dry mouth and throbbing temples. I imagined a glass of water on the nightstand, before I realized I would actually have to move to make one appear. I finally pulled my sorry self to a sitting position and remembered that I didn't have clean clothes in this house; all of my things were at my new place on Broom Street.

"Jo, you awake?" I heard Jilly calling up the steps. A moment later she popped into the room and said, "Ye gods, you need a shower."

"Thanks," I whispered.

"I saved your ass last night," she said, pulling no punches, sitting on the foot of the bed and regarding me with somber eyes.

"I know," I said. "He wouldn't have gotten very far, believe me. For one thing, I reek like puke."

"He is determined though," she said. "Jo, I'm scared he's going to convince you, take you back to Chicago. Don't let him."

"Jilly, oh my God," I told her, aghast that she'd even think such a thing. "Give me some credit. I might have been wasted, but if he'd tried to kiss me I'd have kneed his nuts."

"Yeah right, you could hardly walk. I'm not saying he was going to force you. I was afraid he'd charm you, dredge up the past and make you nostalgic. If anyone could manage that, it's him. I saw his eyes last night. I told him Blythe was coming back, and he was all like, 'Well he's not here now, is he?'"

"But he will be," I whispered. "And Jilly, my heart is his. Jackie could never change that, not anymore."

Jilly seemed to relax a little. "I know," she breathed. "But I'll feel better when Jackie goes home, all the same."

By the next weekend Tish, Ruthie, and I had lived in our rental house on Broom for six days, and the girls were getting the hang of the new routine. And growing accustomed to living in a separate space than their big sister. I missed my oldest with a keen-edged ache. I knew she was only a mile or so away from me, just around Flickertail, under the loving, watchful eyes of Mom, Gran, and Aunt Ellen; Dodge, too, to be fair. Dodge, who considered Clinty and my girls his grandchildren, built Milla a changing table and repaired Clint's old crib like new. I drove the girls over to Shore Leave every day, working lunch for Mom, though we existed under a modified silent treatment since last Saturday; I apologized, but half-heartedly, and Mom had not offered one in return. Only necessity dictated our conversations; Mom told me when I had a new table, for instance, but other than that we exchanged very few words. I was ashamed for being so rude to her; I loved her. But I was simultaneously appalled that she allowed Jackie to influence her to the point that she challenged my decision so openly; couldn't she see through his manipulations? He was transparent as shallow lake water. And that Mom would sink to playing the guilt card, implying that I was doing my girls a grave disservice by refusing to take their father back into my good graces, further aggravated me.

I woke on the morning of my birthday to see a rich spill of rose-tinted light streaming into the bedroom. I lay on my new full-sized mattress, one hand resting on the empty pillow near mine. My fingers curled inward, grasping the daisy-printed case; I'd been in the midst of a strange gray dream and struggled to swim upward, to full consciousness.

Blythe, I thought at once, unduly worried. I sat up, listening hard through the dizzy rush of blood in my head; the sounds drifting from the kitchen caused no immediate concern—I heard the radio, and my girls singing along, clattering things on the stove, clearly preparing breakfast. I pressed a hand to my galloping heart, frightened despite everything. I fumbled for my cell phone and called Christy's number, even though I'd spoken to her just yesterday; no answer. I tried Jilly next, but neither did she pick up; she was probably at Justin's. The sun crept over the apple-green chenille bedspread Gran gifted me with only a week ago, a familiar quilt long in my grandma's possession, and I tried for a calming breath. A lovely day was lifting into existence outside my window—and I just needed to get through the party tonight (which Jilly and the kids were really thrilled about, and therefore I must be, too), and then tomorrow I meant to drive back to Oklahoma. Blythe would be out on the second of September, which was next Tuesday.

Christy told me last night that she'd been to visit him and he'd appeared in better spirits; she assured me three times that she would tell Blythe that I'd be there when he was released. His cell block was still not allowed phone calls unless there was an emergency, and so likely I would not be allowed to hear his voice until then. The way I longed for him felt like an emergency to me, but I breathed deeply, setting aside my phone and pressing both hands on my belly, reminding myself that I would be with him, actually be able to touch him, in three days. And his parole officer seemed to think that Blythe would be able to come to Minnesota, especially with the excuse of a job.

It's all right, I thought. *It's all going to be all right.*

Then what in the hell is wrong?

"Happy birthday, Mama!" called Ruthie, from the door at the top of the basement steps.

"Thanks, honey," I called back. "You guys are up early!"

"We made you breakfast," Tish announced, and I could smell maple and cinnamon.

They'd prepared French toast with actual French bread, an old favorite breakfast. I hugged them both against my robe, which I'd wrapped over my pajama top. Ruthie snuggled close while Tish ducked quickly from the embrace, explaining, "The bacon's gonna burn!"

"This looks great, you guys," I said, as Ruthie seated me at the table, upon which they'd arranged a tall glass vase full of the Russian sage from out front. They also found a few other flowers I didn't recognize, dark green stalks with spiky yellow blossoms. I ran my fingertips admiringly over the petals as I observed, "You two have become good cooks this summer. And these flowers are really beautiful."

"Well, someone has to cook for us," Tish joked, standing at the stove with spatula poised. "And that guy Jake from next door helped us pick flowers."

"He's nice, isn't he? And I cook," I said, only slightly defensive. I thought back, and then back further, in an attempt to recall the last time we ate something I'd prepared, rather than the food from Shore Leave. I amended, "Well, I'll start cooking again soon, I promise."

The girls joined me and we feasted on the sticky, delicious toast, along with coffee and crackling-crisp bacon. Our little dining room was stationed at the back of the house and caught the radiance of the morning sun. I hadn't put up any curtains, so we all basked in the golden warmth, talking about this evening's party, and how school would start soon, and how Jake apparently asked eight thousand questions about Camille while helping pick flowers this morning.

"We told him she was pregnant," Tish said, dragging bacon through the syrup on her plate.

"Patricia," I chastised. "I don't think your sister would appreciate that."

"Like he wouldn't find out sooner or later?" Tish pointed out, not unreasonably.

"That's not the point," I said, exasperated.

"Will Camille be mad?" Ruthie asked, twirling her fork against her plate, tines-down, concerned.

"No," I said, though I was surely lying.

"He asked who the father was, if he was someone from Landon," Tish went on, and I heard notes of apology in her tone. Her indigo eyes flashed my way.

Who knew Jake was so damn nosy? I said, "Well, it's not his business." Studying my middle daughter, I concluded, "But you told him."

"We're sorry, Mom," Ruthie said.

I decided, "Let's not tell her that you blabbed to our neighbors, okay? At least, not at the party."

"Dad's probably coming," Tish said in a startling change of topic, and my warning bells began clanging, full steam.

"To the birthday party?" I realized I'd infused this question with a great deal of anger and clamped my mouth closed; it was hardly Tish's fault.

"Don't you want Dad there?" Ruthie asked, eyebrows crooked in question.

"Your dad is going home to Chicago," I said, not answering her question. I softened my tone. "Remember like we talked about, honey?"

"But he misses us so much," Ruthie whispered. And then, "Can't Dad move in here with us, instead of Blythe?"

I lowered my fork slowly to the table, hardly able to swallow the coffee I just sipped, horrified to see tears balancing on Ruthie's long lashes. My heart clenched. I noticed Tish kick her under the table, but it was too late.

"Ruthann, Dad is moving back to Chicago," I said again. "He's going home to Lanny, honey. He's going to marry her."

Ruthie nodded as though her throat was too jagged to speak. But then she sobbed in a plaintive wail, "I don't *want* him to go, Mom. I want Daddy to stay with us. Don't you still love him?"

I felt as though I'd been hit by a truck. Metaphorically flat on my back, I tried to regroup. I said faintly, "I loved your dad very much once. But I don't…"

"Don't say it!" she yelled suddenly, my Ruthann, who never raised her voice. Tears splashed over her cheeks. Tish's mouth fell open. Ruthie cried, "You won't even see how sorry he feels!"

She then proceeded to throw her fork onto the table, bolt from her chair and streak up the steps to her room. Her door slammed with a vehement thud we felt at the table.

"Holy shit," Tish muttered.

"What do you know about this?" I demanded.

Tish tipped her chair on two legs, bracing both hands on the table. Uncharacteristically quiet, she admitted, "I knew she was upset, Mom, but I swear I didn't know she would freak out." Studying my face, she assured, "Ruthie likes Blythe just fine, I know she does. But you know how Dad is…"

"It's all right," I said at last, as Tish faltered to silence.

And as much as I hated to acknowledge the fact, I knew exactly how Jackson Gordon operated.

Chapter Fifteen

Shore Leave dazzled beneath the evening sun. Mom and Aunt Ellen closed up after lunch and spent the afternoon, along with Dodge, making the yard and the porch festive. I parked in my customary spot, Tish in the front seat beside me, Ruthie silent and sullen in the back. But even she couldn't completely maintain the despondent attitude at the sight of the party preparations. The girls hopped out and ran for the fire pit, where Clint and Liam were busy decorating the lawn chairs with balloons.

"Hi, guys," I said, approaching with only a little hesitation.

"Hi, sweetie," Aunt Ellen called, and Mom smiled with genuine warmth. Apparently my birthday allowed for a ceasefire.

"Everything looks great," I said.

"It does, doesn't it?" Mom murmured, reaching to straighten a hanging paper lantern to her satisfaction.

I stood and leaned one hip against the big charcoal grill we hauled out for special occasions, such as our Fourth of July Eve party.

Ellen added, "Happy birthday! Your gran made a humdinger of a chocolate cake for you two. It's like the old days all over."

I smiled and smoothed the skirt of the pale blue sundress that Tish insisted I wear. My hair had not been cut once this summer, due for a serious trim. It hung well past my shoulder blades, and the sun had bleached it almost as light as Jilly's. I looked around for my sister, figuring she was still getting ready; I headed for her apartment, but hadn't walked more than a few paces when I saw Gran moving slowly along the lake path, leaning over her cane. I jogged to her, realizing she was slightly out of breath. She held out her free hand for my elbow, saying, "Well, look at you. What a sight you make, you pretty girl."

"Oh Gran," I said, loving her so much. I decided to tell her so, right there. "I love you so much."

She gave me her prune face in return, crinkling up. She insisted, "Help me up to the porch, girl. My back is aching today."

"You shouldn't be walking this far without someone," I said gently, easing my arm around her waist.

"Sure I should," she bitched, holding tightly nonetheless. I studied her hands as we walked together, her dear, worn old hands with their brown spots and wrinkled skin and pointy nails painted with the shiny-clear toner she'd always favored.

I thought about how those same hands touched and taught me in myriad ways ever since the day I'd been born, thirty-six years ago to-day—cupping my head, smoothing my cheek just for love, wiping my face with edge of a handkerchief she'd licked to moisten. I'd watched her hands pat dirt around seeds dropped into the soil, and pull back on a fishing line, and later clean and fry up those same fish. Stirring cake bat-ter in the yellow celluloid bowl with the chip on the rim, with one finger extended as she skimmed down the words of a recipe in some ancient food-splattered book she and Minnie shared. Or with fingers spread on the table as she painted her nails. Her hands appeared so different back then, lean and capable and strong; it hurt me to see how frail they ap-peared under the August sun.

"Here we go," I murmured as we reached the steps and I guided her up to a table. Ellen and Mom drifted over to the fire pit to direct opera-tions.

Gran settled into the chair, rested her cane alongside it, and thumped the tabletop with both fists. "Joelle, I know it's your birthday, but go and grab me a drink, will you?"

"Of course," I said, ducking inside the cafe. I slipped behind the bar to the beer fridge and grabbed Gran a light one.

"Thank you, doll," she said. I joined her at the table, studying her face for a long moment, until her eyes flashed to mine, golden-green and somber. Blunt as always, she said, "Don't choose Jackie. He'll let you down, honey."

"I know," I whispered, aching as I thought about Ruthann's words at breakfast. I looked out over Flickertail, brilliant as sheet metal under the gloss of the late-summer sunshine. Gran studied me with uncharacteristic somberness.

"But what about the girls?" I asked, low and painful. I felt like my soul was tearing along a fault line as I whispered, "What if by choosing Blythe I'm letting them down? Doing them wrong? Cheating them out of their parents being together?"

"Joelle, stop that. That is a bunch of hokum," Gran said, rapping her beer bottle on the table. "If Jillian was sitting here she'd agree. And you know it in your heart."

I nodded, tears prickling in my eyes. My grandma caught one of my hands in both of hers, holding tightly.

"I do," I admitted, and knuckled my eyes with the other. "I do, Gran."

"You go tomorrow and get your man," she said, and squeezed my hand. "Promise me, Joelle Davis."

"I promise," I whispered, and later wondered if she'd somehow known.

Everyone showed up and as far as I could tell a wonderful time was had by all. I felt pushed to the periphery, though of my own accord, watching from the outskirts. Drinks flowed, there was enough food for a dozen parties, and Eddie Sorenson and Jim Olson were rowdy on the guitar and fiddle, respectively. High school friends, regulars at the cafe, my family, all were present. I danced a little, not wanting to disappoint my girls. And it brought a smile to my lips to see Camille appearing to enjoy herself as the evening wore on and stars flickered to life above, and reflected below, the unblemished surface of the darkened lake.

Mom had invited Curt and Marie Utley; of course Noah failed to accompany them, but his parents were kind and gracious to Camille, and she didn't seem embarrassed at their presence. I watched, covertly, as Marie chatted with my daughter at one of the picnic tables, occasionally patting her arm, keeping a conversation rolling. Noah's father smiled and nodded, nursing a beer, periodically messing with his hearing aid. I remained grateful that Jake McCall was not in attendance—I'd debated inviting him before this morning's disastrous breakfast. I talked for a spell with Tina and Glenna Carter, Diana and Bull's two oldest daughters, who'd arrived with their husbands. I enjoyed their company tremendously; they still knew all the juiciest gossip in the greater Landon area.

"Oh God, I know just how she feels," Tina commented, nodding at Camille. The three of us sat in the lawn chairs closer to the fire pit, angled so that Tina could sneak a cigarette without her kids noticing. She blew a perfect smoke ring and elaborated, "Preggers in high school. And her boyfriend has been AWOL, huh? Just like Beth's dad was, back when."

"Beth's dad isn't in Landon anymore, right?" I asked. Tina's ex had disappeared from her life shortly after word of her pregnancy; I'd already moved to Chicago by then, as Tina was in Jilly's grade, but I knew the story.

"He hasn't been around since the decade before last, the asshole. Here, you could use a light," Tina said, shaking one from the pack for me, grinning around the smoke in her lips. She teased, "Smoke up, Grandma!"

"Don't," I groaned, using the lighter Glenna offered.

Tina gestured at Camille and asked, "How's she doing? She's adorable, Jo. I could beat that kid's ass for leaving her in a lurch like this. Who would have thought Ben Utley's little brother could be such a coward?"

"I know," I sighed, exhaling smoke.

"It's great to hear that you're sticking around, though, Jo," Glenna said. "I hate losing one of us to big cities, you know?"

"Like Matty," Tina said, referring to their younger brother, Mathias, who attended college in Minneapolis.

"You don't think he'll move home eventually?" I asked, continuing to study my oldest daughter; the firelight gilded her lovely face, shining over its delicate contours; almost as though she sensed we'd been discussing her fate, she glanced my way. Immediately I held the cigarette near my thigh, so she wouldn't catch a glimpse.

"God, I hope he comes home after college," Glenna said. "It's not the same without him around."

"Someday," Tina said. "We won't give up on him." She tilted her head at me, tucking a strand of bright red hair behind her ear. She said, "And Jo, I was sorry to hear about you and Jackie. I mean, you two were always together. But on that note, can I just say that you were always too good for him?"

"Yes, and thank you," I said.

"What about you and Blythe Tilson?" Glenna prompted, poking me with the toe of her sandal. "Scuttlebutt says you two were pretty hot and heavy this summer."

Tina's eyes gleamed with the joy of such a topic. She winked at me and said, "Mama's still got it, huh?"

I giggled a little, in spite of myself. "Sure, *now* I'm Mama. A second ago I was *Grandma*."

"Hey, if the orthopedic shoe fits," Tina said.

By the time Mom lugged out the enormous chocolate birthday cake with about a million candles glinting on the top, the crowd was ripe to sing "Happy Birthday" to Jilly and me. I managed to pry my sister from Justin's arms, catching her hand in mine as we blew out the mass of lights on our cake, grinning at the flashbulb as Dodge took pictures. But once the pictures were snapped and cake eaten, I intended to sneak away to the dock. The mood of the whole gathering had mellowed, everyone partnering up as Eddie and Jim switched to a slower tune. They played their own version of songs, giving everything a sort of bluegrass feel. But they were good, and it was the music of my childhood. I was about to make my escape, planning to enjoy the music from afar, when I looked up and saw Jackie coming through the crowd, his eyes pinned on me.

My heart fell through my ribcage and sank to the ground.

I knew he hadn't been here all evening. I was sure of it. From the corner of my eye I saw Ruthann light up like a struck match. I spared a look her direction to see her grinning from ear to ear. Camille and Tish seemed to be in on something, too, observing from the sidelines as their dad approached me, and a panicked flock of birds took sudden wing in my stomach. My heart thudded, in dread.

"Happy birthday," Jackie said, reaching me, his handsome face beaming with his warmest smile. Once upon a time, that grin would have caused my entire insides to melt away. But now I felt wooden. My gaze flickered around in desperation, searching for Jilly, for help. But she was on the opposite side of the huge crowd of dancers, locked in Justin's arms. Jackie reached me, clad in jeans and a sport coat. I opened my mouth, but he was faster, saying with sincerity, "You look so beautiful, Joelle."

I blinked as though in slow motion, watching mutely as he reached into his pocket; before I could react he produced a small silver package, tied with a glistening green bow.

"What's this?" I whispered, throat dry as a drought year.

"It's something I want you to have," he said, looking intently into my eyes. "But first, will you dance with me?"

Ruthie edged over to us, and her eyes absolutely glowed with happiness. She wheedled, "Come on, Mom, dance with Daddy."

I swallowed, with great difficulty, feeling the trap spring closed over my leg. I started to say no…but then I caught sight of my girls, mine and Jackie's daughters, all suddenly clustered together, watching with such hopeful expressions.

"All right," I relented, and Jackie grinned and handed off the wrapped package to Ruthie.

Despite the fact that he'd been in my arms more than just about anyone else in my life, his shoulders beneath my left arm felt somehow foreign. Jackie gathered me close with no such evident compunctions, the same way we'd danced together a thousand times since high school. His chin was just at my forehead. His right hand pressed low on my spine and he curled our fingers tight. I looked over his shoulder, distracted, my stomach jumping with nerves. One dance and that was it.

"This feels so right," he said, low, lips brushing my ear.

Wisely I did not reply. I would be lying if I said I didn't have a moment's pang that Jackie was trying so hard. His hand had once been so welcome holding mine, skimming all over my body. Sudden, clutching regret for our failure gripped me, the fact that this was the last time I ever planned to dance with someone I'd once loved dearly; the father of my three beautiful children and the man with whom I had planned to spend the duration of my life.

"God, I miss you," he said, and I could tell he meant these words… or at least, he did right now, swept up in the wistful atmosphere of our unchanging hometown and the memories it evoked, the love we'd once shared. And our girls. It was so hard to deny them what they wanted, and I could tell they were part of this whole scheme. They loved Jackie still. They just wanted their parents to be together, like any kids.

"Jackie…" My eyes grew teary without my permission. People danced all around us, smiling, talking, laughing, and yet it was as though he and I stood suspended in a small, amber-tinted bubble, crystallized as versions of our former selves, the couple we'd once been. I recognized this moment as a fork in the road, as critical a decision as any in my life. Part of me danced in Jackie's arms and another hovered, poised, shivering in a sudden breeze, at the juncture of a divided path. It would be so easy to sink into his words and let myself believe him.

"I want you to come home with me," he said then, driving the final nail into the coffin, and I closed my eyes, not allowing any tears to fall. I'd known this was coming. Trust him to do this in a crowd, with our children as witnesses. But he was a lawyer, accustomed to getting his way, and it was a tactic. "Your wedding rings are in that package, Joelle, and I want you to put them on again and come home." His voice was full of feeling. "I have never been so face to face with regret as I've been this last month. I've been so wrong. God, please believe me. Please, baby, come back with me."

No.

My entire body rebelled against all of this, but most especially the endearment. Only one man was allowed to call me *baby*, and that was the last straw. Thankfully the song ended on a drawn-out note, and I eased from his arms.

Jackie kept my hand and brought it to his lips, kissing my knuckles before releasing me. He said, "Think about it, Jo. I'm going home this week."

I remained silent. It stunned me to hear him say these things, to allow such vulnerability.

He said, "I'll come back in the morning. Sleep on it, Jo." And then, as a final lowdown blow, his eyes bearing into mine, he whispered, "I love you. I do. And I'll spend the rest of my life showing you."

He turned and walked back through the crowd.

"Here's your present," Ruthie said, passing me the small silver package.

"Thank you," I whispered. My lips felt numb.

The girls went to sit by the fire, where a large group of their friends gathered. Jilly was undoubtedly somewhere having incredibly hot sex with Justin; I hadn't seen either of them for the past half hour. Mom and Ellen carted food back into the cafe. Two-thirds of the guests headed home, though a couple of Gran's friends, women around her age, remained sitting with her at a porch table, enjoying coffee and slices of cake. I walked briskly away from all the merriment, to the sanctity of the dock, where I kicked off my shoes and took up my customary place at the end, letting my feet sink into the water. In my hand was the wrapped box containing my engagement diamond and gold wedding band. Before last spring, I'd never removed these two rings from my finger.

I set the box on the dock boards and looked out over Flickertail. It was pleasant down here, and so blessedly familiar. My soul was etched with the contours of the scene before my eyes right now, the constant ripple of the water, the shapes of the trees lining the far shore, the way the lake curved out and around a natural bend. The scent of the water, musky and green and tinged with fish. Above me, against the darkened sky, flapped the small, unmistakable shapes of brown bats in their choppy, erratic flight. Gran and Great-Aunt Minnie years ago built bat houses to attract the creatures, which ate their weight in mosquitoes on a nightly basis. I drew a deep breath and held it, and when I exhaled, I murmured Blythe's name like an incantation. Tomorrow I would be on the road to Oklahoma. My bag was packed; Tish and Ruthie brought their overnight bags, as they'd be staying at Shore Leave in my absence. Tish filled me in on several of the shin-digs they planned for this last week of summer; school would begin in just a few days. I would be home by then, and Blythe would be with me.

It hurts you about Jackie, though, admit it.

I didn't hate my husband. In fact, he'd successfully manipulated me into feeling sorry for him. Inadvertently my fingers went to the silver box, tied with a bow. It may be over between us in my mind, but I wasn't totally heartless. He'd said all of the things I would have given my eye teeth to hear last winter. But I'd finally comprehended the basic insincerity, realized that Jackie would not have meant those words back then; if I opted to believe him now, in a few months he would no longer mean them. I understood this clearly. Give us a while in Chicago and his restless eye would rove back in Lanny's direction, probably sooner than later. Or if not her, then some other readily-available woman. Jackie was a handsome man, well-built, charming, not to mention wealthy. He'd long for greener grass, and there was plenty of such grass in the city.

And yet, if not for Lanny, I would never have come home to stay, would have continued living in Chicago, half-alive, my soul trapped behind a barrier I'd never even known was there. I could never go back to that.

But you'll have to hurt Jackie. And the girls.

And far worse than any empathy I may dredge up for Jackie, it tortured me to think about my girls wanting so badly for our family to remain intact. I wanted my daughters to be happy, I knew they wished I would choose their father—but I could not grant them this wish; it would cost me my soul, and that was a price I realized I was not willing to pay. They would understand in time. A strange flicker of awareness sent a shiver rippling over my spine as I thought of my girls, simultaneously studying the starry night sky. And a sense of *knowing* filled my mind with the suddenness of a summer thunderstorm, overtaking me as I sat there on the dock, rapid and intense. I stared out over the surface of Flickertail, momentarily transfixed by the notion of a white-hot lightning bolt striking the water; I could nearly hear its crackling, dangerous sizzle, could see the water broiling in a widening circle in response—I inhaled the sharp scent of ozone.

They will find love. They will love and be loved, deeply and absolutely. It's in their souls, Joelle. It's their destiny.

Why, then, was I so scared?

Much later I curled up on the couch in Jilly's place; I'd intended to wait up for her, but exhaustion and lingering disquiet dragged me under and I fell asleep before she came back. I needed sleep; I intended to head out early, get on the road to Oklahoma before dawn.

But that didn't happen. It just wasn't in the cards on this last morning of August.

I came awake reluctantly, snatched from a restless dream, and realized Mom was bent over me in the pale gray light of early morning. The incongruity of Mom in Jillian's apartment at this hour further disoriented me.

I whispered, "What's…"

Tears wet my mother's cheeks, her hands soft on my shoulders. Fear entered my throat like a knife point. I sat up too fast and demanded, "Oh God, what's wrong?"

Mom knelt, putting her face level with mine. She said in a small, hoarse voice, "It's Gran. Oh, Joelle, she's gone."

"Gone? Gone where? Oh, Mom…*oh no…*"

My voice died out to nothing as everything inside of me swelled with despair. Tears sprang into my eyes as I pitched forward and into the comfort of Mom's warm arms. She held me and sobbed against my shoulder. Her hair was loose and smelled of her pillow. I clung to her, sorrow ricocheting through my body.

"But she was just…having cake…last night," I wept, my forehead on Mom's neck. "She was just having cake."

"She loved you girls so much," Mom whispered after a time, stroking my hair. "You and Jillian, especially. You two were the light of her life."

I passed a hand over my eyes.

Mom drew away, cupping my face as she had when I was small. She said, "Everyone's at the cafe. Dodge is here, Jilly and Justin are on their way, and Rich is coming home."

I sat straighter at her words, my thoughts racing ahead. This meant I couldn't leave. I couldn't go to Blythe, not in the wake of this. My heart panged with new despair.

"Mom, when did you talk to Rich?" I asked.

She scooped her long hair into one hand and blew out a breath, cheeks puffing out. Her eyes and nose were red, her lips swollen. She said, "Not long ago. He's flying home as soon as he can. Surely you're not thinking…"

I shook my head. "No, of course I'll stay here." But the words tasted bitter in my throat, like iron.

"Good," Mom said, patting my shoulders. Her expression changed markedly and she said, "Honey, Jilly is going to have big news."

"News?" I parroted dumbly.

"Just yesterday morning Justin asked me for permission to propose to her. He was going to ask her last night after the party. Gran was so happy about it."

I felt I couldn't quite handle one shock on top of another, but I whispered, "Of course she was."

The morning sky appeared heavy, its underbelly of indigo rain clouds scuttling across a darker backdrop of steel gray. Intermittent rain slashed over the porch and the air was chilly, almost autumn-like. But inside Shore Leave the lights glowed brightly and kept a little of the gloom at bay. Coffee and then food, as those who'd come yesterday to celebrate birth came now in sympathy as news of Gran's death spread through Landon, toting casseroles and breads, plates of cookies, cakes in dented aluminum pans with rollaway tops. Hugs and murmured words, all around. At one point I found myself wondering why Gran wasn't in the room, enjoying the company. For a second I even thought about going to get her. My eyes circled the familiar space with a sense of painful disorientation—I'd never been in Shore Leave without Gran nearby. It was unimaginable that she wouldn't be, ever again.

Just before noon Cal Price, whose family ran the funeral home in Landon, pulled into the parking lot; their ancient hearse, ominous as death, rolled over the blacktop, coming to rest near the cafe. My stomach surged; I felt sure I would be ill in a violent spray across the dining room. Surely they weren't here to take my grandmother away from us; Gran wouldn't dream of leaving. Jilly appeared at my side, tucking close, her weeping emerging as half-choked sobs, deep in her throat.

"They can't…take her," she gasped, leaning on me for support, reading my mind.

I hugged my little sister, holding fast to her, as Mom and Aunt Ellen moved as one, out onto the porch, to speak to Cal. Jilly and I followed, the rain as fine as a mist on our skin. Ellen's knees sagged a little, and Mom bolstered her. Cal, who was only a little younger than Gran, came right up onto the porch and hugged all of us in turn. He said, "I'm so very sorry, girls."

His two sons carried Gran from the house, her motionless form covered carefully with a sheet. I was immeasurably touched to see Cal holding an umbrella over her body as they wheeled the stretcher through the gossamer rain. I stood in a tightly-woven knot with Mom and Jilly, Ellen and the kids, joining us outside with downcast lips and eyes. We grew soaked to the skin, but there was no question of moving. At the last moment Clint broke free and darted to the back of the hearse, where the younger Prices opened the back hatch to place Gran inside. They looked at him with mild surprise, but I knew what he was doing; Clint bent and kissed the sheet covering Gran's face. Dear, sweet Clinty. He murmured something to her. Jilly's weeping escalated and she ran to join him, and then we were all there, clinging to each other and touching Gran with gentle, loving fingertips, bidding farewell to the woman who gave so very much, whose love shaped each of us in countless ways. And we all stood and watched the ruby taillights of the big, cumbersome car as it crunched away over the gravel, bearing Gran down the lake road from Shore Leave for the last time.

Much later, Jilly and I slumped at table three, eating leftover birthday cake, the last ones in the cafe. It was nearly midnight, both of us depleted; Jilly's eyes were so shadowed she appeared to have been punched. I'm sure mine looked the same. We'd run through the gamut of emotions today and sat here relieved to simply be in one another's presence, alone. The kids fell asleep in sleeping bags on Jilly's living room floor, needing one another as much as Jilly and I did right now. Outside, the stars winked on full-force, the clouds having shredded up and blown away to parts unknown. Mom, Dodge, and Ellen sat around the fire; Justin, too. He was so worried about Jillian (after all, it was her birthday and they were newly engaged). I noticed that his lawn chair was angled so he could watch the screen door for the moment she came back outside.

I took my sister's left hand into mine, cupping her slim fingers and admiring her new ring all over again. Despite everything, I was thrilled for her, and for Justin, and tilted her delicate hand side to side to admire the sparkle. I said softly, "Don't put anything off for your wedding. You know Gran would never want that."

She nodded, wiping stray tears, whispering, "I won't, I promise. I'm so happy, Jo, underneath."

A little later I said, "Mom thought Gran mentioned a memorial service once, like way back when we were kids. Mom said Gran didn't want a funeral."

Tears glistened on Jilly's cheeks as she whispered, "She wants to be scattered over the lake, just like Minnie."

The bite I'd just eaten lodged in my throat, but I was determined not to cry anymore tonight. My head already ached. I swallowed, though with difficulty, and then said, "Mom and Ell want to hold the service on Wednesday."

"Rich will be home by then, that's good," Jilly said. And then her expression changed into one of intense concern, lips parting, golden brows drawing inward. She caught my hands into hers. "What about Bly? Oh, Jo, I forgot you were going to drive down there today."

"He's supposed to be released on Tuesday. I haven't talked to him in weeks," I said, trying not to let my agony over that supersede the agony of today. "When Rich gets here I'll find out what's going on. Oh, Jilly…"

"Jo, you're trembling," Jilly said, pressing a soft palm on my forearm. She whispered, "It's all right."

"I didn't get to tell you about last night," I said, clenching the muscles in my arms in an attempt to still the quivers; no use. My thighs took up the jittering. I explained, "About what Jackie said."

"I heard you danced. Clinty told me," Jilly responded. Her eyes grew sharp with distrust. "Why, what did he say?"

I summarized, including the incident with Ruthann at breakfast yesterday morning. And then I told Jilly about the conversation with Gran, just yesterday and about a million years ago.

Jilly said adamantly, "You listen to Gran. You promise me, Jo."

"There was never a doubt in my mind," I said. "And you and Justin go right ahead with your wedding, will you promise me?"

Jillian nodded, swiping at her eyes and then her nose. She looked out the wide front windows, to the group at the fire pit, her gaze finding and holding Justin. She whispered, "Come on, Jo, let's go sit with them."

Justin's dark eyes caressed Jilly as we approached and without hesitation she moved to sit on his lap, where he curled her close within the strength of his arms. She settled her head against his wide shoulder. As I took my own seat, across from them, I smiled. And knew Gran would have, too.

Chapter Sixteen

Monday passed in a haze. We'd closed Shore Leave for the time being. I was useless; we all were. We spent the intermittently rainy day crowded around albums and piles of loose photos that Mom and Ellen carted down from the attic, pictures of Gran in all the seasons of her long, fruitful life. Mom wanted to make a couple of collages for the memorial service on Wednesday.

"Oh, look at this one! Gran looks so young," Camille said, holding aloft a black and white snapshot of Gran and Great-Aunt Minnie, sitting outside by the fire pit, bare feet propped up on wooden stumps, both grinning and holding beer bottles in a salute to the camera. Or maybe just life in general. The year on the back of the picture, 1948, was scrawled in faded black ink.

"I wish you could have known Minnie," I said, leaning over her shoulder to examine the picture. "She was quite a woman."

Camille placed her free hand atop the small swell of her growing belly, almost unconsciously, and whispered, "Me, too."

"Look, I remember that bathing suit," Jilly said, gesturing to another picture, in which Gran wore a polka-dotted number, her golden hair hanging loose over her bare shoulders. She held a cigarette clamped between her teeth, her hands cupped around the heads of Jilly and me, around ages four and five.

"Yeah, she always loved polka dot prints," Ellen said, lightly tracing over the image of Gran.

"And big hats," Mom added fondly, and then lifted from the box of loose pictures a small, brown-toned snapshot. She studied it for a moment before exclaiming, "Ellen, look, it's Dad. I *knew* there was at least one photo of him."

We crowded each other to examine the photo; I could not remember ever having seen a picture of this man, my grandfather. I didn't even know his name, truth be told; Gran had always been a Davis, through thick and thin, never mentioning a married surname. Whatever his name, the man in the picture was handsome and bearded, squinting into the sun of a long-gone afternoon in the 1940s, standing near Gran down by Flickertail Lake; his right hand rested upon Gran's back in what appeared a tender touch, as he pointed out over the water with his left. Gran stood with hands clasped beneath her chin, both of them in profile.

"That's a great shot," I murmured. "What were they looking at?"

"Lord knows," Mom said. "But it's a good picture of the two of them. We should get this enlarged."

"That's our grandpa?" asked Ruthie.

"No, he's your great-grandpa," Mom corrected. "Aaron Owens."

"No shit?" I asked, a little stunned by this revelation. "Since when does he have a name?"

"Joelle, don't swear in front of the kids," Mom admonished, and Jilly and Tish both dared to laugh.

Tish said, "*Yeah*, Mom."

Camille asked, "Did Gran ever date anyone after this Owens guy left?" She sat with another box of pictures balanced on her thighs and there was a layer of vulnerability in her question that I wondered if only I detected. She looked pale beneath her naturally olive skin, her curls tucked into a hastily-tied ponytail. She'd lived apart from me for nearly half a month now, my pregnant baby. I moved to sit at the booth across from her.

"Mom dated a little, now and again, but nothing too serious," Ellen said, but then she pursed her lips in speculation. "Wait, though, I remember when Jilly and Jo were maybe three and four there was that man who came to replace the phone lines. Remember, Joanie?"

"Ooh, what's this?" Jilly asked, her ears perking. "An illicit romance? I don't remember this!"

I dearly hoped Gran took advantage of a relationship like that.

"*Eww*," said Clint.

"Nothing that dramatic," Ellen said, sounding amused. "But they did see each other for a few months. What was his name?"

"Mitchell," Mom said at once. "I can't remember his last name, but I do recall one night Ma came back from dinner with him and her hair was wet. And I knew she hadn't taken a bathing suit!"

The kids made a collective sound of surprise while Jilly and I laughed heartily; it felt good.

Clint gaped at us, truly shocked, and asked, "You mean Gran was *skinny-dipping?*"

Jilly and I laughed even harder.

"She was a woman way before she was your great-gran," Camille chided.

"Yeah, but…" Clinty was at a complete loss.

I headed for the pass-through door between dining room and kitchen, meaning to grab a plate of cookies. Thanks to the generosity of the housewives of Landon, we probably had food enough to get us to winter. I didn't notice Ruthie behind me until I turned around and she said, quietly, "Mom, did you talk to Daddy at all?"

I set down the plate and looked into her beautiful eyes, my youngest and sweetest child, the one who would no doubt take the news of our failed relationship the hardest. She couldn't see her father's faults, nor mine if truth be told, and I wasn't going to elaborate in that fashion. But she needed to know that it wasn't to be. I chose my words with great care, saying, "Yes, we did talk a little."

"Did you open up your rings?"

I pushed aside any anger that Jackie would dare to lift her hopes in that way and said, "I did, but Ruthie…"

She burst into tears before I could say another word and I gathered her in my arms. She clung, wrapping her slim little arms around my waist. My heart ached for her pain. She was so little, when it came down to it, and there was a part of me that truly considered sacrificing my own happiness for hers, the me who would have returned to Chicago and tried again. And then I imagined that, standing here in the kitchen at Shore Leave with my lips pressed to the top of Ruthie's head, her dark curls that smelled of Jilly's coconut shampoo, imagined returning to Chicago and our townhouse, and the fairly privileged lives we all lived there. For a moment I let last weekend play out in my mind…had I slept with Jackie in that old twin bed and gone that route. I shuddered and rocked my daughter side to side, thanking the powers that be that I would never have done such a thing.

Finally Ruthie calmed down and whispered, "But Daddy loves you, Mom."

I said against her hair, "He might think he does, honey, but he really loves the memory of us. He loves what we *used* to have. We were really happy here, a long time ago. He misses our past lives. But we're both so different now."

"But why?" she asked plaintively.

I smoothed strands of hair from her golden-green eyes that were still wet with the aftermath of tears. She looked vulnerable as she questioned me and I gulped a little, suddenly remembering the intensity of the storm that I imagined while sitting on the dock. With effort, I submerged the strangeness of that and finally said, "Because we changed, honey. Sometimes people do that. In fact, it's good for people to change sometimes. But I want you to know that whatever I feel for Blythe in no way changes what I feel for you girls. I will always love you girls with all my heart and nothing could change that."

"Okay," she whispered at last, barely audibly. I squeezed her close. She said, "I'm sorry about Gran, Mama."

Tears slid over my face and I wiped them roughly on my right shoulder. I whispered, "I know. And I'm sorry that I can't make things work with Dad. Will you forgive me?"

Ruthie nodded against me and for that moment it was all I needed.

Jackie stopped out in the late afternoon and asked if the girls and Clint wanted to go into Bemidji with him for dinner. It was kind of him to realize they needed distraction. To his credit, he didn't mention any of what had occurred at the birthday party. He hugged everyone, including me, and told us how sorry he was and that he'd have the kids back before too late. I watched them drive away in Jackie's familiar car and then rejoined Mom, Jilly, and Ellen as they chose pictures to showcase the important moments of Gran's life. I knew I would have to talk with Jackie, sooner than later certainly, since he intended to return to Chicago. But I was relieved not to face that particular conversation tonight.

The four of us worked through dinner, eating from the various casseroles lined up in the fridge, making sandwiches later when we were hungry again. Finally Ellen made a big blender full of grasshoppers to congratulate our hard work; we filled five large poster boards with artfully-arranged pictures. They were roughly chronological, and Mom and Ellen lined them up across the tops of the booths for safe-keeping.

"We'll have to get a couple of easels," Mom mused.

"And flowers. She'd want that," Ellen added.

"Who will be here?" Jilly asked, coming up behind Ellen and hooking her arm around Ellen's waist.

"I would expect anyone who wants to pay their last respects," Mom said. "But just us for the…"

She choked up and I went immediately to her side, Jilly the other. We put our arms around our mother and she was able to finish, saying, "The scattering of her ashes."

Ellen joined our hug and whispered, "I just can't believe she's gone. It doesn't seem possible. She hadn't left this place in almost all of her adult life."

"I'd get so short-tempered with her," Mom said, punishing herself. "But she only ever meant well."

"Aw, Joanie, there wasn't much Ma loved more than a good argument," Ellen said.

Mom sniffed agreement. "I know. Thank God for Dodge."

Jilly eased free and nodded at the window. "Kids are back."

My sister went outside, clicking on the porch light as she did. I folded my arms and didn't budge and Mom observed, "I saw you and Jackie dancing, Jo."

"He told me he still loves me and that he wants us to come home with him," I confessed quietly, seeing both my own defensive reflection in the window and the kids hugging their dad good-night in the dark parking lot.

"Oh, Jo*elle*," Mom said. But then she lifted her hands, palms up, and retreated. Her eyes clearly told me what she thought.

I watched Jackie climb the steps behind the kids, who were carrying leftover boxes from a seafood restaurant. Unable to hide out in the dining room, I clacked out the screen door, telepathically (I hoped, anyway) ordering Jilly to remain on the porch with us. The girls and Clint headed into the warm glow of the cafe, where Mom pulled a dishtowel from a pan of brownies. Jackie hesitated with one foot on the top step, gripping the rails on either side. In the semi-darkness he looked young and lean, his cheekbones sharply defined, like the Jackie of my youth. He kept his eyes steady on mine.

"Thanks for taking the kids," I said, hoping he would just go, and soon.

"Of course," he said and shifted his gaze to include Jilly. "I'm so sorry, you guys. Jo, I'm staying through Wednesday."

I nodded.

"Have you been thinking about…everything?" he asked.

"Jackie, I'm staying here," I said, crossing my arms.

He inhaled sharply through his nose and said, "Don't do this, Jo."

"What about Lanny?" I asked, keeping my voice low. I felt no kinship with the woman, but was compelled to ask the question.

"What about her?" Jackie demanded, all but gritting his teeth.

"The woman you plan to *marry*, remember? What does she have to say about all of this?" I suddenly realized he'd said nothing to Lanny; surely if I refused to return to Chicago he would avoid that conversation altogether, and would expect Lanny to be waiting, none the wiser.

"Jackson Gregory Gordon," I said, and his name sounded like a curse.

He narrowed his eyes at my deeply accusatory tone.

"Grow the fuck up," Jilly finished for me, the two of us standing side by side. She latched her hands on her hips and muttered, "*Jesus*, Jackie."

"It's over with Lanny," he said, grasping at straws now. "But not between us, Jo. It's not over between us."

"It's over between us, too," I said, not without a certain degree of sympathy.

"Not if I have anything to say about it," Jackie said, but he backed up and turned away. At the last moment, just as he reached his car, he looked up at me on the porch and added, "I love you. And I'm not giving up."

"Oh, boy," Jilly said as he drove away.

"I'll be on the dock," I whispered.

Chapter Seventeen

The day's rain passed over Landon and the sky shone satin-clear, the air brisk. I wrapped into an old cardigan and sat on the dock in a sort of emotional stupor, thinking about my last conversation with Gran, when my cell phone began vibrating. I jumped a little, nearly displacing it into Flickertail, hoping beyond all reason that it might be Rich, with news of Blythe. But then I saw the name on the screen and almost dropped it a second time in my haste to answer.

"Joelle, it's me," he said, his deep voice filling up all the emptiness in my heart and soul, my senses absorbing the sound like the precious gift it was. He rushed on, "I'm out, love, I'm here at Mom's. Rich told me everything. I'm dying to get to you."

"Blythe," I whispered, cradling the phone, his voice, as close to me as possible. I began weeping, unable to help it. Everything within me reached out for him, longing and need and desire and love. Oh, how I loved him. My heart throbbed the force of it through me.

"Sweetheart, I'm so sorry I'm not there," he kept saying, his voice tortured. "Oh Joelle, honey."

I drew a ragged breath and my words poured like water from a tipped bucket. "Blythe, I'm so glad to hear your voice. I've missed you so much. I've been so worried about you. Are you all right? Rich said you looked rough the last time he'd seen you. I should be there, I want to be there so much…but Gran…"

"Honey, Gramps told me. I'm so sorry. I'm coming tomorrow, we're flying up there. But I'm going crazy here. Mom keeps telling me I can't just jump in my truck and go. I love you, baby. God, I love you. I have all of your letters right here. They're all ragged from me reading them so many times."

I laughed a little then, so unbelievably happy to have his voice in my ear, the prospect of him being here tomorrow. It was almost too much to bear. I said, "I have all of yours, too, and I sleep with them every night. Rich told me he and your mom couldn't touch you when they came to see you. I plan to never stop touching you, *just you wait*."

His voice was hoarse as he said, "Baby, I will take you up on that. I'm a little starved for touching right now."

"I'll make up for all of the last month," I promised, cradling the phone as if it was his hand against the side of my face, hot little flutters in my belly. "Did you get out early? I thought tomorrow morning…"

"They released me twelve hours early. I'm lucky they allowed it. And Dale said if I have a job in Minnesota the state should allow the move."

"Oh, thank God," I breathed.

"And happy birthday. I'm so sorry I missed it." His voice grew even softer with tenderness as he asked, "What happened with Gran? I can't believe it, Jo. I can't imagine her being gone. She was the one who hired me up there, who decided I was a decent person just by looking into my eyes. I'll never forget that."

"She died in her sleep," I whispered. "It was peaceful. But I'll miss her forever."

"Sweetheart," he breathed. "I know you will."

"She told me something so important on Saturday. It was mine and Jilly's birthday party that day, and Blythe…" I trailed to silence, frantically wondering if this was the time and place to tell him everything. But I refused to hang up and part from his voice before morning light, at the earliest. I wrapped the cardigan more tightly around my shoulders and moved from the dock boards onto the glider.

"What is it, honey?" he asked. And as though reading my thoughts, he added, "I'm not letting you go tonight. You're going to keep the phone open on your pillow so I can hear you breathing even after you've gone to sleep."

As always, his words touched me to the core. He felt and said just what I needed to hear. I whispered, almost shyly, "You always say things like that and I feel so special. So safe in your love. So important to you."

His voice was husky as he replied, "You are important to me, baby. The most important part of my life. And I mean to show you that every day. All the nights this last month I spent lying in that cell imagining that you were beside me, that I could feel your heart beating and hear your breath. I mean to hear that every night for the rest of my life."

My heart caught and lifted up into the sky and fresh tears prickled into my eyes, spilling down my face. I whispered, "I'm holding you to that."

"Don't cry, baby, it breaks my heart if I can't be there to hold you," he said softly. "Tell me instead about your birthday. Was it a good party?"

"No, because you weren't there," I said, swiping roughly at my tears. "Gran baked her famous chocolate birthday cake. Jilly and I always used to have a double birthday celebration. But something else happened… something shitty…I mean, at the party. Before everything with Gran." I refused to hesitate and forged ahead, determined to tell him everything. "I have to back up. Blythe, Jackie has been in town all month. You know he brought divorce papers. But he's been reconsidering the whole divorce. He's been spending all this time with the girls. They've missed him. They love him, I can't…I mean, I *wouldn't*…change that. I'm glad they do. But they don't seem to understand that it's over between their dad and me." I drew a deep breath. "And on my birthday he told me…" Suddenly I felt terrible. Why did I think this would be anything Blythe would want to hear? But he deserved my honesty.

"Told you what?" Blythe asked, his voice so close and rough with emotion that I felt as if I turned my head I would see him sitting beside me, here in the darkness.

"Told me that he didn't want a divorce. That he still loved me."

"He did." Blythe's voice was flat. Almost despairing.

"But don't you see?" I begged into the silence. "It doesn't matter."

He didn't speak, though I could hear him as he breathed. I pictured him sitting on the steps of the trailer, the hand not holding the phone braced in his short hair.

"Blythe!" I implored. "Please tell me what you're thinking."

He said brokenly, "Promise me, Joelle, that if you…still feel anything for him that you'll take that into consideration."

My heart squeezed inward on itself. I could sense that he was terrified, that he thought I would tell him I wasn't sure and that I needed time to think, thereby giving me an out. I was appalled that he thought I might be on the fence. My throat hurt as I said, "You know that I don't. You *know* that, Blythe. Don't doubt it for a moment."

"I hate him," he said then, fiercely. "That he would do this to you. After *everything* he's done to you. And now he has the fucking gall to tell you he wants you back?"

"He's jealous," I said, clutching the phone with both hands, the way I wanted to be clutching Blythe. "He's petty and jealous, and the moment I went back to Chicago with him the entire tune would change." I implored, "Please don't think I want Jackie back. Oh, Blythe, since the moment I met you, I started forgetting him."

"I know," he whispered, and relief poured over me to hear that he sounded more like himself, less like he'd just been fisted hard in the gut. "And I know you love me, sweetheart. I don't doubt it. But you scared me there."

"I just wanted you to know what happened. I don't want us to have secrets. And I don't want you two to fight, ever again. That was so horrible."

"I'm sorry it happened like that, baby. But I'm not sorry I hit him. Especially now."

"I know," I said, repeating his words. "And I would only ever tell *you* this, but I love that you stood up for me, that you protected me when you thought I'd been hurt."

"I would do that and more," he said passionately. "Joelle, just wait. I'll be there tomorrow. And Wednesday is the service, right?"

"Yes. We put together all these pictures today. There are so many more pictures than I remembered. There was even one of my grandfather. Gran looked so happy. I think she was happy, here all these years running the cafe. I hope she was. I don't know what my life would have been like without her."

"Sweetheart, she was happy. Being around her even one day showed me that. She loved you guys so much. You should have heard her talk about you before you and the girls got to Shore Leave last May. I'd even go so far as to say that you were her favorite."

"Nah, but I'd like to think so," I said, smiling. I bent my knees and wrapped an arm about my lower legs.

"How are the girls doing? How's Clinty? I can't tell you how much I've missed everyone. And the cafe, and Flickertail, the whole place. Sometimes when I was lying there in jail I'd feel like all my time at Shore Leave was just this beautiful dream. Like I'd only imagined all of it."

"You most certainly did not," I said, with asperity. "I'd like to think that eventually Jillian and I will be running the cafe. And you and Justin can help. But we have final say."

Blythe snorted and then laughed. "Oh, well, as long as that's clear. How's everything between those two?"

"Good, so good. I'm so glad to see it."

"What else have I missed this month? Tell me everything."

When Jilly found me hours later, I lay on my side upon the glider, sound asleep but still clutching the phone. Jillian laughed a little, waking me. I blinked, immediately bringing the phone to my ear. The last thing I remembered was curling up with Blythe's voice and whispering good-night.

"Was that your man?" my sister asked as I sat up. She wrapped her arms around my waist, snuggling her chin against my shoulder.

"Yeah," I said. "It was my man. He'll be here later today. I'll see him." She squeezed me and I put my arms over hers. I asked, "You okay?"

"Yeah, I'm okay. Mom finally went to bed. I told her that she needed to rest."

"Good, she does. I didn't mean to fall asleep. Blythe must have fallen asleep, too. I wanted to hear him breathe all night." I sighed, cradling the phone even still.

"Oh, barf," Jilly teased. But I knew she understood.

Blythe called me back at first light, just an hour or so later.

"I didn't mean to fall asleep," I said. "I don't remember falling asleep."

"I do," he said, teasing me a little with his soft, warm, sleepy tone. "You said you were going to lie down for just a minute. Down by the lake, too. You're probably covered in bites, baby. Don't worry, I'll inspect you when I get there."

"What time?" I murmured. "Hurry. Blythe, hurry to me."

"Aw, sweetheart, I will. We'll be there by early afternoon, I hope. We're leaving for the airport in just a few hours."

Restless with energy, I showered and went to find my kids. Of course everyone was already at the cafe, Tish stationed in the kitchen scrambling eggs, while Ruthie fried bacon. Camille sat at one of the booths, feet propped on a nearby chair, holding what looked like a sheet of notebook paper. I poured a cup of coffee, marveling at my girls, how they'd changed over the summer months. I realized it was September now and moved to tear August from the calendar hanging on the wall, the same style we'd always featured at Shore Leave, a locally-made one featuring images of southern Beltrami County businesses. In fact, we'd been the July image if I remembered right.

"That smells good," I said, leaning against the counter to stir creamer into my mug.

"Morning, Mom," Tish said, peering through the ticket window. "Aunt Jilly said Blythe is coming back today."

"He is. I hope that you guys are excited to see him. He's really missed you."

Tish nodded enthusiastically. "Yeah, we missed him, too."

Leave it to her to take things in stride; I appreciated that very much about Tish. Jackie and I named her Patricia Joan (after our mothers) and envisioned calling her Patty Jo. It was only when tiny Camille began lisping 'Tisha' in an attempt to speak her sister's name that we realized she would never be a Patty Jo. Certainly someone with that nickname would have a much different personality than my outspoken Tish.

"Where are Grandma and Aunt Ellen?" I asked.

"They drove into town to see about something at the funeral home,"

Ruthie explained, expertly flipping the bacon. "Aunt Jilly's out on the dock on the phone with Justin, and Clint is still sleeping."

"Thanks for making breakfast," I told them.

"Ready in five!" Tish heralded, imitating Rich.

I joined my oldest at the booth, asking, "What's that?"

Camille's cheeks took on a slightly scalded appearance as she tilted the paper, angling it so that I could see the image.

"White Oaks," I murmured in surprise.

"It's from the calendar," she said, setting the image flat upon the tabletop and gently smoothing her fingertips over its surface. White Oaks Lodge stood in all its old-fashioned grandeur just around Flickertail; she and I could have seen it in person, had we jumped from the end of the dock and proceeded to swim into the lake about fifty feet, then looked left. She said, "With everything that's happened this summer, I still haven't been out there to see it."

"The old homesteader's cabin is really something, you'd love it," I said. "The Carters were all here at the birthday party."

"I talked for a while with Bull and Diana," she acknowledged. "They are great, actually. And Bull is hilarious."

"And you talked to Noah's parents," I prompted carefully.

She nodded without speaking, caressing the glossy photo from the calendar. I marveled anew at her beauty; pregnancy lent her face an additional softness. Of course she would interpret this as a suggestion that she was growing fat, which was completely untrue; wisely, I said nothing of her appearance. She looked abruptly into my eyes and said, "Marie asked if she could see the baby, if she could be part of her life."

"Well, I would certainly *hope* so," I said, lacing my tone with sarcasm at Marie's presumption that Camille might not allow this.

One side of my daughter's lips lifted as she said, "Right?"

"Did she say anything about Noah?" I asked, hating to see the way Camille's lips compressed into a tight line, her fingers curled into loose fists; frustration and pain crossed paths over her face.

"He's back at school in Madison," Camille whispered, gouging the tabletop with her right thumbnail. She didn't have to say, *He never said good-bye, never called, doesn't appear to give a shit about how I'm doing.* I knew all of these things, and far worse, so did she.

I wanted to tell her to forget him, that he wasn't worth her pain, but I couldn't say such things—not when she carried his baby and would therefore be unwittingly connected to Noah Utley for the rest of her life.

"Hey, I heard you picked paint colors for the nursery," I said, hoping to provoke at least something resembling enthusiasm, heartened when she nodded and proceeded to give me the details.

Just after noon, I found Mom out on the dock, where she stood staring reflectively over Flickertail Lake, having a smoke. Though she certainly felt my footsteps, she didn't turn around. I reached her and gazed in the same direction. The lake was in a petulant mood today, reflecting a sky that couldn't make up its mind. Fat white clouds with smooth silver undersides raced along in a brisk wind, creating alternating bursts of sun and shadow. Out on the wide surface beyond our small bay, Flickertail was laced with miniature whitecaps. I wore cut-offs and a cream-colored tank, my hair loose over my shoulders and blowing into my face, and wished I'd grabbed a sweatshirt. Mom flicked the last of her ash and finally looked over at me; I couldn't exactly read her expression, but I offered a tentative smile.

"Joelle, I'm sorry about everything," she said, at last. "I think you're making the wrong decision, but I won't mention it again, deal?"

I felt my jaw tighten. She had offered an apology, and I realized I should leave it at that.

I finally muttered, "Deal."

At last, in the early afternoon, I gave up all pretense of doing anything but watching for the rental car bringing Blythe closer to me; he called to tell me they were an hour away an hour ago, and from that point onward I could not remain sitting. Mom, Ellen, and the kids converged on the house, helping Camille with some pre-painting work, and probably I should have been helping them, but when I said as much to Jilly, she replied, "They have plenty of help without us. Besides, you'd be zero help just now, and you know it."

Jilly had long since given up trying to make conversation with me and sat at the counter doodling on a napkin. The clouds swept away as afternoon advanced, the wind slacking off, leaving a mild, pleasant day out the windows. I resumed pacing and received a pointed look from my sister. But suddenly her expression changed markedly and she gestured behind me with her pen; I whirled around just in time to see Blythe climb out of the driver's side of a car I didn't recognize and sprint for the cafe.

I flew. We crashed together with enough force to send Blythe quick-stepping backward, my legs around his waist as he went to his knees and then all the way to the ground at the edge of the parking lot with me clinging like a monkey, laughing and crying at the same time. Blythe dug his hands in my hair, rolling us to the side and commandeering me for a kiss. I couldn't touch him enough, my hands sliding over his torso, back to his face, into his short, thick hair; at last I gripped his ears, lifting my face just a fraction, enough to look into his beautiful, dear, blue-gray eyes. He kept his fingers in my hair and traced my cheekbones with his thumbs. Our hearts beat crazy rhythms against each other.

He whispered, "Hey, there," and tears washed my face, even though I was smiling. He added, "Missed me a little, huh?"

In response I kissed him again, thoroughly. He wrapped his arms possessively around me, so solid and strong against my body; I draped myself over him like frosting on a cake. It wasn't until I heard a very pointed *ahem* that I noticed Jilly's feet, clad in her red flip-flops and with bright orange toenails, just inches from our heads.

She said, "You know, some of the rest of us would like to say hello to the guy, too. Some of us have *also* missed him."

I shaded my eyes and looked up at her. Blythe kept me in his arms as he rolled gamely to his knees and said with complete composure, "Hi, Jilly. How are you?"

She grinned at us and threw her arms around his neck for a good squeeze, kissing his cheek before she said, "Well, way better now. Joelle can quit being so damn moody now that you're back. I couldn't take another minute of her talking about how much she missed you, seriously."

"Is that so?" he asked. He held me like a bride going over the threshold, and I tightened my arms around his neck.

"Yeah, that's so," I said.

"Wow, what happened to your hair?" Jilly asked, hands on hips and one eye squinted as she studied him.

"I'm finally getting used to it. But I shaved off the beard yesterday," he explained. "I wanted to keep it, but Rich and Mom conspired against me."

I couldn't stop smiling at him. I couldn't stop touching him. God, he was here, he was really in my arms again.

"Rich," I realized, managing to drag my eyes from Blythe to look around for him. "Where's Rich?"

"He's inside," my sister said. "He could tell you were a little…preoccupied. A beard, really? Like, how much of a beard are we talking?"

Blythe laughed, getting to his feet and letting mine touch the ground. But he ordered, "Stay right here," and kept me against his side. I wrapped my arms around his waist and breathed against his red t-shirt. He smelled so good, just like himself. In response to Jilly's question he said, "I'm not talking ZZ Top or anything. You don't exactly get a lot of time to shave in the mornings, where I was."

Rich came out onto the porch then, a mug of coffee in his hand, his kind brown eyes crinkling at the corners as he smiled fondly at us. He told Blythe, "Well, I guess you found her."

Blythe bent and kissed my hair. He murmured into my ear, "Yeah, I found her."

"Rich, I'm so glad to see you," I said, hurrying into his open arms. He wasn't my dad, but I loved him just as much as I could imagine loving a father. I whispered, "Thank you for bringing him back to me."

Rich hugged me with one arm, holding his hot coffee out and away. He rested his cheek on my hair and said, "I'm so sorry about Louisa, honey."

Blythe climbed the porch steps behind me. I couldn't bear to stop touching him either, and curled myself back against his warm side.

Jilly rolled her eyes at us but even she couldn't resist one more hug, squeezing both Blythe and me into her exuberant embrace. She said to Rich, "Come on, let's go find everyone. They're up at the house."

The two of them linked arms as they made their way over the lake path, and at long last I was alone with my man. I grabbed his hand and hauled him inside Shore Leave, where the sun drifted in lazy beams. The screen door hadn't finished clacking shut before he gathered me close and kissed me the way I'd dreamed of being kissed, all those long nights we'd been apart. His mouth was made for mine and I moaned with soft pleasure at his taste, kissing him with total abandon, our heads tilting one way and then the other, his hands in my hair and mine sliding over his back. Everything within me became a river, flowing to him. He kissed my nose, my chin, my neck, our words flooding on top of one another.

"All those nights I dreamed of this…"

"I missed you so much, I was dying…"

"Nothing was right without you…"

"I love you…"

"God, I love you…"

I pulled his mouth back to mine, making up for lost time. He lifted me in one effortless motion, my legs around his waist. I rested my hands on his wide, wide shoulders and looked deeply into his eyes.

"You're here," I rejoiced.

"I'm so sorry about Gran," he said softly. "I'm sorry I wasn't here right away to hold you."

"But you're here now and that's all that matters."

"Joelle." His tone was one of reverence. "All those nights I pictured your face just the way it looks right now." He stroked through my hair, murmuring, "You're so soft. I want your hair draped all around me. I know this isn't the time or place…"

"I wish the same thing," I whispered, pressing firmly against him.

He groaned and claimed my mouth, clamping both hands around my backside, hauling me even closer. But out the windows we spied not only Jilly and Rich, but my whole tribe, making their way back to the cafe. They would be upon us in just a minute.

"Here comes everyone," I said, my lips on his neck.

He growled into my hair, risking a last touch, gliding his big warm hands beneath my tank top, cupping my breasts and shivering almost violently. He said hoarsely, "You feel so good."

"Later," I promised, before leading the way outside so that my family could welcome him home.

Ellen and Mom prepared a second lunch in no time flat. Clint, Tish, and Ruthie all but danced around Blythe and Rich, excited to inform them of everything that had happened since July, talking over one another and vying for attention as the men ate plates of food. I disciplined myself and tried to keep my eyes from Blythe's lips whenever he answered questions.

Camille was polite but remained distant, though she seemed glad enough to see them both; she shared Jilly's prediction about the baby being a girl, which I found endearing.

Rich said, "I thought the same thing when you said you were having a baby. A little girl for you just seems right, don't it, honey?"

After lunch I showed Blythe all of the pictures we collaged for Gran.

"Look at you, Gramps," he said to Rich. "Wow, your hair was long back when."

Rich asked Mom and Ellen, "You want me to say a few words tomorrow?"

"I was thinking that anyone could share," Mom replied. "But Ellen and I have something prepared for when we scatter her ashes."

Blythe rubbed my back and I leaned against him, so goddamn glad he was here; I felt whole. He smiled down into my eyes and I noticed how shadowed his were, with simple exhaustion.

"Baby, you need sleep," I murmured.

He kissed the top of my head and admitted, "I'm about ready to collapse."

"C'mon," I told him.

Ruthie walked over to the house with us, holding my elbow, still a little shy around Blythe after his absence; she kept quiet until we neared the front door and then said, "You make my mom really happy," before darting ahead and flying through the door, as though embarrassed at her words.

"Thank you," Blythe whispered to her retreating figure. I looked up to see tears spangling his lashes; his strength and height belied his dear, sensitive soul. He threaded our fingers and said, "Their opinion means so much to me. I don't want them to think of me as the guy who punched their dad."

"They don't," I whispered, my heart still resonating at Ruthie's sweet words. "They think of you as the man who makes their mom happy."

"I intend to, always," he said, hugging me close.

No more than a minute later I settled him in the twin bed where I'd slept all summer. It was ridiculously small beneath him, but he bent his legs and snuggled his jaw into the pillow, saying, "It smells like you in here, sweetheart."

I sat by his hip and he wrapped one arm around my waist.

"I'm letting you sleep…for now," I whispered.

He opened one eye and gave me a lopsided grin. "I'm holding you to that, baby. Come here and kiss me."

He cupped my jaw. I made a small yearning sound and he tightened his grip around my waist, but this wasn't the time or place. For one, I knew he truly needed sleep, and for another, Ruthie was puttering around downstairs, waiting for me.

"I love you," he said, his voice husky with emotion.

"I love you," I told him back, and let him rest.

Later in the evening I crept back over to the house and found him snoring, feet hanging off the end of the bed. For a long time I just watched, sitting close but not touching. He lay on his back with head turned to the side, long lashes fanning his cheeks. He looked power-ful even in repose, but peaceful, mouth soft, lips slightly parted, palms resting upon his chest. At last I couldn't resist the temptation and knelt near the bed, brushing my lips over his. He stirred a little, sighing, and I kissed his chin, the corner of his lips, his left temple. I inhaled his scent, closing my eyes, and in the next moment he hauled me onto the bed, curving his body to make a space for mine.

"That tickles," he whispered, eyes still closed.

"I thought you weren't ticklish," I murmured, running my hands over his ribcage, biting his earlobe.

"Maybe a little," he conceded, kissing my neck, tasting my skin with ever-hungrier strokes of his tongue. He groaned softly, "But I have a much bigger problem right now."

I giggled, muffling the sound against his chest. I could feel what he meant and whispered, "Big *is* the word."

He groaned as if in pain, crushing me close, and was in the process of kissing me quite absolutely when the door downstairs banged open and Clint called, "Aunt Joey! Grandma sent me to tell you dinner is ready!"

Blythe groaned again, his lips on my neck, arms in a vice grip around me.

I called back to my nephew, "We'll be right over, Clinty!"

"Shit," Blythe murmured, peppering my skin with little hot, wet kisses. I shivered and bit the side of his neck. He muffled another moan against me, making me giggle and squirm. He said with feeling, "I'm gonna die. But we can't make love with your family waiting for us."

As if in response, Clint yelled from downstairs, "C'mon, you guys!"

"We'll eat fast," Blythe murmured, cupping my breasts, gently closing his teeth over my right nipple. "And then maybe we can take a walk."

Clint ran ahead on the lake path; Blythe and I followed more slowly, Blythe swinging our joined hands as we walked. Dodge and Justin were over, grilling steaks on the porch, which beckoned in the gathering twilight, the glimmer of the candle lanterns warm with welcome as Blythe and I approached. Rich and Mom sat at a table sipping bottled beer, and I thought of the way Mom had said that Rich was one of her dearest friends, nothing more; as I watched, Mom reached across the table to touch his wrist, both of them smiling as they chatted. The girls were clustered around another table with Jilly, Clint and his best friend Liam sitting balanced on the backs of two nearby chairs, laughing about something; they all held frosty mugs, probably root beer floats, Ruthie stirring hers with an ice cream spoon. Ellen and Dodge argued with their typical good-natured banter, Ellen pointing out something on the grill. The air seemed dusted with intoxicating indigo light; indeed, the entire lake-shore glowed with a dusky-blue hue, gorgeous and almost otherworldly in appearance.

"Joelle," Blythe whispered, stopping us perhaps twenty paces away, and I looked over to see him caught in the moment, just absorbing the sight. The expression on his face sent my heart beating faster in simple gladness. He didn't need to speak a word to convey his joy at being here, being part of us again. I knew he would never take it for granted. I wrapped my arms around him.

"Tilson! Is that you?" Dodge bellowed, coming down from the porch to catch Blythe in a hug, thumping his back. Justin wasn't far behind, shaking Blythe's hand, everyone telling him how much they missed him being around Shore Leave. Tish ran inside the cafe to grab him a root beer float, Mom drew him a chair at her and Rich's table, while I leaned against the porch railing, smiling, letting my family flow around him like an exuberant springtime river.

"You look happy," Jilly said, coming near and hooking my waist with her arm.

"You, too," I said, squeezing my little sister close.

"It's good to have him home," Jilly said. "It seems right, doesn't it?"

Blythe looked our way, though he couldn't have heard Jillian's comment what with all the noise between us and him, but he blew me a kiss, which I proceeded to catch and press to my heart, just as he'd done with mine last summer.

"We decided two weeks from Saturday," Jilly said then, and I didn't even have to be looking at her to see the warm, delighted flush bloom across her cheekbones.

"For your wedding," I whispered, smiling at the notion.

"For our wedding," she repeated, caressing Justin with her gaze; he looked her way and winked, and then grinned, wide and happy, and Jilly threaded her way to him and proceeded to jump into his arms.

After dinner I told Mom that Blythe and I were going to take a little stroll over the lake road, praying that the heat in my body didn't flood onto my face. I said, as innocently as I was able, "It's just so nice that we thought we'd enjoy a walk."

"It is an especially nice evening," Mom agreed, tipping to study the stars.

And so we left the cafe behind; I held his elbow against me this time, needing to be closer than joined hands allowed.

"It's so good to be here with you, to be home," he said as Shore Leave receded around the bend. Flickertail lapped the shore, as though in agreement. He murmured, "My heart feels whole again. I feel like I should pinch myself, like I might just wake up at any moment."

I realized where we were and said, "This is right where you pulled over to pick me up that first night, when we watched the fireworks."

Blythe grinned down at me. "It was my lucky night," he said, tugging me close, lowering his lips to mine. He stroked my hair as we kissed here on the dark lake road, deep, hungry kisses that burned a path straight between my legs. His breath shallow, he whispered, "I don't mean to be impatient…but I can't wait much longer…"

No sooner had he spoken when I heard a car engine, the vehicle headed slowly our way on the lake path. Blythe immediately moved us closer to the edge of the road; I did not release my hold on him, hoping, however uncharitably, that the car contained no one who might want to brake and chat for a spell, that it would instead drive quickly past.

"Oh, no," I despaired, my heart sinking down, down, as the headlights appeared and I realized it was a car I knew all too well. My pulse took up a frightened rhythm and I pressed even closer to Blythe.

Not tonight. I can't deal with this tonight.

"What's wrong?" Blythe asked, protective concern heavy in his tone; before I could speak he realized exactly what was wrong, the two of us silently watching as Jackie parked and climbed from his car, leaving the engine running, headlights beaming into the darkness, illuminating Jackie's thunderous expression. I felt all of Blythe's muscles tense, his entire posture becoming threatening. I truly believed he didn't intend to act, but his body was preparing just in case. My eyes darted between my lover and my husband, whose shoulders squared, his chest inadvertently popping out as he strode our way. In high school Jackie loved fighting, taking great pleasure in getting into what he'd call a rumble. I hated it then and hated it even more now. I would not watch Blythe get carted away in a police car ever again, so help me. I would go with Jackie before I'd let that happen.

Jackie stopped in the middle of the road, about ten feet from us, his gaze unwavering. Tense energy crackled into the air all around the three of us, nearly audible. I could barely breathe. But I understood I must take control of this. I stepped around Blythe, who'd edged me behind him; as I moved he seemed to collect himself, gently touching my elbow as though to ask what I intended. I sent him a silent plea, *It will be all right, let me handle this.*

Before I could speak, Jackie observed, "So you're back from jail."

"Jackie," I implored. "This is enough."

His eyes darted from Blythe to me, glittering angrily, half of his face lit by the glow of the headlights. Jackie shifted slightly, almost like he meant to pounce, and from the corner of my eye I saw Blythe's jaw tighten.

"Do you think I'm going to stand by and watch you throw yourself at a criminal just to get back at me? To get revenge? What about the girls, Jo?" Jackie all but hissed, steaming angry, just barely containing his temper. It occurred to me that Jackie's intent may very well be to provoke Blythe into striking him—likely Jackie could think of no better way than to ensure Blythe's return to jail.

"You don't know what you're talking about," I said. Tension cut a razor through me, but I kept my voice steady.

"Don't know what I'm talking about?" Jackie stormed. Patronizing sarcasm drenched his tone as he demanded of Blythe, "So, what's your education, buddy? What's your career? Where're you planning to work to support *my wife*, huh? Or do you just fuck her, jail bird?"

My teeth went on edge, a buzzing fury bursting into existence in my skull. Blythe spoke then, low and dangerous, but exerting control; he would not allow Jackie the upper hand. He said, "You need to walk away, right now."

"Or what?" Jackie challenged, stepping closer just to be a fucking asshole. I hated him more in that instant than I ever had—even the night I walked in on him with his pants around his ankles, screwing Lanny on his office desk.

I sensed the rage stretched taut across Blythe's chest, flowing into his arms and hands, his desire to smash a fist through Jackie's contemptuous face. But he remained motionless, saying only, "Walk away."

"I will, but only if you come with me, Jo," Jackie said, abruptly changing tactics, imploring me now. "I meant everything I said the other night. You belong with me. I can give you so much more than this loser. And our girls deserve better, even if you won't admit it."

My fingers curled to fists, my lips dropping open to shriek something along the lines of, *Fuck you, you self-righteous son of a bitch*, but Blythe responded, his tone deceptively light. He asked, "Better than a husband who cheats on his wife? Better than that, you mean?"

"It's none of your *fucking business*," Jackie seethed. He looked again into my eyes and ordered, "This is your last chance to rethink this."

"Let me tell you something," Blythe said, maintaining control with herculean effort. "Joelle is an amazing woman. She loved you once and you *threw it away*. You fucking stomped on her love for you, so don't call me a loser when the only *fucking loser* I see is the one standing in front of me."

There was a beat of stunned silence, before Jackie said in a completely different tone, one with perhaps a note of humbleness, "I still love you, Jo. You're my wife and I will ask you one last time to come home with me."

Part of me wanted to tell the bastard that he had no right issuing ultimatums to me. Another part of me wanted to go to him and hug him one last time, tell him I was truly sorry for many things. I hesitated for a long moment. Blythe remained motionless, watching me like a hawk. At last I said to Jackie, "I know you do." I tightened my grip on Blythe's arm and added quietly, "But it doesn't matter. I don't love you anymore, Jackie. I haven't for a long time."

The man I did love seemed to draw a breath for the first time in minutes. I looked up at Blythe; his expression was a combination of relief and tenderness. He swallowed hard and I felt just the smallest of trembles run through him, like an aftershock.

"Don't do this," Jackie said.

I looked his way and said, "The girls are at the cafe if you want to see them. They can come and visit you anytime, Jackie. You know that. I would never keep them from you."

"I know," he said at last. His voice was rough as he added, "Good-bye, then."

And he got in his car and drove away without another word. It was only then that I whispered, "Bye, Jackie."

"Come here," Blythe said, his voice gruff with emotion. I moved swiftly into his arms and let him pick me up off the ground, clinging to his neck. I pressed my face against the cords of muscle along the top of his right shoulder. He held me like I needed, close to his heart, his lips pressed to my right temple. The quiet darkness of night surrounded us once again, melting the angry tension from the air. After a time he whispered, "Are you all right, baby?"

"Yes," I whispered, and pressed my mouth to his neck. "Thank you for being here."

"There's nowhere I'd rather be," he told me. "You know that, crazy woman."

I tried to keep my voice light, but failed as I ordered, "Never leave me again, okay?"

He drew back enough to look into my eyes and said, "I won't. And promise me you won't worry about it ever again."

"I promise," I said, hugging him as hard as I could.

"Let's go home," he said.

"I'll give you the grand tour tomorrow," I said as I unlocked the door and led him inside, clicking on the overhead light in the kitchen. We'd walked to our house on Broom Street; I figured Jackie was over at Shore Leave saying good-bye to the girls and didn't want to infringe on that.

Blythe turned in a slow circle before resting his eyes on me with a certainty that made my knees begin to tremble. He said, "I love it already, Joelle. And I'll take you up on the tour. But the only room I want to see right now is ours."

I led him through the kitchen and down the basement steps, then clicked on the lamp in our room, lending the dimness a rosy glow. My heart throbbed with love and desire and simple gladness. I whispered, "I've imagined you here with me so many times."

He gave me his slow, smoldering grin, and I reached to free my hair from the clip holding it up, but he moved and caught my hand in his, bringing it to his lips.

"Let me, baby," he implored. I shivered a little at both his tone and the way he studied me, his eyes dark in the lamplight, sensuous with longing. He curled his fingers into my hair and loosed the clasp, catching its heavy length and settling it over my right shoulder. With deliberate slowness he cupped my bare upper arms, letting his fingers stroke softly. I shivered, almost feverish with need.

He bent and kissed the side of my neck, breathing lightly against me. I pleaded, "Blythe…"

"Not yet," he whispered. "I dreamed about this so many times. Undressing you, the way your eyes look when you want me…"

"The way they look all the time," I said, reaching for him, but he wouldn't be rushed.

"Your soft skin," he murmured, running his palms down my arms. He was so tall if I tipped my forehead against him it would be cradled against his huge chest. He murmured, "You feel like warm silk."

I closed my eyes as he tasted my neck with soft, suckling kisses. His hands worked down my spine, freeing the small pearl buttons on my tank top. Once undone he let the soft cotton slip down my waist, unhooking my bra and easing the straps over my arms with deliberate slowness. I moaned, my nipples round and full against his palms as he cupped me, closing his teeth over the tendon that ran along the top of my shoulder.

"You feel so good in my hands," he said. "And you taste so good, Jo-elle, I need you in my mouth." So saying, he sat on the bed, drew me into the vee of his legs and opened his lips over the peak of one breast and then the other, cradling me close, drawing my nipples into his mouth with slow, sensual strokes of his tongue. My knees went weak. I fell over him and he took us to the bed, rolling me to my back. I dug my hands into his thick hair and he rested his chin between my breasts; his voice low and hoarse, he whispered, "Your heart is beating so fast. I can't get enough of you. I need you so much, Joelle."

"I need you, Blythe, I need you so much. Don't stop," I begged, and his eyes caught fire at the expression in mine, sending a heated pulse all the way to my tailbone. "Get this off," I demanded, and he yanked the shirt from his body, moving back over me like the most gorgeous predator in existence, lavishing my breasts with his tongue, frantically removing the last of our clothes. My throat arched in wordless pleasure, though I was far from quiet. He kissed my collarbones, my belly, my pelvis. His breath pelted my skin and sweat slipped down his huge chest as he spread my thighs farther apart on the mattress. I gripped the sheets with both hands as he bent his head between my legs.

Later, when he moved back up my body with hot, sweet kisses I was scarcely aware of space and time. My head tipped weakly to the side; he pressed his warm, smiling lips against my temple. I lay drenched in sweat, my body limp. He was harder than any rock against my right thigh but he held back and whispered, teasing me, "Baby, the neighbors will call the cops if you get any louder."

"*Mmmm*," I managed to articulate. He murmured against my skin, soft sounds of love, his long fingers stroking me until I regrouped my strength and reached to grip him, shifting my hips to impale myself on his flesh.

"Holy God," he groaned, overcome. I rolled him to his back and found a new well of energy.

"Now who's…being loud?" I managed to gasp. His hands clutched my hips and I was pleased that he was the one now unable to speak.

"Don't come yet. Not till…I say," I ordered. "Not yet…let me make you come *so hard*…"

He made a sound like his heart was being torn out, moving back above me without breaking the connection of our bodies. For the last few strokes he plunged so deeply that the line between pleasure and pain grew thin. But I clung to him, would have died if he'd stopped. And after he came I cradled him on top of me, the small tingling aftershocks of our lovemaking shivering through my insides. He pressed his warm lips against my hair and whispered, "You always make me come so hard, sweetheart."

"Good," I mumbled back, hooking a thigh over his hip. "I love you, Blythe Edward Tilson."

"Fuckin' right," he whispered, his voice a soft, teasing murmur. "G'night, my sweet Joelle. Let me hold you while I sleep. That's all I need in the world."

In the morning light, I woke to find him braced on an elbow, smoothing a strand of hair from my forehead, studying me. I rocked against him and kissed his chest.

"Morning," I said, breathing against his skin.

He kissed the side of my neck and said, "Mornin', baby. Your phone was ringing a minute ago."

I was unwilling to move from his embrace, certain there was nothing critical that demanded my attention—but then a creepy little jolt hammered at my spine. I slid on my stomach to the edge of the bed and leaned over the mattress, catching up my phone, seeing a missed call from Camille.

Oh God…

At once inexplicably terrified, I pressed the voicemail button and heard Camille's message, her voice frantic, "Mom, call back as soon as you can. It's Aunt Jilly."

…THE STORY CONTINUES IN *A Notion of Love*

Excerpt from A Notion of Love

Landon, MN - August, 1984

OUR NEW PINK RADIO WAS PLUGGED IN AND POSITIONED ON the back of the toilet tank, blaring my current favorite song, "Sunglasses at Night" by Corey Hart. I swayed my hips to the beat as I carefully curled my bangs; last week I hadn't been paying enough attention and burned the crap out of my forehead. Seconds later my older sister Joelle flew into the bathroom and slapped her hip against mine, grinning as she effectively bumped me over and then leaned close to the mirror to reapply her new lip gloss. She'd just picked it out yesterday, on her seventeenth birthday. I watched her critically before saying, "It *already* looked fine."

Jo rolled her eyes at me, rubbing her lips together and then miming a kiss in the mirror. Everyone is always saying we look so much alike, and I guess we do, but I always thought Jo, being older, had an edge on me in the looks department. I mean, she's my best friend and I love her like crazy, and I'm happy with how I look—mostly. It's just hard when your older sister is tall and has D-cup boobs, and you aren't tall and yours are still (hopefully) growing. We both have long hair and good tans from being on Flickertail Lake all summer, and I know looks aren't supposed to be important in the long run. Gran is always telling us that it's far better to know how to catch and clean a fish, make a proper margarita, and be a considerate human being. And Great-Aunt Minnie says looks fade but spirit always glows. But *still.*

"Happy birthday," Jo said for the hundredth time today, meeting my eyes in the mirror, a smile crooking her glossy lips. "You look so pretty, Jilly Bean. What time is Chris getting here?"

I couldn't help but grin at the mention of my boyfriend, Chris Henriksen. His sixteenth birthday was back in June and his mom was letting him drive her car until he could afford his own, which would probably be around the time he turned twenty-five or so. I shook out my hair, fluffed my bangs one last time and said, "Pretty soon. How about Jackie?"

"I think I just heard his truck. Here, let me fix your shirt before I go."

She reached and turned my hips so I faced her, then hiked up the bottom of my hot-pink tank top and tied it in a knot, exposing my belly, just like hers. Then she tugged my jean shorts down about two inches and stepped back, satisfied.

"I hate showing my belly button," I grumbled, but Jo slapped my hands from adjusting her handiwork.

"But you have such a cute little belly," she teased. "Now leave it!"

There was no point in arguing. I asked, "Did Mom say anything else about the tattoo?"

Jo rolled her eyes again, complaining, "No, still no. Even though it's all I wanted for my birthday. I mean, it would just be a little daisy, right near my hip. I could cover it up anytime I wanted. I don't get why it's such a big deal."

"Yeah, but what about what Gran said, about when you have a baby some-day, and it would get all stretched out?" I reminded, leaning to click off the radio before following her out of the bathroom.

Jo thumped down the stairs, calling over her shoulder, "Believe me, that's something I'm not doing for a *looooong* time! Shit, Jills, can you imagine?"

"No," I said honestly. "Not really."

Outside, the late-afternoon air was clear and mellow, scented by the camp-fire that Dodge was tending over by the café. Jo, spotting her boyfriend Jackie Gordon pulling into the parking lot, sprinted ahead. He climbed down from his rusty F-150 and pushed back his sunglasses as she jumped into his arms and they kissed like it was months since they'd seen each other, instead of just a few hours.

"Lookin' good, babe," I heard him say, his hands all over her.

I would have considered this obnoxious except that when Chris got here I planned to cover him in kisses, too. My heart sent a rush through my blood as I thought about Chris, who'd been my boyfriend since last spring. I'd known him forever, of course, like basically everyone in Landon. I hadn't paid any attention to him in middle school, but all of a sudden in tenth grade we had four classes together and he just seemed to be in my mind…a lot. *A lot*, a lot.

I would think of him as I lay in bed with my headphones on, trying to block out Jo, talking incessantly to Jackie on the phone in our room, at least until Gran would get on the extension from the kitchen downstairs and tell her it was time to quit yakking and go to bed. Gran thought that was funny, rather than just sticking her head in our bedroom door. But every song I heard as I lay there in my twin bed somehow reminded me of Chris. His eyes were brown, with a gold sheen and flecks of green sprinkled throughout. It wasn't something you could see unless you looked directly into his irises.

The first time he'd asked me to hang out was last March, after geometry but before lunch. He was with a group of his buddies and I was walking with my good friend Jenny Hull, and he pushed off from the locker he was leaning against and followed behind us.

"Hey, Jills," he said, the nickname just about everyone in school used, but for some reason when Chris spoke it I felt a little extra thud in my heartbeat. I turned and walked backward for a couple of steps so I could look at him, until he laughed and grabbed my elbow, the one not cradling a pile of books, and said, "Don't crash!"

We all stopped, Jenny included, and Chris shot her a slightly flustered look, but then his eyes came back to me and he asked, "Hey, you wanna swing by Dairy Queen with me this weekend?" His voice cracked just a hair on the last word. I found myself studying the face that was so often in my daydreams. He'd grown about six inches between the beginning of the year and March. His hair was chestnut brown, cropped close to his head. He had a square jaw and the kind of laugh that made everyone around him want to laugh, too. His eyes seemed to be sparkling at me as he waited, though I could sense he was really nervous.

"Sure," I heard myself say, and the smile that spread over his face was surely mirrored on mine in the next moment.

"Cool, I'll see you," he said.

And we'd been pretty much inseparable ever since.

"Hi, honey!" Dodge called as I came near. He was one of my favorite people in the world, someone who was such a part of Shore Leave that sometimes, in my most secretly-guarded thoughts, I pretended he was my dad – even though he was married to Marjorie, with two of his own kids, Justin and Liz. Justin was in Jo and Jackie's grade and Liz a year behind me. Dodge ran the filling station and engine repair shop about a quarter-mile around the lake, but he was still here at the café all the time, helping out with the things Mom and Aunt Ellen couldn't manage. He stopped in for coffee every morning of the busy season, without fail, sometimes bringing Justin, who helped him in the summers. Dodge's bushy salt-and-pepper hair was held under control only by the aviator sunglasses perched on the top of his head. His full beard and mustache seemed like a continuation of his unruly hair.

"Hi, Dodge," I said, burrowing against him and squeezing tightly. He couldn't hug me back because he held his drinking mug in one big hand and a long, tapered stick in the other, which he used to poke at the blazing fire. Though the sun wouldn't set for a couple hours, the bonfire was already alive and kicking. He kissed the top of my head and I smelled his familiar, comforting scent, a combination of wood smoke, motor oil, tobacco, and Jim Beam.

"Happy birthday!" he said, sounding jovial as always. Truly, I'd never seen him in any other mood. And then he hollered, "Boy! What's taking you so long?"

"Shit, Pa, I'm coming," Justin said, giving us a grin as he staggered up to the fire bearing an enormous armload of wood. "Where do you want this?"

Dodge pointed with the stick and Justin grunted as he deposited the burden on the ground. He stood and brushed debris from his flannel shirt, which flapped open over his tan, bare belly and damp swim trunks.

"Hey, Jilly," he said to me, offering an easy smile. Justin was tall and lean and wiry, with wavy black hair that hung past his shoulders in back, though the sides were shorter, and a face that Gran always said was too pretty for a boy. I was glad she'd never said that directly to him. I'd known Justin forever; the two of us, along with Joelle and Justin's sister Liz, played like siblings every summer as far back as my memory stretched. He treated me like a little sister, teasing me mercilessly when we were kids. Since high school we'd drifted apart, but now he added amiably, "Happy birthday."